STORM ISLANDS
Ann Quinton

PIATKUS

Copyright © 1985 by Ann Quinton

First published in Great Britain in 1985
by Judy Piatkus (Publishers) Limited of London

British Library Cataloguing in Publication Data

Quinton, Ann
  Storm Islands
  I. Title
823'.914[F]   PR6067,U5/

  ISBN 0-86188-337-3

Typeset by Phoenix Photosetting, Chatham
Printed in Great Britain by Mackays of Chatham Ltd

To my husband

Foreword

Anyone who has visited the Isles of Scilly will recognise the locations described in this book, but the characters of my plot are entirely fictitious. To the best of my knowledge there never was a Dutch East Indiaman called the *Maria Johanna*, but many similar ships have come to grief in those waters, some already salvaged, many as yet undiscovered.

I wish to thank the following people for the help they have given me:

Mrs Enid Malec, Hon. Sec., Isle of Scilly Museum Association; Mrs J. M. Phillips, Librarian, St Mary's; Mr Roy Graham, Marine Study Centre, St Mary's; Sergeant Adrian Ridley, St Mary's Police Station; and last but not least, Mr Terry Hiron of the Isles of Scilly Underwater Centre, who answered my many queries with unfailing good humour and helpfulness and who first told me the story of the *Merchant Royal*.

Chapter One

I knew that I had made a terrible mistake the moment the ship edged imperceptibly away from the quay. No, that is a lie. I had known right from the beginning when the project was first mooted that it was a crazy idea, and that I would be mad to even contemplate it. How had I managed to get myself into this situation? Against the good advice of friends and the realisation that I would be doing the wrong thing I had let myself be persuaded into going back. Back to those beautiful, enchanted islands where I, Bethany Carr, a widow of eighteen months' standing, had spent an idyllic honeymoon just three years before.

Now that it was too late to turn back, the enormity of my return to the Scillies hit me like a visible blow. But was it too late? For a few seconds I clung to the rail with the desperate idea of leaping ashore. But even as I hesitated, gathering courage, the narrow gap between ship and pier-head widened; the wedge of oily water gaining proportions that no human agent could bridge. As I watched with a sick feeling the ship seemed to pause; then with a thrust and surge she swung slowly round in a broad arc and headed out towards the empty horizon.

An elderly woman at my side eyed me with sympathy. 'Bad traveller, dear? It's going to be a rough crossing.'

1

She took my silence for acquiescence and continued, 'You should have gone by helicopter, it's much quicker.'

I gave her a weak smile and moved away. Quicker! When all I wanted now was for the journey to continue for ever; to never make landfall. Already Penzance was slipping away, flattening out to a grey-white frieze on the edge of the ruffled water, a single church tower reaching up into the turquoise, cloudswept sky. To the left, St Michael's Mount loomed, shining in the morning sun, to be passed and pushed back to merge with the retreating landmass.

I made my way to the stern and hung over the churning wake. The mighty screw cut through the water like a ploughshare, turning the blue, green depths, and overhead the gulls wheeled and hovered over the hissing furrows that creamed out behind. I had forgotten how different the gulls were in this part of the country; bigger, more vociferous; haunted and haunting with their plaintive, half-human cries. Trim and gleaming, her pristine whiteness broke only by touches of ochre paint, the *Schillonian III*, modern and stabilised, though still capable of rolling horribly as I later discovered, plunged through the white-capped waves to her home port of St Mary's.

I moved back along the deck, seeking shelter from the freshening wind, and let my thoughts drift back over the events of the last eighteen months; an exercise I normally tried to avoid as I struggled to forget the past and to face the future without my beloved Martin. Martin, my darling, handsome, witty, tender husband; suddenly dead as the result of an accident one foggy November day.

We had been living at the time in a flat at Hampstead. A large rambling apartment on the top floor of a house that had known better days; and from certain of the windows

2

one had a quite breathtaking view of the Heath. My studio had had such a view and I had never been quite sure whether it had been a good thing or not; inspiring perhaps, but too distracting. I am a free-lance artist specialising in botanic illustration, and that day I had found it hard to concentrate. My attention had kept wandering to the scene beyond the window where the mist-enwrapped trees stood sentinel against the amorphous grey and mauve background. I had had a great urge to stop work on the rather dull biology textbook I was illustrating, and instead paint the scene before me. Pastels I had thought; pastels were just the medium to capture that ephemeral light shot by a hazy, autumnal sun that swum through layers of fog.

Twilight had put an end to my painting by four o'clock and I was preparing our evening meal when the doorbell had rung. At first I had been unable to take in what the police constable was telling me. When he had finally got through to me that Martin had been knocked down and killed by a hit-and-run driver I had refused to believe him. Later, when I was able to look back on that horrific day with more equanimity, I realised how marvellous he had been. Although not much older than myself, he had coped with my shock and hysteria and extracted enough information to enable him to summon my family and friends.

For a few days I had lived in a nightmare world in which my father, an Anglican priest who had rushed to my side, strove in vain to comfort me. Then the true horror of Martin's death became known. The police had told me that he had been knocked down and killed instantly whilst crossing Ashby Street near Northampton Square. The fog had been particularly bad in that area, it had happened at twilight, and there had been no witnesses.

Then, just as I was assimilating these stark facts, a

witness had come forward. He was a boy of eight and what he had told opened up frightening vistas. He had seen Martin walking down the middle of the road clutching his briefcase and had heard the car approaching. So the occupants of the car had been unable to see him because of the fog and had struck him down? asked the police. Oh no, the boy had said. The car had drawn alongside him and the two men inside had leaned out of the window and had appeared to be having an argument with him. They had been trying to get him inside the car and there had been a struggle and Martin had fallen violently against a nearby lamp-post. He hadn't moved again and one of the men, after examining him, had snatched up the briefcase and scrambled back into the car. Then – and he had had difficulty in getting out the next bit – the car had reversed and deliberately run over the inert body.

The police had queried the boy being able to see anything at all in the fog, but he had simply replied that it had happened under the street lamp that had lit the scene, even to the extent that he insisted that the man driving had had red hair. That was the first mention of a red-haired man and at the time it had held no significance for me. The boy's statement had opened up a whole new line of police enquiry. To their questions I could only reply that I knew of no-one who had a grudge against Martin; that I had no idea what he had been doing near Northampton Square and that I only knew that he had had an important meeting that day, about which he had been somewhat secretive and excited; but with whom and about what I did not know.

The car was never traced but a couple of days later Martin's briefcase had been found about a mile away tossed over a churchyard wall, its contents scattered across the tombstones. At first I had refused to believe that Martin had been deliberately killed, then I had had the unnerving experience of being followed by a red-haired man as I went about the morbid business of winding-up Martin's affairs. I had gone straight to the police, still shaking with reaction and probably not making much sense. How well I remember that interview. The sergeant had been soothing but firm and what he had had to say shattered me still further. 'Mrs Carr, we have news for you. I was coming to tell you myself. The boy's story was a hoax. Well, not exactly a hoax, but let's say a case of a vivid imagination taking over from reality. The scene he described so carefully was lifted complete from a television play he'd been watching the night before.'

'But are you sure?'

'Oh yes, we checked as soon as the possibility was raised. One of my young policewomen got suspicious when she was reading his statement. She'd actually seen the play. It was surprising that no-one else had picked it up; but it was an obscure thing, on late at night.'

'And the boy had seen it?'

'Yes, he admitted it when he realised we had sussed him but he still insists on sticking by his story that it really happened.'

'And is it possible?'

'No way. He is an only child with elderly parents and apparently lives half his time in an imaginary world. His teacher says there is no real harm in him but that he has difficulty in differentiating between fact and fiction. He actually believes it really happened.'

'But what about the red-haired man who followed me today?'

'Well, ma'am, you are in a state of shock still and I think it is preying on your mind. There are a lot of red-haired men about . . .'

'But was there actually a red-haired man in the television play?'

'Well, no, there wasn't. We reckon he must have embellished the story a little.'

'What will happen to him?'

'He's had a severe reprimand. He won't go around misleading the police again in a hurry. Now, ma'am, you must try and forget this horrible episode. Your husband was killed by accident and I don't suppose we will ever find the culprit.'

But much as I had wanted to take his advice, yet something niggled at me. Perhaps it had been Martin's recent behaviour. He had been evasive and restive over the last couple of months and I had thought it was connected with a discovery he had made in the course of his work. But he had not seen fit to enlighten me and I had been somewhat piqued; especially as this mood had seemed to stem from the time of his last visit to the Scillies on business, just two months previously and unaccompanied by me. I was sure that I had not imagined the red-haired man even if the boy had. I felt that the police were too eager to close the case.

'What about Martin's briefcase?'

'Easily explained. The driver probably did stop to see what he had done. When he found that he had killed a man he panicked and drove off at random; then realised that he had picked up the briefcase in his fright so he threw it over the nearest wall.'

There was nothing more to be said. After postponements and long delays an open verdict was brought in at the inquest and I was left to pick up the pieces of my shattered life.

A sudden lurching of the ship recalled me to the present. I leaned against a doorway and fought back tears. Why had Martin died? I sighed and opened my eyes to find a man standing nearby who was regarding me rather strangely.

6

He was tall and rangy with a lot of untidy brown hair. He made as if to speak to me, probably thinking I was feeling ill, but I hurriedly turned away and plunged down the companionway. I really must pull myself together. Why, even this man seemed vaguely familiar to me as if it wasn't bad enough being haunted by a red-haired man. I was getting quite paranoid. My best friend Lisa had been right about me getting away though she had tried hard to dissuade me from going back to the Scillies.

Lisa is everything I am not: witty, sophisticated and always one step ahead of the current fashion. We had been at school together and for a short time had even shared a flat – until Lisa moved on to higher things in the form of a penthouse apartment, jetting round the world on an expense account and live-in lovers. I suppose we each supplied something that was missing in the other. As a writer of amusing, pithy articles on modern living she was well thought of in journalistic circles and commanded an awesome salary, but we had never lost touch. Months would go by without a word from her, then she would suddenly arrive out of the blue like a homing pigeon, and we would spend a few days exchanging news and catching up on each other's lives. From time to time she would concentrate on the problem of 'bringing Bethany out'. I am sure that she thought of it in captial letters and felt it was her duty to try and drag me into the modern scene.

'You really must sell yourself more, Bethany,' she commanded. 'You are just as successful in your line of business as I am' (false modesty was not one of her faults), 'and you could be really attractive if you applied yourself'; and she would whisk me off to some sophisti-cated party where I would listen fascinated to the brittle, insouciant conversation flowing around me, and marvel at the witty small-talk, the easy way in which beautiful, dashing girls, my own contemporaries, brushed off or

7

accepted the sexual advances of the equally trendy young men. Nobody propositioned me. It was as if I had a large label round my neck announcing 'country parsonage upbringing; dull, conventional, out-dated morals.'

It was at just such a function that I had first met Martin. Taking pity on my wallflower status Lisa had whisked up to me with this man in tow. He was tall and dark and only saved from being incredibly handsome by a decidedly crooked nose and pale blue-grey eyes instead of the dark ones which should have gone with his hair and complexion.

'Bethany, this is Martin Carr. He goes around discovering fantastic valuables in the earth's surface – you know, minerals and metals.'

Startled out of my usual shyness I had said: 'You mean you are a diviner?'

'Good heavens, no! Trust Lisa to disappear on a cryptic statement like that.' Lisa had indeed wandered off. 'I'm a geo-physicist employed by M. & K., currently working on the discovery of new sources of fossil fuels.'

'North Sea oil and gas?'

'I've been closely involved with the North Sea fields but the potential of the Celtic Sea is engaging our interests very much at present. I'm also into nuclear energy in the form of uranium deposits.'

'Your work must be very exciting.'

'Mostly dull routine, but I can assure you that I have actually prospected for diamonds in South Africa and panned for gold in Australia.' A quick grin had flashed across his face, and I had been so interested in him and his discourse that I had forgotten my usual shyness.

And that was how it had all started. By some extraordinary coincidence he had seemed to find me as fascinating as I found him, and our friendship had developed quickly. Before long I had been head over heels in love, and he had seemed to reciprocate my feelings. I couldn't believe my good fortune. How could I hope to hold someone as attractive and ambitious as he? I, Bethany Woodrow, who sat at home and painted like a Jane Austen heroine. When he had suggested getting married my doubts and fears had all erupted and I had possitively flooded him with reasons why he couldn't possibly marry me. He had listened in astonishment and then hugged me to him. 'Good God, Bethany, I want a real woman for my wife, not a painted, fickle doll who'll jump into bed with my best friend the moment my back is turned!' After that I had been content to continue wearing my hair in a long, straight curtain, although Lisa insisted that that style had gone out with the Flower People; and I did not feel the need to experiment with pink eyeshadow and plum blusher.

We had been married in May in the little country church where my father had the living; he had officiated at the ceremony and my two older, married sisters had been matrons of honour. We had honeymooned in the Scillies, which Martin had fallen in love with on a previous visit on business for his company. His enthusiasm for the islands was soon shared by myself as he unfolded their unspoiled beauty before my eager eyes. Afterwards we had settled in the flat at Hampstead. He had been away a lot, as was inevitable in his job, but he had encouraged my painting and I was gradually making a name for myself in my particular field. If there had been any cloud on the horizon it was what I felt was his excessive secretiveness in respect of his work. I knew that he worked on highly secret projects, often of an international delicacy, and that I couldn't expect him to regale me with all the details of his work; yet he seemed to positively enjoy keeping me in the dark, and I often had no idea where he was when he went off on one of his frequent journeys.

But I had known when he had made a return journey to the Scillies just two months before he was killed. I had been hurt when he had not suggested that I accompany him. No, I had been very upset, and the expression of outrage and reproach on my face when he had first mentioned the proposed visit had got through to him.

'This is a business trip, Bethany, there's no way you can accompany me. But we'll go back together another time, I promise you.' It was a promise he was never to keep, but now I was remembering his behaviour on his return; the repressed excitement and speculative gleam in his eyes as he paced the flat and drawled, 'Thar's gold in them thar hills.'

I had decided to play it cool and not heap reproaches on his head, so I had said lightly: 'Don't tell me Piper's Hole is stuffed with diamonds or Shipman Head is really solid uranium.'

'Much more prosaic than that, but they're certainly treasure isles. I'm saying nothing more for the present until I'm more certain, but Bethany girl, you'll soon be using gold-plated paintbrushes.'

'And is the boat also coming in for M. & K.?'

'This has nothing to do with M. & K.'

'But I thought you were there on official business . . ?'

'Don't look so worried Bethany. I am not committing industrial sabotage. This . . . this discovery,' he had hesitated. '. . . has nothing to do with my work. It was a happy coincidence. Now don't plague me with questions because I refuse to answer. Here's a souvenir for you from the Scilly Isles,' and he dug two small objects from his pocket and flipped them towards me. They rattled against the lid of my art box and slid to a halt amongst my tubes of paint. They appeared to be two

10

small encrustations of rock embedded with tiny pebbles and pieces of dull metal.

I had shrugged and left them where they lay. 'You appear to have been beachcombing.'

He had raised his eyebrows in a pained, droll way. 'There are some bulbs in my case.'

'Bulbs? Soleil d'Or?'

'Soleil d'Or, Monarch, Paper Whites. Don't ask me how I juggled the weight restrictions on my baggage.'

'Oh, Martin, thank you. I'll plant them in the window boxes and in the spring they'll remind us of the Scillies.'

I never saw those bulbs bloom. Long before they had put forth their first tentative buds I had left the Hampstead flat for good.

It was getting rougher. The *Scillonian* had left the shelter of the lea shore, lapped Lands End, and was now ploughing across the open Atlantic towards the Scillies that are situated roughly twenty-five miles south-west from Lands End. The main island of St Mary's is the largest although only two and a half miles long and one and a half miles across at its greatest width, and Hugh Town, its capital and my destination, is built on the sandy isthmus between the two hills forming the main contours of the island. The sea forms a shallow lagoon around St Mary's achieving incredible colours of turquoise, azure and jade shading to indigo and viridian where it deepens, and dotted about this lagoon are the off-islands: St Martin's to the northeast, Tresco, Samson and Bryher to the north and St Agnes and Gugh to the south-west and a galaxy of other smaller islands, some named, many more too numerous and minute to achieve this status; just jagged teeth rearing up from a treacherous sea. St Mary's, Tresco, Bryher, St Agnes and St Martin's are now the only inha-

11

bited islands. According to legend the Scillies could be the lost land of Lyonesse or the famed Casseritides where the Phoenicians mined for tin. I hated to think what the journey might have been like in an open longboat at the mercy of the elements and the wild Atlantic breakers.

I have always been a good sailor but the long, shuddering rolling combined with the oily throb from the engines was beginning to get to me. I decided to have a drink to steady myself and then get back on deck and the fresh air. I pushed my way towards the bar then froze. Ahead of me, glimpsed through the milling people, his elbows propped up on the bar counter, was a red-haired man. *The* red-haired man. I told myself not to be so ridiculous, that there were hundreds of red-haired men about, and it was extremely likely that there were several aboard the *Scillonian* on this very voyage. But something about the tilt of his head, the way his hair was slicked back over his ears made my stomach turn over. He mustn't see me. I turned and fought my way back to the other counter where tea and coffee were available. I bought a cup of coffee and made my way to a table at the far end of the saloon. As I gulped the hot liquid my teeth chattered against the rim of the cup. So I had not imagined seeing him at the station last night.

I had booked a sleeper on the overnight train from Paddington. Fortunately it had not been crowded and I had had the two-berth compartment to myself. After stowing my luggage away I had idled away the half-hour before the train left not wanting to settle for the night. In fact, to be truthful, as the time of departure drew nearer I viewed my coming journey with great reluctance and was poised to abandon it. Then I had seen him again, the red-haired man. He had been walking down the platform carefully scrutinising each carriage. The overhead artificial light had whitened his features but could not bleach the gleam

12

of ginger hair. I had bolted back into my compartment, slammed the door and pulled down the blinds with shaking fingers. I must get off the train, I had thought, but even as I panicked there was a gentle jolt and we were in motion, sliding inexorably out of the station.

I had not known whether the man had actually boarded the train but he could easily have got my name and compartment number from the reservations list. I had tossed uneasily all night and as we approached the West Country I had watched the grey light filtering through the gaps at the sides of the blinds as the train stopped more frequently – Exeter, Plymouth, Liskeard, Bodmin Road – and finally, as we sped along the home run through Camborne and St Erth to Penzance, the sunshine had struck invitingly against the dark wood fixtures announcing a brilliant day outside.

My dash from Penzance station to the quayside where the *Scillonian* was berthed had been an undignified scuttle dragging my case and hand-luggage. And now it appeared that I had been followed. Or was I really getting paranoid or suffering from persecution mania as I'm sure the police believed? They had listened patiently to my reports and complaints over the last eighteen months but had not come up with any evidence that I was being persecuted or was in any danger apart from an over-worked and neurotic imagination.

About a week after Martin's funeral I had been asked to attend a meeting at M. & K. The chairman of the board of directors himself had greeted me and taken charge of the proceedings, and I had been escorted to a very plush office where a couple of other important personnel were waiting. After condolences and inquiries into my well-being they came to the point. Had I any idea what Martin had been up to in the months preceding his death? Immediately I had been plunged back into that nightmare

13

world that had opened up to engulf me the day it had been suggested that Martin's death might not have been accidental.

A weak, wintery sun had shone through the large plate-glass window embellishing the executive scene, and I had been concious of another man sitting behind me at a table pushed into the corner. He seemed more engrossed with the pyrotechnics of lighting his pipe than in my answers, so I ignored him and made the obvious reply to the men before me. 'What do you mean?'

'Mrs Carr, I know this has been a shattering blow to you, and I don't wish to distress you further, but we feel obliged to make these enquiries. Had Martin been approached by another company?' He mentioned a couple of well-known international companies, rivals of M. & K.

'You mean, was he working for anyone else on the side?' I was astonished and then the anger had taken over. 'Of course not, how can you suggest it? He was completely loyal to M. & K.'

'Please don't misunderstand me. Your husband was a very talented young man with a brilliant future before him. It is not unknown for men of that calibre to be lured by a rival organisation.'

'If Martin had decided to work for another company he would have resigned from M. & K. first. Are you suggesting he was secretly working for someone else whilst still drawing a salary from M. & K.? That's quite pre-posterous!'

'I'm sorry, Mrs Carr, I'm not trying to blacken Martin's reputation. We are just as much in the dark as you appear to be. I'm just trying to suggest a reason for his behaviour.'

'What behaviour?' I had been feeling quite belligerent by then.

'In the last couple of months before his death Martin took a great deal of leave, some of it unofficial, and he certainly was not giving his full attention to his work.'

'Martin took leave? But that's ridiculous. He had no holiday for at least nine months. He was always away on this company's business.'

The three men had exchanged looks and the chairman had tapped his pen against the table and looked thoughtfully at me.

'The last time Martin was away on business for this company was in September when he was based in the Scillies whilst working on our project in the Celtic Sea.'

'But he went to Plymouth only ten days before the accident.'

'Plymouth? Excuse me a moment.' He pressed a button and fired a series of questions into the intercom. The answers seemed to satisfy him. 'Martin was not in Plymouth on our behalf, Mrs Carr. We have no office or business in Plymouth.'

'But I don't understand. What exactly are you accusing him of? That he neglected his work during his last few months? Even if this were so, he is dead now and incapable of furthering your research. Or are you accusing him of having stolen industrial secrets and having sold them to the highest bidder?' I had been quite overwrought by then, not least because I had known that there was some truth in what they were suggesting. Martin had been up to something, but what and how it related to his work with M. & K., I did not know.

'Please calm yourself, Mrs Carr. We are not accusing him of anything. Why, you are in receipt of a handsome company pension; that surely speaks for itself.'

'Then what exactly is all this about?'

'Two days after Martin's death his office here was broken into.'

15

'Was anything taken?'

'As far as we know, no. Of course, all papers relating to confidential work are filed in our central security files, but someone had forced Martin's own office file and done a very thorough job of searching it. Are you sure you cannot help us?'

I had decided to be honest. 'Martin had discovered something . . .' I had paused and had had the full attention of the three pairs of eyes facing me. Behind my back a fourth pair had bored into my shoulder blades. '. . . He was excited about something he had turned up, by accident, I think. But he was very mysterious about it; he would tell me nothing more, only that it had nothing to do with the work for M. & K. Is there anything else I should know?'

'His secretary was approached.'

'His secretary? Sarah Barnard? How do you mean?'

'A few days before he was killed she was at a party. She was accosted by this man, he "chatted her up" is the phrase used, I believe.' He had looked disdainful. 'He showed an inordinate interest in the work she did, and in particular was angling for information about your husband. She was amused at the time and had intended mentioning it to Martin. When the circumstances of his death became known and foul-play was suspected, the whole incident assumed sinister proportions to her, so she came to us.'

'The police have closed the case. It was all a ghastly mistake – Martin was killed accidentally.'

'Quite so; well, I am sorry you cannot throw any more light on the matter to enable us to close *our* files. If there is anything we can do . . ?'

'But I'm in receipt of a handsome company pension. What more could I want?' He had had the grace to look a little embarrassed and on that small victory I had swept out. The man in the corner had still been having difficulties with his pipe. A week after this interview the flat in Hampstead had been broken into and turned upside-down.

It had not needed much persuasion after this to move house. My family had urged me to return to Suffolk, pointing out that I could paint just as well there as in London, but though the idea appealed to me, I had fought to retain my independence. I had moved to a smaller flat in North Finchley. It was further from the city but I was unknown there. I lived quietly in a small apartment in a tall, grim Victorian house overlooking a school, and I tried to shut out the immediate past and to carve out some sort of future for myself. Then the anonymous phone-calls had begun.

It was always the same voice; male, low and throaty with hidden amusement in it and a hint of intimacy that chilled me. The caller always asked for me by name and then went on to suggest a meeting 'to discuss things to our mutual benefit'. At first my reaction had been to slam down the receiver and spend the rest of the day in a state of nervous apprehension; but by about the fifth call my anger and curiosity were aroused and I had challenged the caller.

'Who are you? What do you want?'

'Come, Mrs Carr, don't hold out on me. Surely Martin told you about me?'

'If I don't know to whom I am talking, how can I tell? Are you a business acquaintance?'

'Let's say a prospective one. I'm beginning to get a little impatient with your unfriendliness.'

'Have you got red hair?' I had blurted it out before I could stop myself. There had been a chuckle from the

17

other end of the line that had frozen my blood.

'So you do know about me, Mrs Carr. Actually it's my colleague you're referring to. I suppose you could say he had a touch of the "Titians".'

'You were responsible for Martin's death,' I had croaked into the phone.

'There you are, gross unfriendliness. Believe me, Mrs Carr, I have every reason for wishing him alive. As it is we'll have to make do with you.'

'I don't understand, what do you mean?'

'Just a little cooperation. I'm sure we can do a deal. I suggest a meeting later this week.'

'I don't know what you're talking about. I don't know who you are and I don't want to know. Please stop pestering me or I shall inform the police.'

I had put the phone down and I had rung the police but they had shown very little interest. As little as they had shown over the break-in at the Hampstead flat as soon as it was known that nothing appeared to have been taken. I was sure that by now I was firmly listed on their books as a hopeless neurotic. I had even rung up M. & K. and told them about the calls, but they had shown no interest either, firmly insisting that it was a police matter and nothing to do with them.

The phone calls had still come but I had hung up as soon as I had realised who the caller was. Each time it had happened I had got in touch with the police but they didn't want to know. It was as if they had inside information which was not available to me; information which put me in the wrong rather than my unknown caller. I had felt that I was up against a massive wall of conspiracy, a conspiracy in which the police themselves were involved, although that idea in itself was ridiculous. Maybe I was going mad or had Martin really been involved in something criminal? Something the police had known about and therefore I had been labelled as a criminal accessory, not a persecuted innocent?

I was also quite certain that from time to time a red-haired man dogged my steps, particularly when I had a change of routine and went somewhere different. The first time this happened I had been on a visit to a friend who lived in Wimbledon. As I had left the tube station, one of the very few passengers who had left that particular train, I had been aware of footsteps following mine. When I hurried, these footfalls hurried, when I slowed down, they dropped back to my pace. As I had reached the corner of the road in which my friend lived I had paused and risked a look back. My follower, a few yards behind, was at that moment directly under a street lamp. It lit upon the glint of red hair and I had bolted the short distance to my friend's house, too panicked to take in whether he actually pursued me. I had done nothing about that first incident, having managed to convince myself, once safely inside, that I had imagined the whole episode; but when it happened a second and third time I knew that I really was under surveillance and I had panicked. I had gone into the local police station, trembling and incoherent, and had poured out my tale to the sympathetic officer on duty at the desk. He had soothed me and promised to look into the matter, and for a short while I had thought my complaint would be investigated.

I was soon disillusioned. Before long the curtain of silence and disbelief had descended once again. I was politely but firmly fobbed off. I began to wonder if the police could possibly be nobbled – but how and why? What on earth had Martin got himself involved in? The red-haired man continued to put in intermittent appearances. Just when I thought I was rid of him and was lulled into a false sense of security, he would pop up again and all my fears would come rushing back. I had stopped pestering the police. It was obvious that they were not prepared to believe me and I feared that if I became too much of a nuisance I would find myself under medical restraint through the instigation of the police. I was in such a state that I almost believed my sanity was in question.

As the months passed my grief over Martin's death seemed to get worse. I missed him terribly and mixed up with my loss was the fear that I hadn't really known him. That the man I had loved and lost was not the man I had thought, but a criminal mixed up with an unsavoury coterie. I longed for him and some mad, unstable element in me made me look for him in crowds, hoping to catch a glimpse of him over my shoulder in the street or in the rush-hour on the tube. I saw instead the red-haired man.

I suppose, looking back, that at any time he could have accosted me. The very fact that he didn't, that he just continued to monitor my movements without any personal confrontation, made the whole affair even more sinister. I was haunted by a red-haired man with a sly, crooked grin and I had recurrent nightmares and blind daytime panics when I feared for my life and my sanity.

Amazingly enough my painting didn't suffer. I had become so engrossed in my work that I actually managed to occasionally push the matter to the back of my mind, to forget it for a few hours.

It was my agent who had first suggested a one-man show of my paintings and I had quickly been fired with enthusiasm. Besides my flower studies, usually executed in gouache or water-colour and the finely detailed line drawings of botanical specimens, I also painted regularly in oils, breaking out into large, vivid compositions where colour and feeling for a subject took over from my finicky, painstaking observations from nature. Landscapes, still-lifes, one or two portraits and quite a few abstracts had flowed from my brush over the past two or three years and

20

it was these that my agent used for the backbone of the show with a small selection of my 'bread-and-butter' work in an adjacent gallery.

The preview had been the usual affair. Mass of people; friends, critics, a scattering of professional people from the art world mingling with what had appeared to be a far larger number of hangers-on, strangers and weirdos. Clutching my sherry, a rigid smile fixed on my face, I had been propelled from one group to another by my agent who really had been working for his money that day. I suppose that I had made the right responses, ignoring the gushing, ignorant remarks that had flowed around my head, and trying to concentrate on the genuine admirers. My mother and father had been there, managing to look at one and the same time embarrassed, bewildered and smug about the achievements of their youngest daughter.

A lapse in the excitement had found me, momentarily alone, standing beneath a group of oils that I had painted from rough sketches made in the Scillies whilst on my honeymoon. I had eased a foot surreptitiously out of a shoe and stared blankly at the canvases. Martin had encouraged me to paint these pictures. Martin, who should have been here now, he would have been so proud of me. A voice at my elbow had startled me out of my bleak recollections.

'Is that the location?'

I had recognised the voice at once and spun round, spilling sherry down my new silk dress. He was of medium height, thickset, with dark hair lightly tinged with grey at the temples, and pouchy eyes. He had been dressed in a well-cut dark suit that sat uneasily on his heavy frame.

'Who are you? What do you mean?' My voice had cracked and wavered.

'You know perfectly well who I am, Mrs Carr. This constant denial is beginning to annoy me.' It had been said in such an affable tone but the humour beneath the surface had frightened me far more than any displeasure could have done. I had looked round wildly seeking for help and he had grasped my arm and swung me back to face the paintings.

'Don't forget your public, Mrs C. This is a social affair. A gracious smile to left and right would help your image.'

'How did you get in here? It is by private invitation only.'

'I've long been one of your admirers. Let us discuss this picture. I repeat the question: is this the location?'

'I haven't the faintest idea what you're talking about. What location?'

'Where your late, lamented husband made his discovery.'

'What discovery? I really don't know what you are on about. Whatever Martin is supposed to have found he didn't tell me. He is dead and the knowledge is in the grave with him, so please leave me alone.'

He had studied me through narrowed eyes then bared his teeth in a humourless smile. 'You almost had me convinced there for a moment. What are you holding out for – a larger share? I think fifty-fifty is more than generous. After all, the knowledge is of no use to you on your own. You need our help and expertise to profit by it.'

'Listen,' I had spoken forcefully, shrugging off the hand that still rested on my elbow, 'are you from M. & K.? One of Martin's ex-colleagues?'

'Dear me, no. Don't be so naïve my dear. Martin was onto something big and we, his friends, are anxious to see that the chance is not passed up; and to see that his sorrowing widow gets her share.' And he had actually winked at me in a suggestive way.

'Look, I don't know who you are, but you were certainly no friend of Martin's. He would never have had dealings with anyone as suspect as you and your associates appear to be. If you don't stop pestering me I shall inform the police.'

'But you have told the police and they don't believe you, do they? I shouldn't keep running to the police, Mrs Carr. We don't want to blacken Martin's reputation, do we?'

There was an interruption in the form of my agent who had appeared at my side with a query, and when I had dealt with that and turned back to face my persecutor I discovered that he had vanished. I had looked wildly around the gallery seeking him and at that moment my friend Lisa, a vision in leather and hopsack, had whisked up to me.

'Bethany, what on earth's the matter? You're as white as a sheet.'

'Lisa, you did believe me, didn't you, about the red-haired man and the phone calls? Well, he was here just now threatening me.'

'The red-haired man?'

'No, the other one who made the calls. I recognised his voice. He was intimating that Martin had been up to his neck in some shady deal with him and that I knew all about it. Don't look at me like that, Lisa, you do believe me, don't you?'

'You obviously believe it, that's what is important. Pull yourself together, we can't discuss it here. I'll come home with you after this, or what about you having dinner with me tonight?'

'My mother and father are staying over for a few days. I don't want them to know anything about it, they're worried enough about me as it is. Lisa, you don't think I'm going mad, do you? That Martin's death has made me flip?'

'Rubbish, you're as sane as me underneath. Your

bereavement has just undermined your confidence. Look, what about dinner at Luigi's next Wednesday? Eight o'clock?'

Somehow I had got through the rest of that morning. The exhibition had been a great success. I sold a lot of pictures and received several commissions, one of which had seemed like the hand of fate intervening in my future.

The following Wednesday had seen me at Luigi's facing Lisa across a stripped pine table. We had eaten an excellent meal during which we had chatted desultorily about this and that, carefully avoiding my obsession with threatening phone-calls and mysterious men, red-haired or otherwise. We had reached the coffee stage and as I toyed with my capuccino I had wondered what form her attack would take. It came as a surprise.

'Bethany, you must get away. Have a holiday, a complete break.'

'You think I have been hallucinating?'

'No-o.' She had looked worried. 'I think perhaps you have been the victim of a cruel hoax, but you have blown it up out of all proportion. It's understandable – the dreadful trauma of Martin's death, and you have been working too hard.'

'I have to work. Don't you see, my painting is the only thing that has kept me sane?'

'Yes, but you've been doing too much. Get away, go somewhere new and try to forget.' At least I now had some ammunition to counter her attack.

'I am going away, I was going to tell you.'

'Good girl, where?' I had put off telling her. 'It's a working holiday. Now don't look like that, I need to paint. I couldn't sit on a beach all day long and do nothing. That way I really would go mad.'

24

'Perhaps you're right. Tell me more.'

'It's Gerhardt and Frobisher, the publishers. They are doing a series of detailed flora studies of the islands of the British Isles. They have asked me to undertake the illustrations for one of them. It is a great honour.'

'I suppose so. Which island do they want you to do?'

There had been no help for it. 'The Scillies.'

'The Scillies? Now I know that you're mad. You can't really be serious?'

'Perfectly. I can't possibly turn down an opportunity like this.'

'Why can't you do one of the other islands? Arran, Skye, or better still, the Orkneys or Shetlands?'

'They know that I have been to the Scillies and that is the one I have been asked to work on. Besides, I really want to go.'

'No, I can't believe that. It will crucify you, Bethany, going back to the place where you spent your honeymoon and such a short while ago. You will have to turn down the offer.'

'I have already accepted. I have to go. There is some mystery about Martin's death and it is connected with the Scillies. I just know that I must go back.'

Lisa fights hard even when she knows that she is losing. 'You don't actually need to go to the Scillies – surely you can find the same flowers in Cornwall and the West Country?' I had murmured something about hottentot figs and three-cornered leeks. 'That's ridiculous. I saw a whole glade of three-cornered leeks at Versailles last spring.'

Lisa constantly surprises me. She is so urbane, cosmopolitan, that one hardly expects her to know the difference between a daisy and a buttercup and then she comes out with a remark like that.

She pressed home her advantage. 'Surely you've left it

25

a little late? A lot of the spring and early-flowering plants will be over by now.'

'Yes, that's true. It's going to extend over a longer period than we had at first envisaged, but I hope to be there by early June and I shall still catch a large proportion of the flowering season.'

She had argued and pleaded with me but I had been adamant. Although I knew that she was right, yet something, some unnamed compulsion, was driving me back to the Scillies. I would paint every damn flower and plant, known and unknown, and I would come to terms with Martin's death.

In the few weeks whilst I pored over details of my forthcoming trip and made plans to shut up the flat the threatening phone-calls ceased. I still had the feeling from time to time that I was under observation, but my fears had receded to the background, and it wasn't until last night when the red-haired man had swum back into my orbit again, that my fears came crowding back. I *was* still being followed, the red-haired man was aboard the *Scillonian*.

I gulped the last of my coffee and looked warily around the saloon. A few tables away sat the dark-haired man who had witnessed my short burst of lost control up on deck earlier. He was still studying me carefully and when he saw me look at him he raised his cup and silently saluted me. I got to my feet and staggered as the floor rose and tilted sharply. I must get up on deck. I rebounded off tables and chairs as I made my way towards the stairs and it was with relief that I reached the sunlight again. The wind whipped through my hair and snatched at the scarf at my neck and I sat down hurriedly on one of the slatted seats facing the bows. A shadow fell across me and I glanced upwards. The dark-haired man had followed me

26

up on deck. I lurched to my feet and tried to move away but at that moment the ship gave a horrible plunge and I fell against him and together we rolled back against the seat in a tangle of limbs. I struggled to extricate myself, aware of his hands on my shoulders and a pair of golden-brown eyes laughing at my discomfort.

'Are you all right?'

'Yes, thank you', I said stiffly, trying to edge away from the grip he seemed in no hurry to relinquish.

'Do you remember me?' I stared at him in growing alarm as he went on: 'I should like to have a few words with you.' So *he* was one of them.

'I don't know you, please leave me alone.' I managed to pull away from him and fled back along the deck, miraculously fitting my movements to the plunge and roll of the ship.

I spent the remainder of the journey locked in the Ladies, and I did not venture up on deck again until the *Scillonian* rounded Penninis Head and sailed up The Road to St Mary's Harbour.

Chapter Two

It was just as I had remembered it. Rat Island, now firmly joined to the main island by the long arm of the quay with its customs house, restaurant and storage buildings; Town Bay at half-tide, its wide crescent of sparkling water alive with dinghies and craft of all descriptions, backed by the long curve of sand and the grey and white stone houses that rose from the very beach itself. To the left, the lifeboat house and behind it the Buzza Tower and to the right, rising above tiers of granite houses, Garrison Hill crowned by Star Castle.

I waited quietly, well-hidden by a crowd of passengers during the whole paraphernalia of docking, bitter-sweet memories flooding through me. I almost expected to hear Martin's voice at my side pointing out the various landmarks. It was customary for the passengers' cases and heavy luggage to be loaded onto an open truck and dropped off at the various hotels and guest-houses dotted around Hugh Town. I passed mine over and started the trek along the quay. Then I saw the dark-haired man again. He was standing by the truck looking at the labels of the cases stacked that side. I was convinced that he was searching for my case, seeking out my address. He obviously knew my name and I watched helplessly, seething with anger, as he got closer to my case which perched precariously in the back nearside corner. At that moment the truck's engine sprang to life and the man jumped back as it swung away and trundled along the quay. He shrugged his shoulders, picked up his battered old grip, and started off in its wake. I hung back until he was well ahead and only then did I follow the crowd of passengers that was fanning out along the quayside.

On our honeymoon Martin and I had stayed at Tregarthen's, the luxurious, old-established hotel that nestled at the foot of Garrison Hill overlooking the harbour. I tore my eyes away from its gleaming white frontage and hurried past the Mermaid Inn which spilled noise and people from its lunchtime trade out onto the cobbled street. I had a climb in front of me. I had booked to stay at a house in Sallyport, much further up the hill, that offered half-board accommodation. I had been promised, in addition to my bedroom, a large room with plenty of light in which to work.

As I trudged uphill, I marvelled anew at the riot of flowers proliferating everywhere; spilling over from the cottage gardens and cascading down the stone walls. Swags of red and coral geraniums, orange gazanias and pink, peach and magenta mesembryanthemums clashed gloriously in the midday sun, and tall blue echiums stood sentinel looking like something thought up by John Wyndham.

I found the cottage easily enough. It was tucked away under the lea of the Garrison Wall that actually formed its back boundary. It was approached by a series of steps leading up past terraced gardens over which fuchsias dripped their crimson and purple flowers. They were enormous specimens, gnarled and twisted from years of sturdy growth, never cut down by frost like their counterparts on the mainland. Pink geraniums festooned the grey

29

walls reaching from ground level to the roof like climbing roses.

Mrs Pethick, my landlady, was waiting to greet me. I discovered later that she was not a native of the Scillies but had come originally from Cornwall. She had lived in St Mary's for over thirty years, her husband had died ten years ago, and her only daughter had married and moved to the mainland. She was short and stout with grey hair and faded blue eyes but she moved briskly and had soon swept me indoors and shown me to my bedroom to the accompaniment of a constant barrage of comments. She noticed my wedding ring almost at once.

'You've left your husband behind?'

'I'm a widow, Mrs Pethick.'

'A widow? And so young – what a tragedy. But you've come here to work, haven't you?'

'Yes, as I told you in my letter, I've come to make a study of the flora of these islands; to paint them for a book which is to be published.'

'You'll like the upstairs room. I've had artists staying here before.'

'Do you take a lot of guests?'

'Not regularly. My daughter and her husband and family come back a lot. She'll be wanting the rooms in late June.'

'I shall be back and forth between the mainland and here. I can probably arrange my painting sessions to fit in with the times when she is not here.'

'As long as you realise that the rooms are not available all the time.' She ushered me up the stairs and pushed open the door at the top. 'Here's your studio. There's a gas-ring and a sink so you can make yourself a cup of tea when you want.'

But I was not interested in such domestic details. I was staring spellbound round the room. It was long and rectangular, running the length of the cottage from back to front, built into the roof itself with sloping ceilings and dormer windows at either end. It was the window facing east that drew my attention. It had a panoramic view of Hugh Town. To the left was Town Bay spread out in all its glory; to the right Porthcressa Bay with Penninis Light on the far headland and between, on the narrow isthmus separating them, the town spilled out, layer upon layer of granite houses roofed in gleaming slate. Opposite on the hill that climbed up from the other end of the town stood the church with its square tower and behind it the cluster of pines that marked the edge of the airport.

'What a fantastic view. I'm going to have a hard job concentrating on flowers with that before me.'

'It's not bad,' conceded Mrs Pethick grudgingly, 'but don't go out and leave those windows open. The weather changes very quickly here and a storm can blow up and flood half the room before you know it. What time do you want your breakfast?'

'Actually,' I said, looking round the room and taking in the cooking facilities, 'I can manage up here. I don't eat much breakfast, only coffee and toast, and I can brew up when I feel like it, if that's all right with you?'

'Yes, that suits me. I'll cook you your main meal at night or you can have it at midday if you like. Just let me know when you want it or if you are eating out.'

'Thank you, Mrs Pethick, that will be fine. Tell me, has this island altered much in the last couple of years?'

'You've been here before, have you? I don't think you'll notice much difference. A couple more shops perhaps, for the benefit of the tourists, and more cars. No, they still don't allow visitors to bring their cars over,' she had caught my look of enquiry, 'but the locals are getting more and more motorised. It's not necessary.' She spoke disapprovingly. 'And all the young lads are into

31

motorbikes. You can't believe the noise they make roaring around the place.'

I could well believe it knowing how sound carried over these islands and stretches of water.

After she had left me I studied the room more closely. The window at the other end of the room was on a level with the top of the Garrison Wall which blocked almost the entire outlook. As I looked out I saw heads and shoulders moving along above the top of the granite blocks and I realised that the Garrison Path was only a few yards from the back of the cottage. The room was comfortably furnished. There was a large studio couch along one wall spread with many-coloured cushions and a couple of easy chairs. There was a table and chairs near the west-facing window, a low table in front of the east window, and a large desk nearby. The wall which contained the electric fire was fitted with bookshelves and there were plenty of lamps dotted about. It was comfortable to the point of luxury and I knew I could work here happily. I flexed my fingers and itched to start painting. After I had unpacked I decided to venture into town and get a meal; it was a long time since I had eaten. As I ran down the stairs, Mrs Pethick appeared in a doorway. 'I can give you a cold snack – salad and cheese – if you're wanting a meal. I expect you're hungry.'

'Yes, I am actually. That would be very welcome, thank you.'

It was later in the afternoon when I walked down Garrison Lane intent on renewing my acquaintance with the town. I lingered at Mumford's the newsagents, and bought a map of the islands, and wandered along The Strand past familiar shops and landmarks. Towards the end of The Strand, facing across the road to Town Beach, were two shops I didn't remember seeing on my previous visit. One was a ships' chandlers and next to it a shop called The Treasure Cave. The window was crammed with nautical *bric-à-brac*; ships' lanterns, model ships, coins and medallions, books, maps and pictures. I promised myself a thorough browse at a later date and re-traced my steps along The Strand, through Hugh Street, past the Atlantic Hotel and down to the quay. The launches that carried visitors to the off-islands each day were returning to the harbour, disgorging their passengers who displayed a wide variety of suntanned flesh ranging from deep mahogany to boiled lobster pink. I had forgotten how powerful the sun rays were here, reflecting off the blinding white sands through crystal-clear air.

Along the quay, propped up near the booking kiosk were boards advertising excursions to the off-islands – Tresco, St Martin's, St Agnes, Bryher and Samson, and the names of the launches making each trip – *Britannia, Golden Spray, Sea King, Swordfish II* . . . As I ran my eye over the familiar names I felt a lump rise in my throat and I blinked angrily. A tubby little boatman, almost as broad as he was high and several inches shorter than me, accosted me. 'Where do you want to go, me dear? I'm running a trip to St Agnes this evening.'

'Another time perhaps.' I walked back into the town feeling alone and alien amongst the crowd of happy holidaymakers, laden with cameras and rucksacks, that thronged around me.

I enjoyed an excellent meal cooked by Mrs Pethick and decided to have an early night; but first I had another pilgrimage to make, another ghost to lay and until I had achieved this I knew that I could not face the next few weeks in these islands with any equanimity. I changed into jeans and a warm shirt, hung my camera round my neck, and set out. Up the steep, uneven flagstones of Garrison Hill I trod, post the entrance to Tregarthen's Hotel and under the massive gatehouse leading to Star Castle –

built during the reign of Elizabeth I and so called because it was designed in the shape of an eight-pointed star. It is now an hotel and I walked up the hill following the path that led past the castle and becomes part of the Garrison Walk; a rough, well-trodden path that encircles the Garrison Hill, or Hugh, to give it its proper name; and from which one gets superb views of the ever-changing sea and the off-islands.

This is a favourite walk for all visitors, an almost obligatory evening promenade, the culmination of which is to watch the sun setting in all its glory between the twin humps of the island of Samson. Martin and I had been no exception to this rule, and had spent many blissful hours walking along here. If any one place could epitomise for me the true beauty and enchantment of these islands; if one view haunted my memory more than any other, it was this scene now spread out before me. The cliff dropping away in a tangle of bracken, gorse and bramble to the sea which shimmered like a pearly, opalescent mirror now that the wind had dropped. The arching sky glowing pink and gold through which a hazy sun dipped towards the horizon; and the islands themselves silhouetted against the serene sea and sky; whilst behind me the dark mass of Star Castle loomed against the coming twilight.

With grim determination, I picked my way along the uneven path, trying to ignore the courting couples, arms entwined, and the family groups towing children in their wake. Everywhere was the scent of honeysuckle. It rioted in cream and gold abundance amongst the scrub bordering the path, and the air was heavy with its perfume. A thicket of Monterey pines, wind-bent and stunted, the twisted trunks and lower branches covered with grey-green lichen, ran along the landward side of the track and from this spilled the song of a thrush. The liquid cadences soaring into the still air nearly proved my undoing. With aching throat and heavy eyes I forced my footsteps onward. The path curved downwards and soon I was facing south and could see the island of St Agnes across St Mary's Sound. To the right of it was the little island of Annet, glowing faintly pink from its cover of thrift, and beyond that, the Western Rocks and the thin pencil of the Bishop Rock Lighthouse rising sentinel out of the silver sea. How innocuous those rocks looked, just a proliferation of black smudges in the water, but how treacherous they were in rough weather. This area was the worst graveyard for shipping in the whole of the British Isles.

I turned back and re-traced my steps. As I drew adjacent to Star Castle I stopped to watch the sunset again. There would be no sensational dousing of the sun behind Samson this evening. A thin line of purple cloud hovered above the horizon. In all that wide expanse of sky it was the only bank of cloud in sight but it hung low waiting to obliterate the golden orb sinking towards it. This had happened time and time before when Martin had tried to photograph the sunset. I remembered him resting his camera on the very boulder I was now leaning against, fiddling with his exposure meter and alternatively cursing and laughing as the sun fizzled out like a damp squib.

Then I did cry. I leaned back and the tears coursed silently down my face. I had forgotten all about the mystery surrounding Martin's death and my persecution by a consortium of unknown men. I did not see the eyes that watched me from the battlements of Star Castle.

Surprisingly enough I slept well that night, possibly due to sheer exhaustion, and I awoke the next morning to brilliant sunshine. It was going to be a hot day although there was still a stiff breeze, and I determined to start work. I had already drawn up lists of all the various wild flowers that I hoped to find and a corresponding list of their habitats and the most likely islands on which to locate each one. Heading that list was a small, insignificant little flower, which nevertheless had priority. It was the dwarf pansy, *Viola kitaibeliana*, and it grew only in these islands, being unknown on the mainland – so much for Lisa's theory – and its flowering season was just about over. It grows on coastal turf and sand-dunes and is restricted to Bryher and Tean where it blooms in April and early May, though later-flowering plants sometimes straggle on into late May and June. It had been pointed out to me on my previous visit, growing in a valley in the south of Bryher and I decided that I would go over to Bryher and try and find it.

I packed my sketching block, paints and pencils into a small rucksack with some sandwiches and a thermos, and walked down to the quay. The water sparkled blindingly in the crystal air and I hastily donned my sunglasses and tied a scarf over my hair. I bought my ticket at the kiosk and wandered along the quay looking for the launch, *Swordfish II*, which was making the Bryher trip today. As it was low tide it meant a steep climb down to the bottom of the jetty and *Swordfish II* was moored on the outer edge of the pontoon of launches so I had to clamber over the others to reach it. Helping hands guided me and passed me over from one boat to another and I eventually subsided onto a seat near the bows from where I had a good view of the quayside and the holidaymakers trooping along it.

People were coming along thick and fast now and the launches were rapidly filling up. *Swordfish II* would be the first to leave and already the engine was ticking over, filling the air with exhaust fumes. They surely couldn't fit any more people aboard; one of the crew was preparing to cast-off, and then I saw him – the tall, dark-haired man with whom I had tangled yesterday on the *Scillonian*. He was walking rapidly along the quay but he paused as he reached the top of the steps and appeared to be searching each launch. I cringed behind a handy back clad in a plaid shirt but I swear he looked right at me, his gaze homing in and seeming to recognise me despite the sunglasses and scarf. He swung down the steps and across the bridge of launches with surprising agility. Please God let us go, I prayed silently as he moved closer and closer to *Swordfish II*. It seemed as if my prayer was going to be answered, for with a staccato phut-phut we slid gently forward; but there was an exchange between him and the boatmen, and some good-natured bantering, and the stern rope was held close until he managed to scramble aboard.

He settled in the stern, sitting up on the transom and stared at me across the solid phalanx of people seated between us. Like a mesmerised rabbit I stared back, hoping my dark glasses would hide my apprehension. His hair was sticking up in wild disorder and he squinted his eyes against the sun, drawing heavy eyebrows towards a formidable nose. He was dressed in open-necked shirt and jeans with a disreputable-looking denim jacket slung over one shoulder. I imagined he was in his early thirties and there was a suppressed energy about him that belied his casual appearance. He looked dangerous and he was looking for me. The knowledge was not comforting. For the moment I was safe; he couldn't harm me in a boat full of people but as soon as we landed he was going to tackle me. Thank God I was in the bows and should be one of the first ones off. Surely I could lose him on Bryher once safely ashore? Either that or I would attach myself to a group of people and stick to it like a burr.

The boat chugged through the translucent water throwing up a scattering of spray. Overhead a couple of gulls hovered lazily and we passed a line of shags perched blackly on a granite ledge. We beached at Samson to allow four people to wade ashore. Samson is an uninhabited island but holidaymakers are dropped off to enjoy a day of solitude and peace and picked up later in the day. I toyed with the idea of joining them, then realised that I would be a sitting duck if my pursuer decided to follow my example.

As we neared Bryher our skipper announced over the public address system that as it was an exceptionally low tide we would be unable to get in to the quay and he would try and beach us at Rushy Bay at the south of the island. Avoiding as if by a miracle the surging masses of seaweed that marked submerged or barely visible rocks we nosed towards the shore. There was a grinding crunch as we scraped over the rock but our boatman seemed unperturbed. We were asked to move back in the boat to redistribute the weight, and when we complied with this order and the boat was refloated, we crept in closer to the sandy beach.

'Half of you overboard,' announced the skipper jovially, 'then I can bring her in closer.' The people in the forward part of the boat began to take off their shoes and socks. I removed my sandals and rolled up my jeans, determined to be the first one off. A plank was run from the bows down into the clear jade water and I was helped down it.

'Didn't think you'd have to walk the plank today, did you?'

'You certainly don't advertise these added delights.'

The water was cold and came above my knees. I staggered, regained my balance, and picked my way carefully across the rock-strewn seabed followed by more of the passengers wading ashore. The dark-haired man was still wedged in the stern of the boat but he was on his feet watching my progress. I gained the beach and hastily donned my sandals, not stopping to dry my feet or legs and hitched my rucksack more securely over my shoulder. The launch was now backing off. With engine throttled back it reversed slowly into deeper water and was then brought in gently to nose against the line of rocks which jutted out to one side of the beach like a miniature, natural jetty. The rest of the passengers started to pile off. I had to disappear fast, and I hurried up the beach towards a grassy path that curved through a stand of bracken; then I hesitated and looked back over my shoulder.

He was perched precariously on a clump of seaweed-covered rock and he put his hands to his mouth and called after me: 'Wait for me, Mrs Carr.'

I hesitated no longer but ran along the track which led to an expanse of open grass, noting with a professional eye as I ran the sea bindweed with its deep pink flowers striped with white and the matt, fleshy carpet of hottentot fig out of which sprang the startling, artificial-looking yellow and magenta flowers. As I ran I tried to remember the lay-out of the island. My objective, the dwarf pansy, grew somewhere not far from here, near the freshwater pool that bisected this part of Bryher. That would have to wait. I would carry on northwards past Gweal Hill towards Shipman Down.

The island grew bleaker and wilder as I went north over the vast expanse of Shipman Head Down where open heathland was scattered with large outcrops of granite. Surely up here on the cliffs of Hell Bay, so named because of the fury with which the sea hurled itself against the jagged, ferocious rocks, I would find somewhere to hide; some cairn or nook where I could creep and secrete myself. I was getting out of breath and had the beginnings of a stitch. I paused for a quick breather and glanced back. I had far out-distanced the other passengers who straggled in different directions seeking an idle, pleasant day in the sun. All but one, that is, who followed on my heels with alarming tenacity. There was no doubt about it – I was being pursued and the tall, lanky figure was surely gaining on me. I stumbled on, the breath sobbing in my throat. I had long since lost the scarf off my head and my hair streamed out in the wind and whipped in my eyes. I ran across springy cushions of thrift that were now in their full, pink glory and stretched as far as the eye could see; and slipped and slithered along the sandy, rock-strewn path, between rabbit holes and larger formations of weathered granite.

There was nowhere to hide. I was fully exposed as I scrambled up and down that vast, undulating expanse. I would try to reach Shipman Head, the gigantic granite formation that lies at the northern tip of Bryher. Except at very low tide it is cut off from the island by a narrow gully through which a maelstrom of water rages from Hell Bay. It was low tide this morning though the tide was now coming in. I had some mad idea of getting across before it was cut off by the tide-race.

I pounded on along the track that led round the cliff-top curve of Hell Bay. There was a westerly wind today and Hell Bay was living up to its reputation. The sea roared and pounded onto the uncovered rocks, throwing up sheets of spray that scintillated in the sunshine and foamed across the black granite. Even at low tide the noise was deafening, drowning out the cries of the sea-birds who surged backwards and forwards with the flow.

I had reached the summit of Shipman Head Down and before me the ground fell away in dizzying cascades of rock towards the chasm that separated the Head from the Down. I stopped my precipitate flight and sought a way down the rocks and across. A quick glance over my shoulder showed my pursuer drawing ever closer. He waved his arms and mouthed something that was inaudible to me. Fear drove me on to the point of recklessness. I leapt down that spill of rock in a foolhardy way that should have resulted in a broken ankle at least, but luck was with me that day. As I teetered and ricocheted from one slippery rock to another I frequently stumbled and tripped but I kept going. The tide was coming in fast now and the narrow channel was widening. I was never going to get across. A shout and a stream of dislodged pebbles behind me provided the spur. Gathering all my strength I launched myself across that terrifying gap. For a few seconds I didn't think I was going to make it. My outflung hands scrabbled futilely at the rock surface and my feet slipped into the racing water, but I gained a hold and slowly and painfully dragged myself inch by inch up the rockface, my rucksack banging at my side.

I had only just done it. Even as I crawled thankfully to a stop, trembling with reaction, there was a louder roar from behind me and with a crescendo of noise a wall of surging water boiled through the chasm. If I had slipped I would have been swept halfway to Menavour by now. Shipman Head was well and truly cut off from Bryher and I with it. I was also, of course, trapped. No-one could now get to me but neither could I escape. My pursuer made no attempt to follow me, wise man. He had no need. All he had to do was wait. Wait until the tide went out again and he could join me, or stay until I gave up and ventured back again. I could not stay on Shipman Head for ever more. As these chilling thoughts went through me I watched to see what he would do. He swung himself down the rocks agilely, in no hurry now, and as he faced me across the torrent that separated us I declare that he was grinning in genuine amusement. I glared at him and scrambled further up the rockface.

His voice followed me: 'Bethany! Bethany Carr!' The wind snatched the words and tossed them about and the seagulls joined in so that the very air seemed alive with my name, echoing round the headland. 'Bethany, Be-ethany C-aarr!'

I gulped and tried to ignore him but he persisted.

'Bethany Carr, you're a reckless young woman. I'm not staying to argue with you. I'll meet you in the Shipwreck Bar at nine o'clock this evening.' And to my utter astonishment he turned round and proceeded to climb back the way he had come without a backward glance. Very soon I was completely alone. He had disappeared out of sight and I was left with only the seagulls for company; the seagulls and the turmoil of my thoughts.

Who was he? What did he want? Why had he chased me in what had seemed to me to be a life and death pursuit, only to toss out a casual invitation to meet him at a local bar? And why had he walked off without another word leaving me completely marooned?

I glanced at my watch but it had stopped. I guessed it to be around midday. I knew it would be several hours before I could attempt getting back. I clambered up the steep scarp of Shipman Head and settled down in a little hollow that was protected from the wind, facing eastwards across the inland water to the northern point of Tresco. I got out my sandwiches and was immediately mobbed by the seagulls. They plummeted towards me out of the sky shrieking and scolding and strutted around on their ungainly webbed feet, fixing me with their beady yellow eyes and daring me to eat all my food. As I fed myself and them, my fingers at great danger from their snatching beaks, I tried to sort out my thoughts. He must be mad to think that I would go to this assignation like a lamb to the slaughter. But as a secret assignation it didn't really stand up. He could hardly have chosen a more public place in which to ask me to meet him. The Shipwreck Bar was part of the Atlantic Hotel in the main street of Hugh Town. It was very popular with the tourists and was usually packed out. Any information he wanted to get out of me or to divulge would have to be communicated at the tops of our voices. It was most strange and I was puzzled. But I was equally sure that nothing on earth would get me to the Shipwreck Bar at nine o'clock that evening.

I decided to paint to pass the time. There were clumps of thrift and stonecrop clinging to the bare rock and the lichens were superb. I got out my paints and pad and water-jar which I set down on a flat stone nearby and started to work. Now that I was out of the wind it was very hot and the sun burned the back of my neck and shoulders through my thin shirt. I rummaged in my rucksack for my sunhat and accidentally kicked over my water-jar. I snatched at it but the contents had spilt and I watched in an agony of frustration as the trickle of water soaked quickly into the parched ground. After that I sketched the seagulls and grew more and more impatient as the hours slid slowly by.

Somehow, I made that terrifying leap back as soon as the tide allowed and started the trek back to Bryher quay. I moved down the eastern side of the island now, marvelling at the difference in terrain. Here were the cottages and farm buildings of the inhabitants with their bulb fields gently sloping down to the inland water. Across the sheltered lagoon was Cromwell's Castle lapping the water on the western shore of Tresco and, in between, Hangman's Island with its gibbet and noose, starkly visible against the blue and green background. This was where they had hanged pirates in days gone by. The contrast between this side of the island and the fury of Hell Bay was complete; I could have been in a different world. Clouds of meadow brown butterflies dogged my footsteps and a wren whirred in and out of the bracken.

As I neared the quay I wondered just how I was going to get back to St Mary's. It must be after six o'clock and the official launches would have left some time ago. I might even have to spend the night on Bryher unless I could bribe a local man to make the crossing with only one passenger. I reached the quay feeling windswept, sunburnt and decidedly peckish. The tide was well in and a small motorboat was moored to the steps. A man was bent over the engine and he straightened up when I hailed him. 'Can you take me back to St Mary's?'

'I reckon I can do just that. In you get.'

I stepped aboard, pleased at how simple it had been. The boat was a fishing boat, there was a pile of crab pots in the stern and a heap of nets. There was also an overwhelming smell of stale fish. I hurriedly moved forward and the man eyed me thoughtfully as he fiddled with the engine. 'Are you the young woman who got left behind?'

'Well yes, I suppose I am.' I must have looked surprised for he smiled as if secretly amused. 'Have you had a good day?'

'It turned out somewhat differently from what I had planned.'

He shrugged and started the engine. On the journey back I tried to engage him in conversation but he was taciturn to the point of rudeness and in the end I gave up and sat in silence until we reached St Mary's quay.

'Thank you very much; how much do I owe you?'

'That's all been taken care of.'

'How do you mean?'

'Your young man paid when he arranged for me to pick you up. He said I wasn't to mention it the other side in case you decided not to come.' I was speechless. The man grinned and helped me ashore. 'I suppose it was a lover's quarrel? Still, he must think a lot of you – this has cost him something.'

I still could not think of anything to say so I just mumbled my thanks and fled.

At half-past eight, having eaten and showered, I was still convinced that nothing would get me in the Shipwreck Bar that evening. At five to nine I was tripping down the hill to the Atlantic Hotel. I had changed into a cotton skirt and embroidered blouse and I wore high-heeled sandals and a careful make-up. I told myself that I wasn't really going to enter the bar; I would just pop my head inside and see what was happening; that I didn't have to talk to the dark-haired man at all . . .

The Shipwreck Bar was very full and very noisy. I paused just inside the doorway and looked around. It was a low-ceilinged room and the walls were covered with murals and photographs of local wrecks. The bar counter took up most of one wall and opposite it was a wall of glass panels and doors that led onto a balcony built right out over Town Beach. The crowds were very animated; strikingly suntanned men and women gesticulated and laughed and conversed in loud tones, and the air was heavy with smoke. I was suddenly very aware that I was a single unit where once I had been half of a pair. As I turned blindly for the door a voice spoke from behind me.

'What will you have?'

He must have been waiting for me, half-hidden by a pillar.

Against my will I heard my voice replying: 'A dry martini please.'

'Ice and lemon?'

I nodded and he pushed his way through to the bar. I studied him carefully. He had changed into a pair of slacks and a tee-shirt but he still looked as if he had been thrown together somehow. He was so tall he had to duck his head to get under the beams. Whether it was this superior height or some air of authority about him, he managed to get served very quickly. He looked totally out of place amongst his fellow drinkers but this was not to his detriment. As he fought his way back to my side I was filled with panic and a sense of curiosity. Things were moving too fast but would I at long last learn the meaning of my persecution?

He handed me my drink and raised his. 'Well, Bethany Carr, here's to our association.'

I choked briefly and stared at him in perplexity. He smiled, wrinkling up his eyes and I noted irrelevantly that they were the colour of a medium-dry sherry. Around us people clamoured and pushed, intruding and persistent.

'We can't talk in here, let's go outside.'

As I hadn't yet managed to utter a single word, I thought this was rather overstating the fact, but he guided me to the patio door, opened it and we stepped outside. The silence was startling. Inside there had been a constant babel of voices; out here it was quiet and peaceful, the mild evening air lapping our senses and cutting us off from the bustle inside. The balcony was whitewashed with white wrought-iron tables and chairs dotted about. I sat down at one of these tables, clutching my drink like a lifeline, determined not to speak first. Let him do the talking; he had a lot of explaining to do.

He seemed in no hurry to begin. He sat down opposite me, stretched out his legs and dug a pipe out of his pocket. As he tamped and fiddled with tobacco and matches, recognition flooded over me.

'But I *do* know you!' I cried.

Chapter Three

He raised an eyebrow. 'Rory Patterson.'

'But you're the man who was at that meeting! The meeting at M. & K. just after Martin died. You were sitting in the corner, I remember now. You don't seem any more successful now than you were then – lighting your pipe I mean.'

'It's a serious business and needs to be approached with caution.' When he had finally got it going to his satisfaction he gave a long contented draw, then leaned back and gave me his full attention. 'As I was saying, my name is Rory Patterson.'

'And . . ?'

'And . . ?'

'You can't leave it there. What are you? What is your function at M. & K.? Why are you pestering me?'

'Let me just ask you a question first. Why are you so frightened?'

I looked at him in astonishment. 'Surely that's obvious. Ever since my husband died, and in such suspicious circumstances, I've been living in a nightmare world. You must know – you're part of it; anonymous phone-calls, being followed by that red-haired man, accosted in public, threatened; and now nearly chased to my death!'

47

'All I wanted was to have a conversation with you. I had no intention of precipitating that death leap. By the way, you got back safely?'

'Yes, it was most humiliating. You could have chosen some transport that was not quite so – so fish orientated.'

He threw back his head and gave a bark of laughter. Then he became serious again and leaned towards me. 'This persecution you have been suffering has nothing to do with me or M. & K. We are as anxious as you to get to the bottom of it. Tell me all about it.'

'Why should I? How do I know that I can trust you? You haven't told me yet what your connection is with M. & K. and Martin.'

He looked taken aback. 'You could say that I look after their interests in the world of industrial sabotage.'

'You mean you're an industrial spy?' I said coldly.

'Let's say I try and stop other companies from stealing our confidential information.'

'And you think Martin was engaged in some underhand business?'

'I think somebody else thinks so. That's why I want to know everything you can tell me. Start from the beginning.'

And so completely had he disarmed me that I did just that. He heard me out in silence, drawing gently on his pipe. I finally dwindled to a stop, then added as an afterthought: 'I may as well tell you, nobody believes me. Not the police, or M. & K. Even my friends think I am hallucinating.'

'Why should you be?'

This was somehow more comforting than all the false protestations I had received before.

'The red-haired man followed me over here. He was on the boat.'

'Are you sure?'

48

'I sometimes think I am going mad.' I got up and wandered over to the balustrade and sank down onto the stone bench-seat that fronted it. There was a large pot in the corner containing a tall bamboo plant and the fleshy leaves of an emergent agapanthus lily. A light breeze rustled through the bamboo shoots, the only noise on the still air. The water was creeping up the beach and at high tide would lap this balcony. As it was, the beach was criss-crossed by mooring ropes and the runnel marks left by keels. Across the water, above Porthmellon Bay, the moon was rising. It was a thin, crescent moon and a single star sheltered in its curve.

Behind me he got to his feet. He did not refute my statement; he must also think I was unbalanced. Instead, he asked if I would like another drink. He took my silence for acquiescence, picked up the glasses and went back into the bar. I did not want another drink. I wanted more answers. He still hadn't told me why he was here. Why, after eighteen months M. & K. were once again showing an interest in Martin and myself. And there must be some connection with the other men. I decided that I did not want him probing further into my affairs; there was something about him that disturbed me. By the time he returned with the drinks I had pulled myself together and was poised with some pertinent questions. But he forestalled me and took the wind out of my sails.

'I think the police have been got at.'

'What do you mean?'

'You reported the incidents?'

'In the beginning, yes. Lately I decided there was no point.'

'Still, those incidents that you did report coupled with the suspicious circumstances of Martin's death should have alerted them to make further inquiries.

Instead, they closed the case and every time you contacted them they . . ?'

'Made soothing noises is the phrase you want, I think.'

'Someone made a good job of convincing them that you were hysterical and suffering from delusions; now why?'

'Because they didn't want the police nosying about any further.'

'Because,' he took me up, 'whatever they think you know, they and they alone want to be on the receiving end.'

'But I don't know anything – and what about?' I wailed.

'Oh, but I think you do. It's probably locked in your sub-conscious. Now listen', he enumerated on his fingers, 'Martin discovered something of great importance in the course of his work. I know he convinced you and himself that it was nothing to do with M. & K. but I think we must accept that he made this discovery in the course of his research. What this discovery was we have no idea but it obviously meant big money and was important enough for some rival organisation who got to hear of it to have no scruples in trying to get their hands on it.'

'You think Martin *was* murdered?'

'No, I think it was an accident. Somehow he got involved with this unsavoury crowd and when he refused to cooperate with them there was a scuffle and he accidently got knocked down and died. They tried to cover up by making it look like a hit-and-run accident. They must have been appalled at what happened – losing their crucial informant; so they fastened onto the one other person who might be expected to be in his confidence – you.'

'But I wasn't. He told me nothing; nothing of any importance.'

'He must have done, think!'

'Don't bully me!'

'Sorry, try and think back. How did he behave; what did he talk about at that time?'

'Nothing that could be of possible interest to you.'

'You don't trust me, do you?'

'Should I?'

He sighed and ran a hand through his hair which did nothing for his coiffure. 'I'm sorry, I've got off on the wrong foot, haven't I? It's getting late and you're tired. I'll take you back to your lodgings.'

'I'm not tired.'

'Well, I'm positively exhausted. Come on, let's go.'

I resented his high-handedness. 'I'm perfectly capable of getting myself back to Sallyport, thank you.'

I saw by the flicker in his eyes that he had not known where I was staying; and now I had told him. Oh well, what did it matter? I suddenly realised that I *was* tired. The events of the day had caught up with me. It was easier to fall in with him than argue.

We left the Atlantic Hotel and turned in the direction of Garrison Lane. It was almost dark and very warm, and there was a heaviness in the air that denoted a storm.

'Have dinner with me tomorrow night.' His voice quite startled me. We had been walking in silence. 'I'm sorry if I've been pressurising you. Don't let it worry you, but while you're working tomorrow try and think back and see if you can come up with anything significant.'

'You seem to know a lot about me.'

'I've made it my business to. How is the painting going?'

'My output so far is nil, thanks to you.'

'I have got a lot to answer for, haven't I? It must be hell for you, going back over Martin's death; can I ask you to do it?'

'And how. But I will. I am just as eager to solve the mystery as you, but for a different reason.'

51

'And what might that be?'

'To clear Martin's name. I know he did nothing wrong and I'm going to prove it, to you and all your associates at M. & K.'

'Let's hope you don't turn up more than you bargained for.'

'So you *do* think Martin was involved in some criminal activity.'

'Not criminal exactly, but I don't view him through the same rose-coloured spectacles as you, you know. He was a shrewd and very ambitious man.'

'I think you're quite hateful. Why should I help you? You still haven't told me exactly why you are involved.'

'I'm on the same side as you, you know. We'll discuss it further tomorrow evening. In this where you are staying?' We had reached the steps leading up to the cottage and my footsteps had slowed to a halt.

'Yes, goodnight, Mr Patterson.'

'Rory, please.'

'What sort of a name is that, for heaven's sake?'

'My mother was Irish and my father Scottish; they compromised. My mother was more at ease with Rory than Roderick.'

There was a roll of thunder in the distance and a flicker in the sky. I moved away from him and started up the steps.

'I'll pick you up tomorrow at seven-thirty.' I ignored him but he had the last word. 'Goodnight, Bethany Carr, and don't go talking to strange men.'

As I got ready for bed the storm rumbled nearer. Lightning lit the sky and the rain when it came was torrential. It beat down on the roof and poured over the edge of the guttering in a waterfall. I gave up any idea of sleeping yet and ran upstairs to the studio and threw back the curtains. From here I had a spectacular view of the storm. Fork lightning tore in jagged streaks across the sky above the town and the thunder crashed and rolled. I stayed by the window for some time fascinated by the aerial display, then I retired to bed. My last thought before I plummeted into sleep was that I didn't know where Rory Patterson was staying.

I awoke about eight o'clock the next morning, made coffee and toast, and wondered how to spend the day. There was a pink sun filtering through hazy cloud cover, painting the water in the harbour in roseate hues and reflecting pinkly off the rooftops. I did not think it would stay fine for long. There was a thud at the studio door as if something heavy had fallen against it. I started and regarded the closed door with apprehension. There was a silence, then another muffled thump and I cautiously approached the door and opened it a crack. It was pushed open and in stalked one of the largest cats I had ever seen. He was enormous; a black and grey tabby with yellow basilisk eyes set in a flattened head the size of a dinner plate. He regarded me steadily for a few seconds, then dismissed me and padded round the room carrying out a thorough inspection. In vain did I call and try and coax him; he totally ignored me; then he heaved himself onto one of the armchairs and with an almost human sigh flopped down and closed his eyes.

There was the sound of Mrs Pethick climbing laboriously up the stairs and she popped her head inside the door.

'Oh, so Percy's found you. I hope you don't mind cats.'

'No, I'm very fond of them. He's huge, isn't he?'

'Eats too much', she said tersely. 'He likes to come up here but if you don't want him just you push him out.' I seriously doubted if I could push him anywhere and she saw my expression. 'He's very gentle, he never puts his claws out or gets involved in a fight.'

'I shouldn't think he needs to. At that weight he must scare the living daylights out of every other creature; he wouldn't need to do anything. Oh, by the way, Mrs Pethick, I won't be wanting a meal this evening.'

'I'll cook you something for lunch. What storms; we don't usually get storms like this at this time of the year. There's been a lot of flooding and trouble over at Pelistry – electricity and telephone cables down.'

Mrs Pethick left me and Percy slept on regardless.

By ten o'clock ominous black clouds were piling up over Garrison Hill. From the other window the scene had changed from pink to black and white. The sky above Porthmellon had washed out to an almost ivory colour and the water gleamed silver. Below me the slate roofs were gunmetal colour and glistened darkly. It was very still and the horizon was very clear, especially in the vicinity of the airport. A few stray seagulls drifted past the window and I grabbed my water-colours and tried to convey with washes the luminous grey and white scene spread out before me. Then the heavens opened and the rain beat down again and soon the distant buildings and horizon were shrouded in mist.

By the afternoon the weather had brightened considerably and I decided to risk further storms and go out and paint. I walked to Old Town Bay and spent an industrious few hours painting and sketching. I was lucky enough to find a late-flowering wild arum in the lane leading down to the little church and later I moved along the shore and painted mallows and hogweed. I had a real find as I started back along the shore road; a clump of vervain, quite rare in the Scillies, and it was soon added to my sketchbook. So engrossed was I that I forgot all about

Rory Patterson and it wasn't until I glanced at my watch and found it was nearly six o'clock that I decided to call it a day. As I hurried back to Hugh Town the clouds were gathering again and I knew there would be another storm before long.

Against my will I was rather looking forward to my dinner date. It was so long since I had been wined and dined by a man; and a man who, though he could by no means be called attractive, yet couldn't be overlooked. I had nothing to tell him, no half-remembered knowledge that I had dredged up from my memory so I decided to enjoy the meal and forget the more serious implications.

I dressed carefully in a green and blue batik printed dress that had a full, flounced skirt and I piled my hair up on top of my head and skewered it with a barette. A pair of long, jade earrings were added and I went to town with eye make-up. Behind this façade I waited with thumping heart. Percy, after deigning to consume a large saucer of milk, had disappeared.

Mrs Pethick called up the stairs. 'There's a man down here for you Mrs Carr.' She spoke in tones of total disapproval. I snatched up my handbag and descended. Rory Patterson was hovering at the front door, firmly denied entrance by Mrs Pethick. His eyebrows shot up in an exaggerated show of approval as he saw me and I felt absurdly pleased.

'Thank you, Mrs Pethick. This is Mr Patterson. He's a . . ?'

'A friend and colleague,' cut in Rory Patterson; 'you'll be seeing a lot of me in the future, Mrs Pethick, as I shall be working closely with Mrs Carr.'

'You're an artist too?'

'Er – not exactly. More on the administrative side; the text, you know.'

'Oh.' Mrs Pethick was partially mollified but still suspicious. I felt her eyes following us down the path.

'You're a rotten liar, Rory Patterson', I hissed out of the corner of my mouth, 'and how dare you tell her that we're working together.'

'Well, she's got to get used to seeing me around. We shall need somewhere where we can talk and plan.'

'You don't think I'm going to invite you up to my rooms, do you?'

'Why not? We've got to have somewhere to meet. I'm not trying to make you; or would you rather come to my hotel bedroom?'

I glared at him. 'Where are you staying anyway?'

'At the Star Castle Hotel.'

'I wish I had your expense account.'

He responded by holding me away from him and giving me a close appraisal. 'So we go in for the sophisticated touch as well, do we?'

'I try to ring the changes.'

'Very nice, but I'm not sure I don't prefer the windswept, natural look.'

I snatched my hand away. 'Where are you taking me?'

'The Pilot's Gig. Does that meet with your approval?'

'M'mm, sea food. I'll put up with your company a little longer.'

The Pilot's Gig is situated in the basement of a tall stone building on The Bank not far from the harbour. As we walked down the steps the first drops of rain began to fall.

We were shown to a table in the corner near an alcove containing a cunningly-lit old black stove. I accepted a dry sherry and together we studied the menu. I finally settled on crab bisque followed by crayfish thermidor.

56

Rory Patterson stuck to steak and we compromised with a Mateus Rosé to drink.

It was a delicious meal and I did it justice. Rory Patterson was an amusing companion and the conversation was kept on a light, inconsequential plane.

It was raining heavily again outside. The door opened and a couple hurried in bringing with them a flurry of raindrops and a gust of wind. I savoured my coffee slowly, aware that he was watching me carefully.

'You're going to get very wet going back.' He indicated my thin dress.

'It will have stopped by then. After all, we have some talking to do, haven't we?'

'Here?'

'Why not? Nobody's waiting for our table. I'd like another coffee, please.'

When it came I sipped it with pleasure. 'That was a delightful meal. Thank you very much – now I suppose I must work for it.'

'That's unkind. You do me an injustice.' He spoilt the remark by almost immediately leaning forward and demanding: 'Have you remembered anything?'

'No, because I'm sure there's nothing *to* remember.'

'Try and think back. When did it all start?'

'I suppose after he came back from here, about two months before he was killed.'

'How did he explain his behaviour?'

'What behaviour? He appeared to be perfectly normal, apart from being excited about something he had found.'

'And he never mentioned what it was?'

'Only something to the effect that there was wealth lying about and I should be able to have gold-plated paintbrushes.' My voice faltered and he reached over and patted my hand.

57

'So, whatever it was, it sounds very much as if it were a natural deposit of some sort; now what?.

'Oil – gas?'

'But we're already working in the Celtic Sea. There are oil rigs only twenty miles off Scilly. Even if there were large finds in the vicinity I don't see how it would affect Scilly; it's not big enough to be used as any sort of terminal. They work from Milford Haven.'

'You're talking about undersea oil and gas. Supposing he'd found oil actually on one of the islands?'

'I should think that, scientifically speaking, that was not on. But just supposing it were a possibility; there's no way he could have exploited it himself. The big oil companies, including M. & K. would be snapping round like sharks.'

'What a horrible thought – drilling here on the islands. Surely it wouldn't be allowed. The Scillies have been designated as an area of outstanding natural beauty.'

'You'd be surprised what can happen when big business is involved. But I don't think it can be oil or gas.'

'What then? Uranium? Or is that a crazy idea? I've no idea how uranium is found or mined.'

'It's not such a crazy idea. There's uranium lying around.'

'Here?' My voice squeaked in surprise.

'There are uranium deposits in the granite here and in Cornwall, but the quantities are so small that it is not commercially viable to extract it. Besides, at the present time, uranium production exceeds requirements.'

'So no-one would be interested in exploiting it?'

'There's no current formal government uranium exploration programme, but on the other hand, there is no restriction on foreign and private participation in uranium exploration in the UK.'

'So it's a possibility?'

'I don't see how it can be. You don't just fall over lumps of uranium. It is found as a by-product of some other form of mining or in the course of drilling for something else. Martin hadn't set up his own private mining business over here.'

'But that would apply to anything else – tin, copper, silver, gold? I've even thought of diamonds. It's crazy!'

'Completely, viewed in that light, but there must be something. Martin was a very competent geo-phsicist. If he turned up something by accident, he would be able to recognise its potential value.'

'But what? We're back to square one.'

'It would appear so. Don't look so worried, perhaps something will turn up.'

'I don't see how. When are you going back?'

'Going back?' He looked taken aback. 'I've no intention of going back yet.'

'Why not? The trail has come to a dead end here. I don't suppose M. & K. will expect you to hang around any longer wasting company money.'

'It's not as simple as that.' He hesitated and appeared to be choosing his words with care. 'I'm on a sort of sabbatical at the moment, and I'm combining this investigation with my holiday. I intend staying for several weeks.'

'I see.' But I didn't. It all sounded highly suspicious and I thought he was holding out on me.

'How long is your commission going to take?' He asked.

'It's going to be spread out over quite a period – it has to be to catch the entire flowering season. Initially I'm here for a couple of weeks, then I must go back to the mainland to sort out some of my othe work. I hope to come back again.'

'Then we shall be able to keep each other company. You can initiate me into the delights of the Scillies.'

'I'm not on holiday. I have a tough work schedule to get through.'

'In other words, you don't want my companionship. I can't laze on a beach and watch you paint?'

'I can't stop you but I wouldn't be exactly stimulating company. When I'm painting I'm lost to the world.'

'Then I think you need someone to keep an eye on you.'

'You think I'm in some danger?'

'Your red-haired friend and co. are not going to give up now. They've followed you here for a purpose. Perhaps instead of you telling them something, they can enlighten us.'

'How do you mean?'

'They think you can lead them to the source of this discovery. You can't because you don't know what it is; but they must know.'

'I never thought of that. Of course, they must know what it is – so what do we do?'

'They're going to try and make contact again and when they do you must agree to a meeting. We must play it from there.'

'I feel like a sacrificial lamb.'

'I don't think you're in personal danger. You're their only contact; they're going to be especially careful in handling you after what happened to Martin.'

I shivered and he said with an attempt at lightheartedness: 'After all, you've got me around to protect you.'

I wasn't sure what sort of protection he could give me, or even if I should be protected from him. Against my will I found myself drawn towards him but I didn't trust him – yet. He sensed my unease and changed the subject.

'Where are you painting tomorrow?'

'I think I must go back to Bryher and take up where I was so rudely interrupted yesterday.'

'Shall I come with you?'

'No, please. I don't want any distractions.'

'Well, I shall hover round the quay in the morning and make sure you've not followed.' He saw the funny side of what he had just said and grinned.

'I thought you wanted them to contact me?'

'Not when I'm not around.' He suddenly looked rather formidable in spite of his unruly hair and sprawling limbs. 'I'll see you in the evening.'

'It's Friday tomorrow – the gig races.'

'I've been told about them. I understand it's the highlight in the week's social calendar.'

'Don't be so patronising. I certainly intend to watch the end of the race even if I don't follow it in one of the launches. There's great rivalry between the different crews and everyone gets very excited.'

'How many gigs are there?'

'Seven or eight, I think, but usually only five or six compete. I believe one of them is over 150 years old.'

'And they really were used to rescue shipwrecked people; the work of the modern life-boat?'

'Yes, just six oarsmen in an open, shallow boat. It's a terrifying thought, isn't it?'

'Well, as the world and his wife appear to congregate on the quay on Friday evenings I shall endeavour to join them and you.'

'Rory Patterson, hasn't it occurred to you that I might prefer my own company?'

'Why? So that you can wallow in self-pity? That's no way to come to terms with your grief. You're making this stay into some sort of pilgrimage; following the same paths that you took on your honeymoon; doing the same things; trying to relive the past. You've got to let him go and start again.'

'How dare you! How I live my life is no business of yours. Nobody asked for your interference and advice.

61

How could you possibly know anything about it, anyway?'

'You'd be surprised.' He was suddenly at a loss for words and there was an uncomfortable silence as we faced each other across the table. He lurched to his feet.

'Come on, it's time we were gone. You were right about the rain; it has stopped.'

I maintained an offended silence on the walk back to the cottage but as we drew near he spoke urgently: 'Bethany, I'm sorry, that was unforgivable of me. I can't ask you to forget it because I meant what I said but I've no right to preach to you. Can we start again?'

'Please leave me alone.' I brushed past him and ran up the steps. He stayed silently watching me as I fumbled with the key and made heavy weather of opening the front door. He was still standing there, a tall, thin shadow at the bend in the path when I hurtled upstairs and peered out of the window. I wrenched the curtains across and snapped on the light. Percy regarded me from his reclining position, spread the entire length of the studio couch.

'Percy! How did you get in? You certainly know how to look after yourself.' Percy yawned and extended a paw.

'Come on, my boy. It's time you went home.'

Percy didn't agree. He stretched, lowered his head and went blissfully back to sleep. I decided not to argue with him, but left him in possession of the studio whilst I retired to my bedroom. Several times during the night I heard him lumping about above me.

I went back to Bryher the next day. The journey was uneventful; nobody followed me, I saw no sign of Rory Patterson and no-one else showed any interest in my movements. I found my dwarf pansy; a dainty little plant with creamy flowers lightly tinged with yellow and mauve. I also painted sea milkwort found near Bryher

Pool and collected several specimens of more common plants to paint later. It was a hazy day, the sun filtering through layers of mist, though still powerful.

Whilst waiting for the launch back to St Mary's I paddled. The water was icy and I hoped it would soon warm up as I was longing to swim.

By the time I got back to the cottage the mist had thickened and there was a dampness in the air. I ate an early meal and Percy waited to accompany me upstairs.

'He has taken to you,' said Mrs Pethick. 'He ignores most people. Are you coming with me, Percy, and getting your dinner?' Percy regarded her through narrowed eyes, then flicked his tail and ran up the stairs ahead of me. As he reached the door he opened a pink mouth and emitted a very high-pitched mew. I shrugged my shoulders at Mrs Pethick and followed him. For such a large cat he had a surprisingly shrill cry. One expected basso-profundo and got falsetto.

I changed into navy slacks and a scarlet towelling top and pushed my feet into rope-soled espadrilles. At the last minute I grabbed my camera. It was probably going to be too misty for filming but I might be able to get some rather delicate mezzotint effects which could later be translated into paintings. I drifted down towards the harbour. Cinerarias in every shade of pink, blue, mauve and white grew in the gutters; they forced through drain grates and clung to crevices in the grey walls. I supposed that at some time they had been a cultivated species like the ones on the mainland growing in pots; but they had 'escaped' and were now naturalised to the extent that they grew freely everywhere, almost as common as nettles or dandelions.

A pair of herring gulls mewled and squawked on a shed roof like fractious children and as I walked past they took to the air uttering their alarm cry which can only be described as a low-pitched, forced laugh. People are congregating thickly on the quay. The gigs were racing from St Martin's that evening and although the launches had taken many holidaymakers out to follow the race there were still crowds of people waiting ashore to cheer the first gig over the line. The sun was a vast pearl swimming through a milky sky behind Rat Island, lightly describing a rosy path across the opalescent water. It was very still and very beautiful and I was glad that I had brought my camera. I snapped happily away trying to avoid being jostled, and then a ripple of excitement through the crowd indicated that the first gigs had been sighted.

I followed the surge of people to the other side of the quay. As the gigs pulled closer to St Mary's it was a freak sight that met one's eyes. Hovering over the surface of the water was a thick band of fog. Above this band of fog swam the disembodied heads and shoulders of the men and youths rowing the invisible gigs. Behind them in convoy came the launches and many other small motorboats, their crews and passengers in a similar state of levitation above their imperceptible craft. As they got closer, prows, gunwhales and oars took shape, rising ghost-like from a steaming sea.

The gigs *Serica* and *Nornour* were battling it out for first place, and behind came *Bonnet*, *Czar*, *Shah* and *Men-a-vaur* and *Dolphin* a smudge in the distance. There was a burst of clapping and cheering as *Nornour* shot over the line half a length ahead of *Serica* and I looked round to see if Rory Patterson was amongst the crowd; but I could see no sign of him, he must have taken me at my word last night. I shivered; it was getting cold, a damp cold that seeped into me, and I turned to go.

He was waiting for me. Where the quay turned at right angles and led past the Mermaid he stood. It was the perfect place to wait. Everyone walking off the quay had to

64

pass him, there was no other way apart from swimming across Town Bay. I even considered this. I suppose I had known all along that this confrontation was bound to happen. Over the last couple of days I had managed to push it to the back of my mind; had half persuaded myself that I had been hallucinating. Even when discussing it with Rory Patterson last night it had been more an exercise in hypothesis than a real possibility.

But now, when I suddenly saw him, his red hair showing up startlingly against the dark grey stone, I knew that this was the reality and that it was the events of the last couple of days that had been illusory. There was a chill spreading through me that had nothing to do with the dampness. I was shocked into awareness and with the shock came fear. Fear of this red-haired man and his confederates; fear of what they stood for, of what they had meant to Martin and what they intended of me. Forgotten was the need to make contact with them, I just wanted to put as much distance as possible between myself and that sinister figure awaiting me.

With this idea foremost in my head I pulled my hood over my hair and firmly positioned myself in the thickest part of the throng of people now surging back towards the town. It was useless, of course. He had probably had me under observation for some time; had been watching my every movement and had calculated to a nicety how he could pick me up as I walked unsuspectingly along. He even let me get past him. Then, just as I thought I was safe he spoke from behind.

'Mrs Carr, a word with you please.' I bolted. Past the Mermaid, across The Bank and along High Street I ran and I could hear him pounding after me. My one idea was to try and lose him somewhere in the town. I turned left after passing the Steamship Co. Office, down a lane that led into the Thoroughfare. Surely I could throw him off in that maze of little lanes and higgedly-piggedly buildings that backed onto the Town Beach. But he was on my heels and I swung back and tore along The Strand. The fog was swirling in across the water, shrouding the buildings, and I dodged round a corner and found myself under the sheltering bulk of the Methodist Church. I slipped round the back of it and paused. There was no sound of following footsteps. I leaned against the wall panting and gasping. Had I lost him?

There was nothing to be heard except the tolling of the bell bouy on Spanish Ledge out beyond Porthcressa Bay. Its muffled clanging floated weirdly in with the fog. It did not sound like a warning bell; more like the tolling of a death knell; monotonous, regular and infinitely sad. I gradually got my breath back and peered cautiously round the corner before moving stealthily across Church Street into Buzza Street and along that into Porthcressa Road. I could see nothing of Porthcressa Beach; neither sand nor sea, just a grey pall through which the persistent belling from Spanish Ledge could be heard, louder now and more desolate.

He joined me as I reached the car park near the Bishop and Wolf pub. He must have doubled back on his tracks and lain in wait for me. As I passed he materialised from behind one of the parked cars and pounced. I gave a little shriek and made a mad dash for Parsons Field. He shouted something after me as he resumed pursuit but I was in such a panic that I didn't hear. Up Parsons Field I toiled towards the other end of Sallyport, past a garden full of tall echiums that loomed menacingly over the fence. As I ran uphill I realised that I was leading him back to my home. Even if I managed to keep ahead he would run me to earth when I reached the cottage, would know where to find me in future.

I nearly despaired then, but suddenly remembered that

there was access from Sallyport to the Garrison Wall Path. Somewhere along here was the entrance. I scanned the buildings and gardens on the left-hand side as I fled, and almost missed it. A flight of steps led up a terrace to a block of flats through the middle of which was a passageway. I hurtled up these steps and shot through this passageway. My pursuer was right behind me; I could hear his laboured breathing very close to my back. There was a short garden to cross and then the path led through a passage that tunnelled under the Garrison Wall itself and came up on the other side. I plunged into this tunnel. It was dark and smelt dank; the walls, rough-hewn stone blocks, were oozing with moisture and the floor, made of the same stone blocks, was very uneven. it proved my undoing. I tripped and fell heavily and he was on me in an instant. As I struggled to get to my feet his hands were on me dragging me upright against him.

'Mrs Carr, this is getting beyond a joke. You've led us quite a little dance in the last eighteen months but enough is enough. It's time you came clean.'

Even in my panic I wondered if he always talked like that; a poor imitation of a Raymond Chandler gangster. Bereft of words I just stared at him. Close to he was even more sinister looking than my previous glimpses had suggested.

His red hair was slicked down with oil and in the dim light I couldn't see what colour his eyes were except that they were pale and protuberant. He was dressed in black trousers and a black leather jerkin that creaked with his movements. He looked as if he could be very nasty and would derive great enjoyment out of it. He shook me roughly. 'Has the cat got your tongue? Spill the goods.'

I felt an inane desire to laugh, petrified as I was. I gave a choked splutter and tried to escape his hold.

'Let me go or I shall scream.'

'Who's going to hear you in here? You and I are going to have a little talk, lady. It's time we had a heart to heart.'

'I have nothing to say to you. I don't know who you are, and I don't want to know. You're making a big mistake if you think I have some information for you.'

He gave me another shake that made my teeth rattle. 'You'll have to do better than that. What are you holding out for? You've already been offered half shares. I shouldn't be too greedy if I were you; the boss may change his mind. I reckon he's being far too generous.'

'Listen, how can I get through to you? I don't know what you're talking about!' I made a desperate effort to get away from him. I wriggled, broke his hold and made a dive for the end of the tunnel. He threw himself after me and slipped on the wet rock floor. He went down with an almighty crash and a string of oaths that echoed obscenely round the dripping walls.

I took advantage of his temporary immobilisation to make another bid for escape. I reached the steps leading from the tunnel and staggered up them. They twisted at right angles and were slippery and moss-covered. I nearly lost my footing and clutched wildly at the ferns that thrust out between the rock crevices. Then I was up on the Garrison Path and running blindly uphill past the Duchy of Cornwall offices and the cannon embrasures towards the castle gatehouse. Somewhere at the back of my mind was the thought that if I could reach Star Castle I would be safe. Rory Patterson was staying there and he would save me. I didn't think I would make it, but my pursuer must have hurt himself when he fell. I risked a look over my shoulder and saw that he was limping, and he peppered the air with curses as he blundered after me. Up I ran, beneath the archway and up the path leading towards the castle. There was no-one about; no-one that is, until the dark figure stepped out from the castle portals, right into my path.

Chapter Four

I cannoned into it and gave a little shriek that turned into a sob of relief.

'Rory! Thank God!'

'Christ, woman!' He staggered, then narrowed his eyes as he took in my appearance. 'What's the matter? What's happened?'

'He's after me – the red-haired man.' I spoke wildly and clutched at his arm. 'He followed me right from the quay and he's been chasing me for hours!'

'Are you sure?'

'I tell you, he manhandled me!'

'Go inside,' he gave me a little push up the steps leading to the main entrance, 'I'll be with you in a minute.'

'Rory, be careful, he's dangerous!'

He disappeared into the fog and I dragged myself through the doorway. This doorway didn't lead straight into the interior of the castle. There was an inner bailey that curved round the centre keep broken at intervals by the angled niches formed from the eight star points that had once housed cannon but were now furnished with seats and tables. I huddled on one of these seats and waited. It seemed like hours but could only have been about ten minutes before Rory Patterson reappeared.

'Did you see him? What happened?'

'There's nobody there.'

'You mean he's disappeared? The fog. . ?

'I went right down the hill in both directions. There's no-one about.'

'Don't you believe me?' My voice rose in mild hysteria.

'Of course I do. He must have got away.' But he looked at me rather oddly. 'Tell me exactly what happened; but first, a drink.' He led me through a doorway, along a corridor and down a flight of stairs into an underground vault. It was furnished as a bar and he sat me down and fetched drinks from the bar counter.

'What is it?'

'Brandy'

'I don't like brandy.'

'Drink it up.' I sipped at it reluctantly and although I disliked the taste I could feel it warming me as it slipped down my throat. He sat beside me swigging at beer and waiting for me to recover. I glanced round the bar. There was something oppressive about it although it was comfortably furnished and well-lit.

'What is this place, for God's sake? Was it a dungeon?'

'Yes. Don't tell me this is one place you didn't come to with Martin?'

'Actually no. Is your room in another dungeon nearby?'

'It's way up top. Why, are you inviting yourself to my bedroom?'

'It was a purely academic question,' I said crossly.

He laughed. 'I'm glad you're feeling better. Now what exactly happened?'

So I told him, every detail from the time I had

spotted the red-haired man until I bumped into him outside the castle.

'You weren't on the quay,' I ended, hastily adding, 'not that I was expecting you.'

'I was delayed.' He sounded as if he were going to say more but didn't.

'So much for our plan.' I was beginning to feel ashamed of my earlier panic. 'Instead of communicating with him I ran away.'

'My dear girl, I'm not censuring you. I didn't intend you to be accosted in some dark alley. Are you sure you're all right, he didn't hurt you?'

'I've probably got dreadful bruises on my arms but I managed to get away before . . .' My voice faltered and he put his arm round me gently. 'I don't know what he would have done. I was really scared, Rory; he seemed to be the sort of person who enjoyed violence for its own sake.'

'How old was he? Have you any idea where he comes from – had he any accent?'

'I didn't recognise any accent but he had a strange way of talking. He spoke mostly in clichés which he seemed to have lifted from old American gangster films.'

'Did he sound like an American?'

'No, I don't think so. I'm sorry to be of so little help but I was so petrified nothing like that registered.'

'Of course not, I'm sorry.'

I pushed away my empty brandy glass. 'I don't like it in here. There's still an atmosphere.'

'Don't tell me you're psychic as well.'

'I can just visualise what it must have been like in the olden days, prisoners chained to the walls, languishing their lives away with no hope of rescue. . .'

'I'd better take you home, come on.'

We were silent on the way back to Sallyport but I was

71

glad of his protective arm round my shoulders. The fog had lifted a little with the beginnings of a breeze but not many people were about. When we reached the cottage I handed him the key. He raised an eyebrow as he unlocked the door but made no comment, and I led him upstairs to the studio. After a quick glance round he made for the gas-ring.

'I'll make some coffee for us.'

I sank into a chair and watched him. There was something reassuring about the lean brown hands handling mugs and spoons, but he shouldn't be here. What was I doing letting a comparative stranger get so close to me? At that moment he turned and saw Percy who was stretched out in his usual pose on the settee.

'Ye gods! Is it tame?'

'I have been assured he is the perfect gentleman.'

'How ever much does he weigh?'

'About a couple of stone, I should think. Meet Percy – Percy, you have a new admirer.'

Percy opened one bleary eye and there was the merest frisson of movement in the tip of his tail. He was not annoyed, merely giving notice that he might be annoyed when he had had time to consider the matter. Rory handed me my coffee and threw himself down in the other armchair. 'Do you sleep on there?' He indicated the studio couch.

'No, I have a bedroom downstairs which is definitely out of bounds to you.'

'I was thinking more along the lines of sleeping across the threshold as in days of yore; for protection, you understand.'

'That will not be necessary, and Mrs Pethick would certainly not approve.'

I sipped my coffee and studied him furtively. Close to he looked older than I had at first thought. There were

72

lines etched in his lean, mobile face, and a wealth of experience looked out from his brown eyes. In this light they looked an almost golden colour with darker flecks in them. I thought he must be well into his thirties. He was completely at ease and when he had finished his coffee he produced his pipe and tobacco.

'Do you mind?'

'Make yourself at home; who am I to come between a man and his pleasures?'

As he struck the first match Percy suddenly sat bolt upright. I had never seen him move so fast. He stared fixedly at Rory Patterson and when the pipe was going nicely and coils of smoke were wreathing up to the ceiling he started to purr. I had never heard his purr before. It was an experience. If his cry was falsetto his purr made up for it. It rumbled out from the depths of his throat and reverberated round the room.

'Good heavens! You've made a conquest. He must approve of male company.'

'He's got good taste.'

Percy purred louder till his whole body was pulsating with the effort. Just when it looked as if he was going to rock himself completely off-balance he rolled over onto his back, stretched luxuriously and settled with his four paws sticking up in the air like an upturned table.

'He believes in looking after his creature comforts, doesn't he?' said Rory Patterson with a grin.

'Percy is as the lilies of the field. He toils not neither does he spin.'

'And what about you? You're not going to spend every day painting away like a maniac, are you? Take a day off and relax. I thought tomorrow we would go to Tresco.'

The sheer presumption of it took my breath away. Tresco was another rubicon I had to cross. Tresco was perhaps the fairest of all the islands, with its tropical gardens

73

set like a jewel in its crown, and I had been putting off returning there. Martin, our honeymoon and beautiful Tresco were all entwined in a bitter-sweet memory that I had yet to come to terms with. I must go back there, a part of me wanted desperately to, but not tomorrow; not in the company of another man. How could I explain any of this to the unfeeling man who sat opposite me sucking away at a pipe that had now gone out? I took the line of least resistance.

'Is this part of your big plan to lure the enemy?'

'No, it's not. Tomorrow is going to be a real holiday for you and me. Forget about our friends for a few hours. I don't think they'll bother you again so soon. You're looking peaky in spite of the suntan. Give yourself over to the pleasures of showing Uncle Rory around the tropical gardens.'

'I don't think so, Rory, thank you very much.'

'Why not?'

'Well . . .', I floundered, '. . . there are certainly some exotic flowers and plants over there but they don't exactly come under my terms of reference. They are cultivated, not wild.'

'That's exactly what I mean. I'm not talking about your work. Leave your paints and brushes behind for the day and forget about them. May I see some of your stuff?' Without waiting for an answer he got up abruptly and moved over to the desk where my sketchbook lay. He looked through it intently.

'You're good.'

'I'm supposed to be competent at my job.'

'When were these done?' He had found another book of sketches. The landscape ones I had worked up into full-scale oils and exhibited at my recent show.

'On my honeymoon.' The tone of my voice dared him to comment but I should have known better.

74

'You painted on your honeymoon?'

'Why not? Do you think we spent the entire fortnight in bed?' I glared at him, hating the amusement he was not trying to conceal.

'Hardly. In this day and age bed is not the novelty it used to be for honeymoon couples.'

'What do you mean?' My voice was ominously quiet but he ploughed on blithely.

'Well, everyone sleeps around nowadays and participates in trial marriages. The actual honeymoon must come as an anticlimax.'

'How dare you! I didn't sleep around, Martin was the only . . .' I could have bitten off my tongue.

'Martin was your only lover? I do believe you, Bethany, my girl; you're sweet and unique. But Martin?'

'What about Martin?'

'He was hardly the inexperienced type. But no, that was just like Martin. He wanted to have his cake and eat it. He was very much a man of the world but he wanted a pure, undefiled wife. So he took him a daughter of the cloth.'

The hateful voice flicked at me mercilessly. I knew he was deliberately baiting me and I fought for control. I ran to the window and leaned against it, my back to the room.

He came up beside me. 'Go on Bethany, hit me. Shout at me. Come alive!'

I swung round to face him. 'I seem to have run through the whole gamut of emotions this evening.'

'Oh God, Bethany, I'm sorry'. He put his hands on my shoulders but I jerked away.

'What do you want, Rory Patterson?'

'I suppose to get through to you.'

'You'd better go.'

He watched me closely for a few seconds then moved

back to the settee. He ran a hand negligently through Percy's fur and Percy purred, the traitor.

'I'll pick you up tomorrow morning. You bring the picnic and I'll take you out to dinner in the evening.'

'Are you always so unbearably high-handed? Talk about male chauvinism.'

'Of course not, but you seem to respond better if you're told rather than asked.'

I was speechless. I was still wondering whether to slap his face – though he would probably think that yet another example of my Victorian attitude – when he let himself out of the door and clattered down the stairs.

The next day was one of those glorious early summer days that only England can produce and of which the Scillies have more than their fair share, and Tresco spread out her delights before us. Contrary to my expectations it helped having another man beside me, and Rory Patterson was on his best behaviour. We spent the morning exploring the tropical gardens. They had first been established in the middle of the last century by one Augustus Smith, a somewhat despotic philanthropist whose descendants still hold sway on Tresco. The gardens are built of a series of terraces protected by thick shelter belts of ilex, cypress and Monterey pine and are crammed with an exotic collection of sub-tropical plants including many varieties of palms and succulents. The sun beat down on us and the scents and colours were quite overpowering. Blackbirds, thrushes, chaffinches and sparrows, surprisingly tame and unafraid of the human interlopers, flitted along the paths and amongst the jungle of vegetation.

'Look at that!' exclaimed Rory.

A small tree covered with bristly red blossoms bent over the path and nestling on one of its branches only about a foot above our heads was a young thrush. It watched us with bright, incurious eyes and made no attempt to fly away.

'That, I believe, is a *sapinodace*, the bottle-brush, tree.'

'Really? Let's find somewhere to sit and eat your picnic.'

'You're very sure I've brought a picnic.'

'I hope it's food you've been hugging for dear life in that bag, and not paints.'

We walked down the flights of steps leading from the statue of Neptune that crowned the top terrace and sat down on a small lawn under the shade of an apple tree. On Bryher it had been seagulls; here we were mobbed by a pair of golden pheasants. The female, a drab brown, saw us first and made a beeline for us. She snatched eagerly at the food offered her and, impatient at the dainty morsels held out in our hands, waded in and helped herself out of the sandwich box. Then her spouse muscled in having first drive her off with a vicious peck.

'I see female emancipation has not yet extended to the animal kingdom.'

'He's certainly got his pecking order right in more ways than one,' said Rory Patterson tweaking a strand of my hair.

'I'll not rise to that. Have you had enough?'

There was a sudden roar and clattering and a rush of air that disturbed the tops of the palms and pines. It was the helicopter coming in to land.

'You must get a very good view of all the islands from the helicopter,' said Rory Patterson laying back with his hands behind his head. 'I'd like to see a set of aerial photos. It would be interesting to see what shows up on them.'

'You're still thinking along the lines of some sort of

natural deposit? You think something could possibly be detected from the air?'

'It's amazing what shows up in aerial photography. I was thinking more of old mine-workings or evidence of former occupation. But all of that must have been studied already.'

'Perhaps there's hidden treasure buried in some old ruins somewhere,' I said dreamily, 'and a map marked with an X.'

'And a dreadful curse to warn off any who seek to disturb it,' he added, joining in the spirit of the thing.

'Oh Rory, this is quite ridiculous!'

'It's as good as anything we've come up with yet. Do you feel like having another go?' He sat up and studied me, suddenly serious again.

'At making contact? I suppose so, but . . .'

'I promise you, you'll be in no danger, I'll see to that. We'll find you somewhere to sit and paint – quiet and secluded but not overlooked – and I shall be waiting nearby, hidden of course. You just have to act as decoy, I'll take all the action.'

'When? Tomorrow? I was thinking of going to St Agnes tomorrow.'

'And is there anywhere there that would be suitable?'

'Ye-es, up on Wingletang Down near Beady Pool.'

'Beady Pool? What an extraordinary name.'

'It's called that because a ship with a cargo containing Venetian glass beads was wrecked there over two centuries ago and the beads are still occasionally washed up. There's a small string of them in the museum. There are several plants to be found there that I want to paint and it's ideal from your point of view – quite open, I can easily be seen from the surrounding terrain, but there are also plenty of rock outcrops where you

78

could hide. But how can we make our mysterious assailant fall for it? After all, nobody's followed us today.'

'I wouldn't be too sure. I don't think your red-haired friend is working on his own; he probably has accomplices. Don't look so alarmed,' as he saw my face and the frightened way I glanced around, 'I don't think we're surrounded here but there was probably somebody hanging around on the quayside at St Mary's noting where you went and who with. I think we must stage a public scene when we get back.'

'What do you mean?'

'Well, when we land you rush on ahead as if we've had a quarrel and I will shout after you something to the effect that I want to go with you tomorrow, somewhere or other and you will bawl back that you are going to St Agnes to paint and you definitely don't want me with you and I shall accept defeat. Do you think you can manage that?'

'I don't bawl,' I said coldly. 'I don't make scenes normally either, though I have come perilously close to it in the few days I have known you. It must be the effect you have on me.'

'Bethany!'

'All right. I will bawl like a fishwife and if there is anyone in Hugh Town who doesn't know our plans after that it won't be my fault.'

'Don't go overboard. Just a little realistic-sounding quarrel so that anybody listening will get the message that you're going to be unaccompanied tomorrow.'

'That shouldn't be too difficult – staging a quarrel, I mean. Most of the time I find you completely infuriating.'

'That's better than indifference.' He looked at me quizzically and I had the feeling he was going to add something else, something that I was not prepared to hear or think about.

I hurriedly packed away the remains of the picnic and

said lightly: 'Come on, or we won't have enough time.'

'Time for what? Where are we going?'

'You don't think we're going to spend the rest of the day lazing about here, do you? We're going to walk and possibly swim and explore some of the rest of the island.'

'Did you say swim?' He sounded alarmed.

'It's so hot. I can think of nothing better and I want to show you Cromwell's Castle and the northern part of the island.'

'Then let us away.' He got to his feet and pulled me up and I hurriedly disengaged myself and started walking.

We followed the footpath that ran up the western side of the island. The sun shimmered off the water and white sand, and a pair of oyster-catchers piped after us. Rory strode along on his long legs and made no concessions to my shorter ones. I panted after him and when we reached a particularly inviting stretch of beach I called a halt.

'This is the perfect place to swim.'

'You're not serious? You're not really going to swim?'

'Of course. It will be cold but bracing. Aren't you coming in?'

'Most certainly not. I hate water.'

'Then the Scillies were hardly the place to choose for a holiday.'

'I am subjugating my dislikes in the good of the cause.'

He followed me onto the beach, sat himself down and watched me with exaggerated horror. I was wearing my bikini under my shorts and tee-shirt and I quickly undressed and ran down to the water's edge. It was very cold but I couldn't back out at this stage. I plunged in trying not to gasp as the icy water enveloped me, taking my breath away. It was a very short swim but certainly refreshing. As I walked back up the beach he held out my towel with raised eyebrows but made no comment.

The rest of the afternoon passed quickly. We walked

on, round New Grimsby Harbour, along the path that skirted Castle Down, toiling up and down amongst heather and gorse until we reached Cromwell's Castle. We rested there and he took a photograph of me sitting on the cannon outside and then we climbed up through the bracken to the ruins of King Charles' Castle which huddled near the top of the hill. It was wild up there and windy, so very different from the sheltered south, and the curlews reigned supreme. We only just got back to the quay in time to catch the launch. Acting on instruction I sat apart from him in the boat and made a show of ignoring him but during the course of the journey he passed a note to me. It said simply: 'Come up to Star Castle about 7.30. I don't want to be seen escorting you, R.'

The boatman moved down the launch collecting tickets. He was dark and swarthy with light eyes and just for a moment as he passed near me his likeness to Martin was uncanny. For a few insane seconds my whole world shifted; then he moved and I saw that he bore no resemblance to Martin at all. It had just been a trick of the light but it unsettled me. I had a sudden terrible longing for Martin; it completely swamped me, and with it came the stirrings of guilt. Guilt that for a good part of the day I had not thought of Martin at all. I had been quite happy laughing and enjoying the companionship of another man, Rory Patterson.

With that knowledge in the forefront of my mind I had no difficulty in staging a realistic quarrel when we stepped ashore. I did not want Rory Patterson hanging around me, distracting me, during the rest of my stay. I left him and a large audience in no doubt about my feelings before storming off the quayside. I also resolved on the way back to the cottage that I would not join him at his hotel that evening. He had a cheek thinking he could summon me just like that and I would come running.

I had a snack when I got back and settled down with a book but he didn't give up so easily. Mrs Pethick called me to the phone. 'Where are you?' The blunt question without any attempt at social niceties needled me.

'I'm not coming.'

'Why not?'

'I thought the whole idea was for us not to be seen in public together anymore. It seems rather stupid to jeopardise our plan.'

'I don't think you coming here this evening would do that. By the way, your acting on the quay was superb.'

'What makes you think it was acting?'

'What's happened to you?'

'N-nothing.' I refused to say any more and there was a long pause; and then just as I thought he had rung off he said softly:

'Bethany, are you hag-ridden?'

'What do you mean?' I whispered, amazed at his perception.

'Martin's back at your elbow haunting you, isn't he?'

'I don't want to continue this conversation. What do you know about it, anyway?'

'Enough to know that I can't compete with a ghost. You win, Bethany. Stay at home and wallow in self-pity. I shall enjoy a solitary meal here and plan my movements for tomorrow.' I put the receiver down and slunk back to my room, furious with myself, with Rory Patterson, but most of all with Martin, whose untimely demise had led to all this.

The whistling jacks were blooming in the bulb fields. The magenta spikes of the wild gladioli, that had once been grown as a commercial crop but now colonised every cultivated strip and hedgerow at this time of the year, caught the light and glowed floridly as I walked down the lane towards Wingletang Down. Feathery tamarisks dipped over the path and in the distance a tractor rumbled. It was another glorious day, arching blue skies with just a few wisps of cloud and a warm, earthy smell permeated the crystal air.

As I walked I picked flowers from the hedgerow to paint later in the day, and wondered how many pairs of feet, if any, were trailing me. I had been careful on the boat across not to show too much interest in my fellow passengers. I didn't think a red-haired man had been amongst them but I wasn't sure. Rory Patterson had not been in evidence either. I suppose he could hardly have travelled in the same launch as myself; he had probably made arrangements to be dropped off at St Agnes later; he seemed to have the boatmen in his pocket. Perhaps after last night he had shelved his plan altogther.

Wingletang Down spread out before me and I walked south into the sun till I reached the vicinity of Beady Pool. I settled down in a grassy hollow amongst the rocks that swept down to the shore. Anyone looking for me would have no difficulty in finding me and I could see anyone approaching. I did not intend to hide away where I could be pounced on unexpectedly. Around me clinging to the rocky soil were clumps of various flowers, including the delightful little blue sheepsbit; surely one of the prettiest of wild flowers and the bearer of one of the ugliest names. I had plenty to paint and I settled down to some serious work and was soon lost to the world.

A pair of rock-pipits flitting along the tide-line in and out of the seaweed and rocks distracted me a while later. I stretched and stood up to ease my cramped limbs and risked a cautious glance around. Something blue caught my attention near a clump of rocks about seventy-five yards away. I stared harder and the owner of the blue shirt unfolded himself from behind his rock cover and raised an arm in greeting. So Rory Patterson had made it after all. I waved back and he disappeared again and I wondered idly how he would occupy his time on his long vigil. I hoped he had brought a good book with him.

I painted steadily until about one o'clock and then ate the rolls and cheese and fruit that I had brought with me. When I had finished I went down to the cove, kicked off my sandals and paddled and did some beachcombing. I found no beads. Afterwards I went back to my painting. No-one disturbed me. From time to time people would appear on the scene following the nature trail that runs round the coastline of St Agnes, but nobody came very close or showed any interest in me. The afternoon wore on and when I next glanced at my watch I decided it was time I packed up and started back to pick up the launch. Our ploy to make contact had failed.

I could see no sign of Rory Patterson, he must still be lying low behind his rocks. As I walked across the springy heather I put up a little ringed plover and a few yards further on I stumbled over its nest; three eggs laid in a scrape in the ground. As I got closer to where I had last seen Rory Patterson, I called but got no answer. He must have fallen asleep. Grinning to myself and planning how I would tease him about this lapse I rounded the rocks and pounced. There was no-one there. Bewildered, I looked around me. Lying a little way off was a rucksack, its contents scattered over the rough ground, but there was no sign of its owner. Beginning to feel uneasy by now, I retraced my steps and caught sight of a flash of blue out of the corner of my eye. I moved round the clump of rocks. He was lying face downwards, stretched across the rock-strewn ground in a most unnatural position; one arm outflung, the other doubled under him.

'Rory!' I screamed and plunged down the scree. He

looked completely lifeless and as I reached his side I could see a contusion on the back of his head sticky with drying blood. Convinced that he was dead I seized his shoulders and tried to move him. He emitted a heart-rending groan and I nearly dropped his shoulders and head.

'Rory, you're alive! Thank God!'

He gave another groan and opened one eye. 'God! Stop caterwauling, woman; it's enough to wake the dead!'

'I thought you *were* dead. Oh Rory, what happened?'

He tried to sit up. 'Someone must have slugged me. Hell, what happened?'

'Did you see anyone?'

'Nope. I was just sitting there writing, with one eye on you and that's all I remember. Did they get to you?'

'No. I've been sitting there painting all day and I saw nothing. Are you all right?'

'I shall probably never be the same again, but apart from that I don't think there's any permanent damage.' He struggled to a more upright position and flinched.

'That's a nasty place on the back of your head. It ought to be seen to.'

'Don't fuss, woman.' He squinted at me through slit eyes, 'A lot of good I was at protecting you.'

'Don't be silly, what could you have done? Somebody obviously saw through our little game and decided to put an end to it. Do you think they really meant to kill you?'

'It was probably just a warning to let me know that I'm expendable if you're not.'

'Oh Rory, they might have killed you.' I stared at him in consternation and he gave another little moan obviously enjoying my sympathy.

I could not resist asking: 'Are you sure it wasn't my imagination that hit you?'

'That's not fair, to hit a man when he's down and can't

fight back. I was quite definitely slugged very hard by someone who knew what he was doing; undeniably our red-haired friend. I've never doubted that he existed.'

He leaned back against the rocks and closed his eyes again. I hurried back to Beady Pool and wet my handkerchief and started on the task of cleaning up his head injury. He winced as I dabbed at his matted hair and tried to wipe away the clotted blood.

'I don't think you need any stitches. The cut is not very deep but you've got an enormous bump, and you'll have an almighty bruise when it comes out.'

'Leave it for now, Bethany, we ought to be getting back.'

'Are you capable of walking back to the quay? It's quite a way.'

'God, I could do with a drink!' He struggled to his feet and we slowly make our way across the Down. We passed a little cottage café on the way back and I persuaded him to stop and have a cup of tea. We sat outside at a table on the lawn under the shelter of an escallonia hedge. He looked pale and obviously had a thumping headache. After he had drained two cups he leaned back, stretched out his legs and regarded me ruefully.

'Do you know, I don't think I could even manage a pipe.'

'You must be feeling bad then. I think you ought to see a doctor.'

'Nonsense. I shall be as right as rain when I've had a good night's sleep. But we shall have to have a complete re-think about this business.'

'Don't worry about it now. They're obviously content to bide their time before approaching me again.'

'Perhaps they won't approach you any more. I've been thinking about it; in fact I was mulling it over this afternoon just before I was laid out.' He wrinkled up his brow in the effort of concentration and I realised he was very tired and drawn.

'Rory, don't bother about it now . . .'

'No, listen. When you had your little contretemps with our friend in the fog the other night, he said something about you having been offered a half-share in whatever it is if you gave them the information you are supposed to have; but that Big Brother, whoever he may be, might change his mind and cut you out altogether, right?'

'Ye-es, that's about the gist of it.'

'Well, perhaps they've decided not to attempt any more collaboration with you. They'll just keep you under observation and try and discover from your actions whatever it is they want to know and then they'll move in and take over. How does that strike you?'

'It's possible, I suppose. But when they've wasted hours and discovered me doing nothing more sinister than paint, what will they do then? Do you think they will then believe that I told them the truth when I denied all knowledge of Martin's activities?'

'I don't know, that's what is worrying me. For the present let's just concentrate on getting back to St Mary's.'

A strong breeze had got up and the water was decidedly choppy on the journey back. The pitch and roll of the open boat must have caused him agony but he didn't complain. I huddled beside him gasping as the bows dipped every so often and a fine sheet of spray drenched us. I sneaked a glance at him. His hair was plastered over his forehead, his mouth a tight line and his eyes like pebbles, a dirty opaque brown. We didn't speak. I walked up to Star Castle with him but he refused to let me go into the hotel and minister to him.

'I'm sure I shall regret this later but at the moment I'm not capable of really appreciating your services. I shall

87

soak in a hot bath, take several aspirin and collapse into bed, on my own, of course.'

'Of course. Actually that was not one of the services on offer.'

He gave a lop-sided grin and disappeared into the bowels of the castle and I made my way back to the cottage. For once Percy was in an affectionate mood. At least, he wound himself in and out of my legs and purred; but whether this was true affection or simply that he had decided that his food intake for the day was not yet up to par was open to speculation.

I had a nightmare that night. I dreamt that I was plodding endlessly through tracks of bracken and heather, desperately trying to get to Rory Patterson whom I could see in the distance lying lifeless on the ground. When I eventually reached him and turned him over he had Martin's face. I awoke feeling wretched and two large cups of black coffee did little to dispel the gloom. The weather echoed my feelings. It was much cooler with a freshening wind that drove fleets of cloud across the sky and threatened to banish the sun for most of the day. I made some toast and was drinking another cup of coffee when Mrs Pethick called up the stairs to tell me I was wanted on the phone.

'Bethany? How are you?' It was Rory Patterson and I felt a surge of relief. At least he was up and about and not suffering from delayed concussion.

'That's what I should be asking you.'

'Apart from a whopping bruise, as you forecast, and a definite feeling of incipient middle-age, I feel fine. You're not planning to go island-hopping today, are you?'

'I don't think so, why?'

'Stick around here today.'

'Why? Has something new come up?'

'No, let's just say I don't feel capable of "lepping" about after you at the moment and I don't want you to venture far without me.'

'It sounds like a bad case of Mother Hen to me. What do you suggest we do?'

'Bless you for the "we". I feel a distinct need of a gentle hand on the brow and all that. Any ideas?'

'I know just the thing; Vic's Bus Tour.'

'Don't tell me,' he groaned, 'another high-spot on the holiday-makers' itinerary. The death-defying scenic tour of the island, a thrill-a-minute, never to be forgotten.'

'You may take back those words so lightly uttered after you've experienced it. Vic is a CHARACTER in capital letters, and his bus tour is a phenomenon not to be missed.'

'I can't wait. Where and when does this take place?'

'I'll meet you near the Parade just before eleven. If he and his bus are not there his next departure time will be chalked up on a board. I hope you're a good traveller'. I rang off before he could reply.

Feeling in a much more cheerful mood I hurriedly dressed in jeans, tee-shirt and sweater, collected my camera and shooed Percy into his official quarters. I met up with Rory at the bottom of Garrison Lane. He looked none the worse for his ordeal and I think he had probably slept far better than myself. Vic's bus, resplendent in blue and cream, circa early fifties, stood at the beginning of the Parade and propped up against it was the cadaverous figure of Vic himself.

'God! It's practically a veteran!'

'There's no MOT on the island.'

'That figures.'

'You can be certain it's in tip-top condition and perfectly roadworthy.'

Vic unwound himself and waved us aboard, a long

cheroot hanging out of the corner of his mouth. The bus soon filled up; the reputation of his tour ensuring that each trip was fully subscribed. We sat near the front where we had a good view of the road ahead and an even better reception of Vic's running commentary delivered in a splendidly laconic manner, touching on everything from the life history of any unfortunate inhabitant whom we happened to pass, to titbits about the local scene that never made it into the guidebooks. He drove brilliantly in an utterly terrifying manner; mostly slumped one-elbowed against the steering wheel; the said elbow doing the work of hands and eyes, which were apparently completely dissociated with the business of driving. Tele-graph, Watermill, Holy Vale, Normandy slipped past and then we were rounding Old Town Bay and on the home stretch back to Hugh Town. Beside me Rory had relaxed and enjoyed the entertainment, chuckling to himself and attempting to photograph the scenery through the bus window.

It was spattering with rain as we disembarked and we hurried along to the Mermaid where we went upstairs to the restaurant and had lunch, sitting at a table near the end window which had a marvellous view of Town Bay. I tackled my scampi with quite an appetite and sipped at my lager while we discussed the morning's excursion.

'Well, I wouldn't have missed that for the world.' Rory pushed away his plate and produced his pipe. 'What further delights have you got in store for me?'

'The follow-up to that is a slide show this evening.' He raised an eyebrow and I went on: 'They have them on several evenings during the week in the Church Hall or Methodist Hall. They're usually on some aspect of Scilly life – natural history, shipwrecks; a photographic record of the Scillies. In fact, I noticed as we came past the Steamship Co. office a board advertising this evening's

90

show and it is about the wrecks and diving for treasure.'

'It sounds fascinating. Who puts on these shows?'

'They're all done by local experts. The photography is very good and these people certainly know their subject. I promise you you'll find it quite riveting.'

'I can't wait. If we get there early do you think we'll get a seat in the back row?'

'Rory Patterson, don't be so disparaging. There is no cinema on the islands but these slide shows are a most enjoyable alternative. I intend going, you can please yourself. Perhaps you'd rather prop yourself up against some bar and get drunk.'

'Those do seem to be the only two options open. All right, I'm sorry, ma'am, please accept my profuse apologies. I shall be delighted to escort you to the slide show this evening.'

'I don't know why you stick around, Rory. This is obviously not your scene at all. I should imagine you're more into intimate little dinner parties and sophisticated cocktail gatherings.'

'Like the one where you met Martin?' I must have looked flabbergasted, and he went on: 'I don't know where you get your mistaken ideas of me from, but you've certainly described Martin's predilections. It wouldn't have lasted, you know.'

'What wouldn't?' My voice was dangerously cool but he ignored the danger signals.

'Your marriage. This attraction of opposites is a lot of nonsense. It must have titillated Martin to have such an artless, ingenious young beauty as a wife but he would eventually have got bored and looked for pastures new.'

'I see,' I hissed, 'I'm such a simple, naïve, country cousin that I couldn't have hoped to have kept the fidelity of a witty, handsome, delightful man like my husband?'

'Bethany, you've got it all wrong. It's not you I'm

91

getting at. You're everything I admire but your qualities are not the sort to have been fully appreciated by someone as sophisticated and urbane as Martin.' He leant towards me and I glared into his eyes. Today they were like twin humbugs or butterscotch, quite horrible; however could I have thought them attractive?

'Listen, Bethany, you're fine just as you are, don't ever dare change; and don't try to make me into a duplicate of Martin.'

'As if you could ever measure up!' I was deeply hurt and lashed out in my distress, not least because his words had recalled all the old doubts I had had originally when Martin had first showed an interest in me. But they had been overcome and we had had a wonderful, happy marriage.

'I wouldn't dream of competing with your image of Martin. As I told you before, I don't tangle with ghosts. Now, are you going to sit there trying to do a Gorgon all the afternoon or shall we leave?'

'I feel sorry for you, Rory Patterson. You've obviously got such an outsized chip on your shoulder that you cannot bear to contemplate anyone else's happiness.'

'That's cutting a bit close. Put the knives away, Bethany, and smile at me. You're supposed to be humouring me today, remember?'

'I'd rather cajole a gorilla. I'm leaving now and don't you dare to try and accompany me. Thank you for the meal and *Good-bye!*'

'Don't forget the slide show. I'm taking you to the slide show this evening if I have to drag you there by the hair, so it's no use sulking.'

I swept out of the Mermaid and made it back to the cottage before I collapsed in a fit of weeping. I wept for myself, for Martin and for the memory of our marriage, which Rory Patterson, for some devious reason was trying to tarnish.

92

Chapter Five

He came laden down with flowers. Armfuls of them that practically obscured him from view as he stood on the doorstep.

'Beware the Greek bearing gifts,' I said weakly, leaning against the doorpost, overcome with a great desire to giggle as I viewed him through the jungle of wild carrot, honeysuckle, mallow and other massed blooms.

'These are just a small gift to beg forgiveness for having upset you at lunchtime. Picked with my own fair hands.'

'You'd better come in and I'll put them in water,' then, as he thrust them into my arms and I had a closer look, 'where did you say you'd picked them?' There were freesias and ixias and roses mingling with their commoner cousins. He had the grace to look sheepish.

'It's difficult to tell which are wild and which are cultivated here.'

'It's a wonder you didn't get arrested.'

He followed me up the stairs and I looked round for some receptacle large enough to take my bouquet.

'Whew! They don't smell all that nice, do they?' He regarded his gift with disappointment.

'That's because you really did capture some wild ones.

These are the culprits,' and I whisked the white bluebell-like flowers out of the bunch.

'Garlic!'

'Yes, it's the three-cornered leek, almost the badge of these parts. Pretty to look at but not to be recommended for indoor use.'

'Am I forgiven?'

'How can I resist such a gesture? We'd better go if we are not to miss the beginning of the show.'

The hall was already half-full when we arrived and after we had found seats near the middle, Rory Patterson produced a pair of heavy-framed spectacles and put them on. He looked entirely different. Gone was the casual, easy-going man I was used to. Now he looked more formidable; astute, intimidating almost. I was reminded that I really knew very little about him, apart from the image he had chosen to project. Who was the real Rory Patterson? What made him tick? Why had he latched onto me with such tenacity?

'Why are you looking at me like that?' He wasn't looking at me as he spoke and I wondered how he knew I was staring.

'I was just wondering what I'm doing, sitting here beside a man I hardly know, and for what purpose.'

'We're comrades in arms, working to solve the great mystery, remember?'

'By the way, how is your head?'

'Still tender, but improving.'

The lights went out at that moment and I settled down to enjoy the show. It was a fascinating subject and I was soon caught up in the world of wrecks and undersea exploration and treasure hunts. The sinking, re-discovery and salvaging of such famous Scilly wrecks as the *Association, Hollandia, Colossus* and *Schiller* captured my imagination, and the underwater photo-

94

graphy was superb, emphasising the difficulties facing diving teams in these waters. The speaker, himself an experienced diver who had worked on many of these wrecks, gave a witty, lucid commentary with the slides and had a fund of anecdotes which made amusing hearing.

Afterwards we strolled back to the Mermaid. The downstairs bar was crowded so we went upstairs to the Red Drum Bar. There were plenty of people in here too, playing at the pool tables and the dart boards, but we pushed our way through to the bar and I sank onto the wide, red window seat which backed onto a huge picture window overlooking the Road. Rory went to buy our drinks and I stared out at the sunset. The sea was a silver mirror, reflecting the pink sun and dotted with black rock formations like dragon's teeth. A voracious squawking drew my attention down to the water's edge. It was almost high tide and someone had thrown shellfish scraps over the harbour wall. An enormous black-backed gull had found a crab. He banged it against rock and boulder efficiently, breaking the shell, whilst nearby, a group of herring gulls paddled the lapping water and kept a respectful distance. When the larger gull had eaten his fill and lost interest they moved in like a swarm of locusts, churning the water and screaming and squabbling amongst themselves as they fought over the remains.

'What are you watching?' Rory Patterson handed me my drink.

'The law of the jungle in action,' I nodded out of the window, 'the survival of the fittest and all that.'

The barman, who looked like a cross between Spike Milligan and a pirate, was playing old jazz tapes; Chris Barber, I think. I settled back and let the nostalgic music seep through me, enjoying the evocation of a pre-disco era.

'You're surely too young to appreciate this sort of music?'

'Martin was a great jazz fan though he favoured Dave Brubeck and the more modern stuff.'

'So, we're back to Martin again. I suppose tonight's show, which incidentally I enjoyed very much, didn't jog any memories?'

'How do you mean?'

'Well, there's your treasure for you – but lying under the sea, not deposited in rock formations on dry land. You heard what the speaker said; there are still fabulous fortunes lying around on the sea-bed waiting to be found.'

'You think Martin could have discovered a Dutch East Indiaman laden with with pieces of eight? How could he possibly have done? You're back to the realms of fantasy again.'

'I guess so. Well, it was a wonderful idea while it lasted. You're sure Martin didn't produce any doubloons or golden ducats?'

'Don't be ridiculous!' But something was tugging at the edge of my memory. There had been something – something we had joked about and I had thought no more of. What was it?

'Bethany, what's the matter, are you all right?'

'I'm just trying to remember.' I closed my eyes and wrinkled up my brow in concentration. 'I've got a feeling there *was* something; something Martin mentioned or gave to me.'

'Some coins?'

'No, it was only two lumps of some rock stuff.' I suddenly realised what I had said and sat bolt upright. I stared at Rory Patterson and he stared back, excitement sparking across his face.

'*What* did you say?'

'My God! It's coming back. How could I have forgotten? I never gave it another thought at the time. No, it's too far-fetched.'

'What are you talking about?'

'It can't be anything to do with that – can it?'

'What did Martin give you and when?'

I spoke softly, more to myself than to him, excitement raising my voice as I dragged the silent facts out of my memory.

'It was after that trip he made here on his own, not long before he was killed. He brought back some bulbs and also two pieces of – well, I suppose it was some sort of rock; they weren't very big, about the size of a smallish potato, like a mass of pebbles and metal stuck together. He literally threw them at me and said something about treasure lying around.'

'And where are they now?'

I looked blankly at him. 'I've no idea. I don't think I even picked them up or examined them. I thought it was some sort of a joke. They looked like something he'd picked up off the beach.'

'Bethany, try and remember. They must be some-where or did you throw them in the dustbin?'

'No, I'm sure I didn't. I tell you I don't remember hand-ling them.'

'Did Martin take them back?'

'No-o, I don't think so.'

'Where were you, what were you doing when he pro-duced them?'

My mind went back to the Hampstead flat. 'I was in my studio. I suppose I had been painting. He was excited and was talking about this discovery he had made, though it didn't make sense and then he flipped these two pieces of rock across the table to me. I remember they clonked quite heavily against the lid of my box where I keep all my tubes of paint and odds and ends.'

'And then they rolled onto the floor?'

'No, I suppose they ended up in the box.' I stared at him transfixed. 'My God! They can't be . . ?'

'Still there? Bethany, my sweet, where is this box?'

'It's here with me now, up at the cottage.'

'But surely you'd have noticed them if they were still there?'

'There's an awful lot of rubbish in there. I keep meaning to clean it out; old squeezed-up tubes, dirty rags, lumps of charcoal . . . Rory, it's not possible . . ?' My voice was a whisper.

'Come on, what are we waiting for?' We made a dive for the door, our half-finished drinks abandoned on the table, oblivious of the startled looks flung in our direction.

As we panted up the hill towards the cottage I tried to argue with him. 'Rory, it can't be anything important. It certainly wasn't gold coins or anything like that.'

'You heard what that chappie said tonight,' he said over his shoulder. 'Artefacts fished up from the depths are usually enclosed in concretion, crud in other words, and it sounds as if you have or had in your possession two pieces of crud.'

I saved my breath to make the climb. Never had that hill seemed so steep and I was panting by the time we reached the cottage. We charged up the stairs into the studio and I snatched up my art box which had been lying in a corner and emptied it out on the table. Percy, putting in an appearance at the doorway, decided to join in the fun and jumped onto the table blundering in and out of the spilled contents.

'Percy – *out*!' bellowed Rory, and Percy fled.

'My God! I must try that some time.'

We searched frantically, picking through the tubes

and bottles and crayons, many of which should have been thrown away years ago.

'Here's one piece!' I fished out the lump of dark, grey-ish sediment and handed it to Rory. 'The other's gone – no it hasn't, oh heavens!' The second, smaller piece was covered with a thick coating of ultramarine blue which had leaked out of a tube. I snatched up a rag and some turps and scrubbed at it feverishly.

'Well, here's your treasure,' I said staring in frustration at the two pieces of crud lying in Rory's palm. I don't know whether I had expected them to have undergone some miraculous metamorphosis during their long incarceration in my art box – to emerge transformed into gleaming gold or jewels – but they looked as valuable as a couple of cinders.

'Don't look so disappointed. I'm sure we're on the right track; look . . .' he scraped away at one of the protuber-ances with his thumbnail '. . . there's definitely pieces of metal here, though what they are is anyone's guess. Have you got a knife?'

I produced a kitchen knife and a pair of scissors and he scraped and prodded and poked to no avail. They really were as hard as rock.

'It's no good, I need a hammer and chisel, probably a drill as well; hell!'

'Do you think this is really it?'

'Martin's treasure? I think this must be part of it. I think he must have got hold of some artefact or coins which he realised must have come from some so far undetected wreck; probably one that is known to exist but has not as yet been officially found.'

'But where would *he* have got them from?'

'That's the point. This sort of stuff doesn't lie around on the shore', he juggled the two pieces of crud thoughtfully; 'it's dredged up from the deep by divers. I suppose Martin wasn't by any chance an amateur diver? He didn't do any diving around here?'

'No, but he did get friendly with some of the boatmen. He went out on one or two fishing trips with them – and yes, he actually went out once on a diving expedition. He stayed on board the support vessel but he came back full of enthusiasm and said he'd like to have a go.'

'Who were they, did you meet them?'

'No, he went off on these excursions whilst I was painting.'

I looked at him defiantly but he made no comment. 'Do you think perhaps he actually had a go, at diving I mean, when he came back here on that last visit?'

'It's possible, but he can't have been working on his own. There must have been others involved.'

'The red-haired man and his associates? But that means they must be local.'

'I don't see how it can possibly be them. If it were they would know how and where these things were found, wouldn't they? Somehow they must have got to hear about it, realised it was a really valuable find, and are desperately trying to locate the wreck. They must think he told you all about it and that you can pinpoint the site. Didn't he say *anything*?'

'I'm not holding out on you, Rory. He was bursting with excitement, but he said he wasn't going to tell me what it was all about until he was absolutely sure.'

'And you didn't press him? You weren't curious about his behaviour, his discovery?'

'I guess I was still sore because he hadn't taken me with him.' He looked at me speculatively but refrained from comment. He mooched around the studio deep in thought.

'Well, now we think we know what it is, but like your friends we don't know where it was found. We're in the same boat.'

100

'But why are they following me around all the while? If it's what we think it is it has got to be out on the seabed somewhere, not here on dry land.'

'They are expecting you to make contact with someone; the person or people whom Martin must have been involved with.'

'So what do we do now?'

'The first thing is to try and get some sort of positive identification. We must find out just what we've got here,' he held up the two pieces of crud; 'and what sort of wreck they could possibly have come from. I have to go back to the mainland for a few days; there's some business I must sort out. I'll take these and try and get them broken up and analysed. That's if you agree?'

'They're no use to me. When are you going?'

'As soon as I can get a flight to Penzance. I doubt if I'll get one tomorrow. I'll try for Wednesday.'

'You're not going back on the *Scillonian*?'

'No, it's much quicker by helicopter. I shall only be away for a few days. Will you be all right on your own?'

'Of course.' But it was surprising how bereft I felt at the thought of him going. 'I've got to go back myself next week for a couple of weeks. Mrs Pethick wants the rooms and I also have things to do in London.'

'I shall be back before then. In the meantime how about having dinner with me tomorrow night?'

'Only if you're my guest. You've taken me out far too often already. I can afford to take you out to dinner, you know.'

'All right, on one condition; that I choose the venue.'

'I don't see why not, where had you in mind?'

'Tregarthen's Hotel?' He must have seen the expression on my face for he added hurriedly, 'Or is that going it too much?'

'No, I think I can run to that; Tregarthen's it shall be.'

What on earth had inspired him to choose Tregarthen's of all places; my honeymoon hotel, the one place I definitely didn't want to enter again? But I was caught in a cleft stick. If I objected he would think I was mean and didn't think him worth a decent meal; and if I told him the real reason? Oh no, I couldn't do that, not in the light of his already known reactions to my mourning. Unthinkable. I must just grin and bear it.

'I'll pick you up tomorrow evening. In the meanwhile I'll endeavour to find out what diving teams are operating in this area and what the legal position is. May I suggest you paint *very* local flowers tomorrow.'

'No island hopping?'

'Please, Bethany, humour me. There must be plenty of flowers near here you haven't painted yet.'

'Well, I could make a start on your bouquet,' I said brightly.

'I asked for that, I suppose. But *have* you recorded all that lot yet?' he waved a hand in the direction of the staggering flower arrangement.

'Actually no. That should keep me busy for some time, if I'm not snuffed out first by sheer exhaustion or hay fever.'

He was on his feet and raring to go. 'Well, at least we're getting somewhere at last and not just clutching at straws in the wind. I'll see what I can turn up tomorrow. I'll see you in the evening.'

He couldn't wait to get away and I felt oddly piqued.

'This diving business must be a bit of a setback for you,' I said sweetly.

'Why? What do you mean?'

'Your dislike of getting your feet wet, fear of water, whatever you call it. Is aquaphobia the correct name?'

'If you think that I, or for that matter, you,' he spoke coldly, 'are going to troll around on the seabed in snorkel and flippers you really aren't clued up at all. Diving is big business. It involves money and expertise and is a highly dangerous occupation, not for amateurs at all.'

'Well, that let's you out then, doesn't it, Rory? Perhaps my red-haired friend is the man I ought too cultivate after all.'

'Goodnight, Bethany.'

I waved him airily out of the room, but after he had gone I wondered whether I had been right to give him both pieces of crud. They were my only evidence – the only tenuous link with Martin's discovery – and I had entrusted them to someone about whom I was beginning to entertain second thoughts.

I decided to carry out my own investigations the next morning. I visited the museum and carefully studied their section on wrecks. They published a useful little booklet on shipwrecks around the Scillies with the names and descriptions of known wrecks in chronological order which I purchased to peruse later. It was an excellent museum covering every aspect of past and present life in the Scillies, with a very good section on the flora and fauna; everything beautifully displayed in a light, airy, modern setting. Downstairs there was a display table containing a collection of wild flowers currently to be found in bloom. They looked rather jaded and I wondered how often they were renewed. I must find out who perpetuated this display and ask their help in locating some of the more obscure flowers I had to find and paint.

Afterwards I wandered round the town, bought some postcards and a few souvenirs for my family and friends and spent an hour at the hairdressers. Mrs Pethick provided a cold lunch for me and I spent the afternoon sorting out the paintings I had already done; classifying them into family groups and habitat and planning where to go and what to paint next. As the evening grew closer I began to have more and more qualms. Could I cry off with a fake illness, a headache or a tummy upset? How could I possibly walk into that hotel without Martin by my side? Then I had a terrible panic session when I couldn't bring Martin's face to mind. I could describe his features in minute detail but when I tried to recall his dear, remembered face my mind went blank.

I dithered over what to wear and finally decided on a light turquoise dress which swooped low at the back and showed off my suntan to advantage, and I took a lot of time over my make-up. I couldn't think why I was going to all this trouble, unless I looked on my finished appearance as a sort of armour, a sophisticated veneer behind which the real me cringed.

Tregarthen's hadn't altered. There was the same feeling of unostentatious luxury and gracious living. The decor was discreet; in the lounge everything blended happily from the yellow-brown carpet and brown upholstered chairs to the low tables set with dark yellow, brown and green tiles. Nothing jarred. There was nothing blatantly modern in design; rather an air of timelessness that was echoed by the courteous service. It had a relaxed and comfortable atmosphere in which I was the only discordant note. I sat tensely on the edge of my seat with my sherry glass clasped tightly in brittle fingers that threatened to snap the stem.

'Relax, Bethany, you're wound up like a spring this evening,' drawled Rory, eyeing me over the rim of his glass. I sprang up to hide my confusion and wandered round the room looking at the pictures on the walls. Many of these were by local artists and were for sale and were of quite a high standard. By the time we were ready to go into the dining room I had got myself more or less under control. We were seated at a table not far from one of the windows through which one had spectacular views of Bryher, Tresco and St Martin's across the cerulean water. I accepted the menu and chose Sole Meunière.

'Do you always choose the "beasties fra' the sea"?' enquired Rory cocking an eyebrow at me.

'Yes, I suppose I usually do. It has something to do with a secret hankering after vegetarianism but not being prepared to go the whole hog.'

'The white flesh not the red?'

'Uh'mm.'

It suddenly registered with me that Rory Patterson was wearing a suit for the first time since I had known him. True, no self-respecting tailor would have laid claim to it, but it fitted him more or less, and with it he was wearing what looked suspiciously like an Establishment tie. His brown hair still managed to look rakish and undisciplined. I picked at my fish and tried not to look at the table near the end window. This was the table Martin and I had had, but despite myself, my eyes kept straying in that direction. There was a couple sitting at it now: the girl was blonde and beautiful in a healthy Nordic way and her companion was a much older man. I swallowed hard and tried desperately to think of some topic of conversation.

'Is that the table you had before?' I think my mouth actually dropped open as the impact of what he was saying reached me.

'You *knew*?'

'That this is the hotel where you spent your honeymoon? Yes.'

'You're cruel, Rory Patterson,' I whispered.

'It's a case of being cruel to be kind, if you'll excuse the cliché.'

'You've got a damn cheek! How dare you presume to . . .'

'Don't make a scene.' His hand closed over mine and I felt he was holding me pinned to the table.

'I wouldn't give you the satisfaction. Why don't you go the whole way? I'll tell you which room we had, it was on the top floor; and you can hire it and make love to me on the same bed!'

'I thought this was a respectable establishment. You shock me, Bethany. Even I wouldn't presume to go as far as that.' His eyes glittered and I felt threatened and rebuffed at the same time. I looked down so that he wouldn't see the tears in my eyes and toyed some more with my sole.

'For Heaven's sake stop mauling that fish about. You're paying for the meal so you might as well get your money's worth from it.'

'Rory Patterson, you're completely lost to all human decency . . .'

'Then don't try to fit me into a pattern. Don't you want to know how I got on today?'

'You're going to tell me. What did Martin discover? The Queen of Sheba's barge blown off-course by the trade winds or Henry Morgan's cache of ill-gotten goods?'

'Being facetious doesn't suit you, but I will ignore your childishness. I have discovered that our red-haired friend was born and bred in these parts.'

'So he is local!'

'Was. He left for the mainland several years ago. His name is Pete Walmsley; a good old north-country name incidentally; and apparently he was always a bit of a black sheep. He dabbled in a little fishing, boat-hire and diving etc. – yes, diving – and left under rather a cloud about four or five years ago. He was lured to the Big City and got caught up with some dubious company, a little to the left of tax-dodging but not quite into the protection

106

and extortion racket. I gather he is their hit man.'

'How on earth did you find all that out?'

'Never you mind, but he seems to be a thoroughly unsavoury character.'

'How could Martin have got mixed up with somone like that?'

'That is the great mystery, but our Mr Walmsley is definitely knocking around on his old home ground again and the general feeling is that he is up to no good.'

'You should have cackled and shook your bony finger when you said that.'

'I'm giving you the facts for what they're worth. By the way, I've booked on the first helicopter flight tomorrow morning.'

'Would you like me to come and see you off?'

'Don't bother, I should hate you to miss your beauty sleep.'

'It's not that early, is it?'

'No, but I'd rather know you were tucked away safely in the cottage when I go.'

'What do you think is going to happen, a bomb in the luggage hold?'

'I'm hoping my departure will draw the heat off you.'

'But I thought you said they don't think you are of any importance?'

'I hope they'll think that you have confided all to me and I am hie-ing away on your business.'

'Then all I can say is, take care.' I stared at him thoughtfully while I assimiliated this new theory.

'Well' he said, surveying the sweets trolley with a quizzical eye, 'I'm going to have some of that bombe surprise or perhaps Black Forest gateau. What about you?'

'No thanks,' I said with a shudder, 'but I should like an Irish coffee.'

'Good girl. We'll make it two, if you'll indulge me over my sweet first.'

He tackled his bombe surprise with great gusto when it came and I was moved to remark: 'I don't know how you can gorge yourself like that and remain so disgustingly thin.'

'I'm not thin,' he said with indignation.

'Scrawny. A "lean and hungry look".'

'Well, if we're exchanging compliments you're not exactly Rubenesque yourself.'

'I think we'd better change the subject. When do you expect to be back?'

'I'm not sure. I'll keep in touch.'

We had our coffee in the lounge but we didn't linger.

'Will you come back to the Castle for a nightcap?' he asked.

'No, thank you, I've had quite enough already.'

'I'll walk you back to the cottage.'

'There's no need to bother, Rory, I shall be perfectly all right and you're only a short distance from your hotel from here.'

'I'll see you home.' I shrugged and we walked back in silence. He was deep in thought, his pipe clenched between his teeth, his hands in his pockets. I felt rather like a little girl being grudgingly escorted home from a party by a reluctant elder brother. He stopped on the corner where the lane climbed up into Sallyport and removed the pipe from his mouth.

'You should be all right now.'

'I think I can manage the last few yards without getting run-over, abducted or raped,' I said tartly.

He put his hands on my shoulders and swung me round to face him. 'Thank you for this evening, Bethany; I enjoyed it even if you didn't. Now run home before I forget myself'. But he didn't let me go. His fingers dug

108

into my arms and from his superior height he looked down at me with such a strange, embittered expression that I felt frightened.

'You're hurting me.'

'I'm sorry'. He released me abruptly and stepped back, a blank look replacing the previous expression on his face. My heart was thudding and I wanted to get away from him – fast.

'Goodnight and *bon voyage*'. I turned and rushed up the last few yards to Sallyport. He hadn't replied and I didn't look back to see if he were still waiting, watching me.

I felt quite light-hearted when I awoke the next morning, and for the first time in months I felt free. Rory Patterson was no longer around to bully or cajole me; it seemed impossible I had only known him a week, so forcibly had he tried to take over my life. The red-haired Pete Walmsley, now that he had acquired an identity and background, no longer frightened me to the same extent. And Martin? Martin would always be there, occupying an irreplaceable part of my life, but he no longer jostled my elbow. I should never forget him, never love anyone else but I had acquired a separate identity again.

The weather had changed for the better. As I gazed out of the studio window the sharp blue of the water sparkling in the sunlight nearly dazzled me. In Porthcressa Bay a gaggle of yachts had crept in with the evening tide and lay suspended on the gleaming surface like abandoned toy boats. I decided to walk up round the coastline via Porthmellon and Porthloo Beaches and across the Golf Course to Halangy Down. I should find a wide variety of flowers to be recorded; and if I got fed up with painting I would swim and sunbathe or just laze. I hummed to myself as I pulled on a cotton skirt and tee-shirt over my bikini and stuffed my painting things into my rucksack together with my sunglasses, suntan oil, towel and camera.

I tripped lightly down the hill and stopped to buy some food for my picnic lunch, then made my way along The Strand. I seemed to be going against the tide. Nearly everybody was going in the opposite direction, flocking towards the quay to catch the morning launches to the off-islands. My attention was drawn to the shop called The Treasure Cave with its display of coins in the window. I wandered inside.

The interior was quite dark, mainly because the windows and lights were obscured by a myriad of hanging ships' lamps. The walls were hung with maps and charts and tea towels in a nautical design, and the central fittings were hung and stacked with a conglomeration of objects appertaining to the sea; from modern navigational aids to pieces of old cannon and modern souvenirs. It was a glorious mixture of old and new. A large, highly-polished brass diver's helmet that looked as if it had been used in the film *20,000 Leagues under the Sea* stood on the floor surrounded by a pile of rusting anchors, and on the shelf above was a collection of cheap-looking little miniature diving helmets and models of old-fashioned divers.

There were glass-topped display cabinets in one part of the shop containing a vast collection of coins ranging from perfect examples of pillar-dollars and ducatoons, some in silver settings and designed to be worn on chains as medallions, to odd-shaped pieces of metal hardly identifiable as coins at all. I wondered if my pieces of crud contained any such coins and if so, what they signified. So engrossed was I in my contemplation of the contents of these display cabinets that when the voice boomed out at me I was doubly startled.

'Bethany Carr? It is Bethany Carr, isn't it? I recognised you from the photos.'

110

He looked as if he'd just stepped off a Viking long-boat. Blond hair and beard, suntanned physique, brilliant blue eyes; the whole works even down to the gold ring winking in one ear-lobe. I gaped as he pushed his way between fittings, ducking to avoid some hanging nets. He advanced on me with outstretched hand, a grin displaying perfect teeth splitting his beard.

'Well, where's Martin then, the old so-and-so? He's taken his time!' He glanced over towards the dimmer recesses of the shop as if expecting Martin to appear and, God help me, I looked too. Then it hit me and I think I actually cried out.

'What's the matter? Here, sit down.' He pushed a chair towards me. 'Did I startle you? I'm sorry, but what have you done with Martin?'

'He's dead!' I sat down as abruptly as I uttered the words, and he stared at me as if I had taken leave of my senses.

'Hey, steady on! You are Bethany? It is Martin Carr we are speaking of?'

'My late husband. He died eighteen months ago.'

'It's not possible! But that would explain . . . My dear girl, this is quite shocking, I don't know what to say . . .' He looked so distressed that I felt that I had to make the effort to pull myself together.

'Who are you?' I asked as rationally as possible.

'Mike Carberry. Didn't Martin mention me?'

I shook my head but somewhere in the back of my mind a bell rang faintly. I *had* heard the name somewhere before.

'Look, I can't take this in. Martin . . . *dead*? How did it happen? Can you tell me?'

'He was killed in a hit-and-run accident. Or so it appeared.'

'You mean you're not sure?' The brown forehead wrinkled in astonishment. I think he was beginning to think that I was deranged in some way.

'He's dead all right. It's just that there's some mystery about how he actually met his death. I'm sorry I'm not making much sense, but how did he come to know you?'

'He really didn't tell you? We met when he was over here. I say, are you sure you're all right?' He looked at me with concern. I was feeling faint and must have shown it.

'I'll be fine in a moment. You just caught me off-balance.'

'I must have done. Coming out with something like that. In the circumstances I wonder you didn't pass right out. You need a drink, so do I; let's get out of here. Come to my place, it's only across the yard.'

He led the way out through the back of the shop, across a sun-splashed, junk-littered yard to a building with an outside staircase leading up to the first floor. I followed him up this staircase like an automaton. Events were being taken out of my hands and strangely enough I felt no fear or suspicion. The room into which he led me was chaotic in an ordered sort of way. There was a large table littered with maps and charts and a desk against a wall covered with rolls of paper and drawing materials. There were books everywhere, on every available surface and piled up on the floor, and the walls were covered with further charts and tide-tables and pegs hung with an assortment of oilskins and sailing gear. I discovered later that the ground floor was a combined boathouse and workshed.

He waved me to a chair, opened a cupboard and produced a bottle of whisky and two glasses. He poured out a generous amount into each glass and handed one to me. I hesitated.

'I don't really drink at this time of the day.' His reply was to cross over to the sink in the corner and splash some water into the contents of my glass before handing it to me again. Really, I seemed to have met more than my share of masterful men in the past week. I didn't need the drink. I was feeling better already now that the initial shock had worn off, but I was curious and beginning to feel the stirring of excitement. Perhaps at long last I was on the verge of discovering what it was all about. I sipped cautiously at my whisky and studied him.

He was in his late twenties or early thirties; tall with a burly physique. He was dressed in an old Guernsey and shorts and his brown, muscular legs were covered in a matt of blond hairs and his feet, clad in sandals, were as brown as the rest of him. His hair, beard and moustache were dark blond near the roots but bleached nearly white at the ends from exposure to sun and salt. He studied me as carefully as I studied him and there was an expression of open admiration on his face that warmed as much as the whisky.

'Where do I start?' He ran his hand through his short curls so that they stood up like a halo. 'I thought you would have known all about me. Martin and I were going to be partners in a venture. . . . You don't know what I'm talking about?'

'Martin didn't tell me anything, though I think he mentioned your name at some time. But I think I do know what you're hinting at. In fact, I think you must be the missing link.'

'Missing link? You make me sound like some sort of ape.' He chuckled and tossed back his drink. 'Well, do you start or I?'

'You please. I've been groping in the dark for so long; perhaps everything's going to make sense at last.'

'I first met Martin several years ago. He was over here doing some sort of survey for his company and we met entirely by accident; in the Mermaid actually. We got talking, about our respective work amongst other things, and he was fascinated when I told him I did a lot of diving in these waters. We got onto the subject of wrecks and had a long discussion about the known wrecks that had not yet been located and the possibility of finding one. I was quite serious about this but I thought he was just showing the interest any outsider might show in such a, what is to them, glamorous subject. The next time I saw him was about three years ago.'

'Our honeymoon,' I murmured.

'He'd remembered our talk and brought up the subject again, asking me if I'd found anything, and I was able to tell him that I thought it was possible that I was on the track of something really big. Do you know anything about our local wrecks?'

'I went to the slide-show on shipwrecks the other evening.'

'Then you know of the Dutch East Indiamen?'

'You mean you've found one?' I couldn't keep the excitement out of my voice and there was an answering gleam in his eyes.

'Not just any old one. You've heard about the *Hollandia* and the *Princess Maria*? They were loaded with silver bullion and worth a small fortune, but there is another legendary East Indiaman of even greater value: the *Maria Johanna*. She was reported to have floundered in 1744 somewhere not far from the Bishop Rock and there has always been a legend that she went down near Crim though the Dutch Government, who took over the Dutch East India Company, have always denied this. The interesting thing is that she was reputed to be carrying a cargo which included 250,000 gold ducats. This was a most unusual thing. These Dutch East Indiamen sailed from Texel to the Far East – Batavia and places like that – and they always carried silver not gold to trade with. For some

114

reason silver was in greater demand and of more value to the people of South East Asia, especially Mexican silver – your pieces of eight.'

'So what would she be worth?'

'Several millions of pounds by today's standards.'

'Several millions of pounds? And you think you've actually found her?'

'It's even better than that. I can tell you something that is totally unbelievable.'

'I think I am incapable of being surprised any more. Mr Carberry, do go on.'

Chapter Six

He titled back his chair, folded his arms behind his head, fixed me with those brilliant cerulean eyes like a seafarer of old, and went on.

'I had been diving in the area of the Crim Rocks, north of the Bishop and I found this old piece of iron cannon and some coins, some of them contained in bits of crud . . .'

'How do you get them out?' I interrupted. He looked surprised at my query.

'We've found from experience that a small explosive charge is best.'

'Good heavens! Sorry, do continue.'

'When I say I found them, I mean I and two friends who also dive and were working with me. When we had a chance to study these coins we were surprised to find that amongst the very ancient pillar-dollars and ducatoons was a gold coin, very badly defaced and worn, but definitely gold. This alerted us to the fact that there was just a possibility that we'd found the legendary *Maria Johanna*.'

'So what did you do then, and how did Martin come into it?' I breathed.

'The regulations surrounding diving are very strict. Since 1981 the Health and Safety at Work Act completely altered things as far as diving is concerned. Since then,

116

amongst other things, you must have a support vessel with a team of at least four people, a portable de-compression chamber and a stringent training as a diver. One can still dive as an amateur under the British Sub Aqua Club rules, but if you find anything it is illegal to make anything out of it. You'd have to get a commercial diver's licence before you could make any profit and then you're back to those conditions imposed by the 1981 Act. And these cost money.'

'You mean,' I was beginning to see where Martin had come in, 'Martin offered to come in with you with financial support?'

'He was very interested and suggested something of that sort.'

'And he never mentioned it to me!' I was indignant and hurt all over again.

'It was very early days. We had to be much surer before we could do anything official and you have to be very careful – secretive about these things. Any rumour of such a find getting around and the sea around the Western Rocks would be stiff with treasure-hunters, official and unofficial. We decided to keep the facts to ourselves for the time being and I and my friends would go on diving unobtrusively in the area and try to find something that would provide positive proof of the identity of the wreck. Martin went back to the mainland and we promised to keep in touch. Not long after this I was involved in a fishing accident and broke my leg. By the time I'd recovered the diving season was over – the end of September is the limit – so we had to wait till the following summer.

'In the meanwhile, I used to spend a few evenings, especially in the winter months, visiting an old boy up at Holy Vale. He was a local fisherman and boatman, born and bred and knew everything there was to know about these waters. He had suffered a stroke a couple of years

117

previously that had impaired his speech and partially paralysed him. He was still as bright as a button in the top storey but he had a job communicating. He loved to hear of my diving experiences and I got into the habit of telling him all about my little finds; there was no chance of it going any further and it helped to brighten up his life, poor old sod.

'When I showed him what I had found he got very excited, especially about the gold coin. He kept going on about Menavaur. That's a rock out near Round Island and St Helen's, beyond Tresco, and I couldn't seem to make him understand that we'd found them near Crim which is miles away from Manavaur. Anyway, to cut a long story short, we resumed diving the following summer and at first we had no luck at all. We couldn't locate the spot where we had found the stuff – it's amazing how the seabed can alter after a bad winter – and you can only stay down about half-an-hour in each day at those depths. We'd just about given up, it was getting near the end of the season again, when we had another find. This time there was a button and part of a brooch as well as a few more badly worn gold coins and silver ducatoons. We were thrilled and this time took no chances. We marked the spot very carefully with a marker buoy. Then, you'll never believe this; a terrific storm blew up and the bloody thing broke moorings and went adrift. It was completely frustrating – we were back to square one again.

'However, just after that happened Martin came back. When we told him what had happened he insisted that we try another dive and he came with us, as a spectator, of course. Well, we tried but it was hopeless. The weather conditions were against us, it was far too rough and dangerous and we had to give up.

'Martin agreed to come in with us financially the next year and before he went back to the mainland I took him with me when I went on my weekly visit to old Tod Haines, the old man I've just told you about. Old Tod got so excited about our find that we thought he would have another stroke. He kept on again about Menavaur and we decided we'd better go. On the way out we explained to his wife that we thought we had over-excited him and he seemed to have a thing about Menavaur. Then she said a most extraordinary thing. "He don't mean Menavaur, he means man-of-war. He's on about that old ship again." We pressed her about what she meant and she told us that years before he had been fascinated by the tale of an old British man-of-war that could have gone down in these waters and he had done some research into it. She couldn't even remember the name of the ship but she said that there were some papers knocking around the house containing his notes and she'd try and find them and pass them on to us. I never gave it another thought; I just thought the old man had got a bee in his bonnet and that I would have to humour him on my next visit. Martin went back and he took with him some of the coins, intending to try and get further information about them.'

'He also brought back some pieces of crud,' I interrupted.

'He took a few of the smaller pieces we hadn't broken up. You knew about it?'

'He literally threw them at me when he got home and said something about our fortunes being made, but he didn't elucidate further and I didn't take him seriously.'

'About two weeks after Martin left, old Tod Haines had a final stroke and died. It had been expected for some time and no-one was surprised. However, a few weeks after this his widow got in touch with me and passed on a box of papers she had found when going through his stuff. She said it was all to do with this man-of-war he had always been going on about. I brought it home and for a few days

119

I didn't even bother to look inside. When I did I got the shock of my life.' He paused for effect and I looked suitably impressed.

'He'd discovered some evidence about an old man-of-war that was wrecked carrying a fabulous fortune?'

'My dear girl, you've got it in one.'

'I don't believe you!'

'It's true enough except it wasn't really a man-of-war. That's a rather loose term for a fighting ship of an earlier period. The ship he's fastened on was a 700-ton British ship called the *Merchant Royal* and it pre-dates the *Maria Johanna* by nearly a hundred years. It carried a crew of eighty to ninety men and was sailing from Cowles in Spain carrying a reputed 200 million in gold coin, jewellery, silver etc.'

'And who did the fortune belong to?'

'This is where it gets interesting; skullduggery of the highest order with no less a person than King Charles I involved in some very doubtful deal with the Spanish Government of the day. It was coming to the Crown as payment for some unspecified service – the mind boggles as to what it was to command such a reward – and originally being carried on a Spanish ship. This ship caught fire and the cargo was transferred to the *Merchant Royal*. According to eye-witness accounts, the *Merchant Royal* was herself leaking badly and on pumps, and the outcome was that on 23rd September 1641 she sank in deep water ten leagues from Land's End. There had been two other ships sailing in convoy with her, a Spanish ship and a Britisher called the *Dover Merchant*, and they managed to limp into Plymouth harbour.'

'And she actually went down in these waters?'

'There is no positive evidence to support this but ten leagues from Land's End could well be the Western Rocks, and what better place could you find for an already crippled ship to founder? Old Tod had found some gold coins out there and they were with the papers in the box.'

'But what put him onto the *Merchant Royal* in the first place; the coins . . ?'

'Badly defaced and I'd say unidentifiable but something altered him and he's been to Plymouth where the log of the *Merchant Royal* was still housed in the Customs House. Also there were notes about a broadsheet in the British Museum which mentioned that Parliament was interrupted when an announcement was made to the effect that the *Merchant Royal* had gone down; which shows how important it was.'

'So he really thought he had found the *Merchant Royal*?'

'He definitely thought he had found some of her gold bullion, but whether he'd pinpointed the actual location is another matter. For some reason he seems to have done nothing further, which is extraordinary when you think about it; but I suppose it must have been not long after this when he was first taken ill.'

'And now you think you've found it?'

'I really believe we may have. I rang Martin up in London and told him about these latest developments and he was as excited and intrigued as I was. He arranged to go down to Plymouth and look into it.'

I gave a stifled exclamation and he raised his eyebrows so I explained. 'He went down to Plymouth a couple of weeks before he was killed. I thought it was on his firm's business but it wasn't, as I found out later.'

'He rang me back a few days later to say that he'd discovered that the log of the *Merchant Royal* had gone missing about fourteen years ago (this would have been just after Tod Haines had seen it) but that he'd found out some very interesting facts which he couldn't tell me over the phone because he thought he was being "got at" –

those were his actual words. I couldn't understand . . . properly . . . what he was saying, it was a terrible line. Did you say something?'

'Only that it is beginning to make horrible sense. But do go on, Mr Carberry, I'll explain in a minute.'

'Mike, please. Well, he said he would send me all the information in the post and that he would probably need to have the button and broken brooch to help with identification and I agreed to send them to him after I had received his letter. I never heard another word.'

'He was killed on November 15th; they got to him.'

'Christ! No wonder I heard no more.' Then, as he took in my last statement, 'What do you mean "they got to him"?'

'I'll tell you in a minute, but why didn't you try to contact him?'

'I did. I wrote and got no reply and several times I rang his business number, which was the only phone number I had. Each time I was put off by some snooty female saying "Mr Carr was not available."'

'That's odd. Martin was already dead by then; why didn't the secretary tell you? The company must have been really suspicious about the whole affair, and I suppose they were monitoring any calls that came for him, though I don't understand why. They didn't even ask your name and purpose?'

'I thought he had gone away on business,' continued Mike Carberry, ignoring my remark; 'I know he travelled a lot for his firm and at that time something had come up for me. I was offered a job involving diving in the Middle East; the Arabian Gulf. Very lucrative and a handsome way of spending the winter months. There was no possibility of doing any further search for the *Merchant Royal* till the following summer, so I went out to the Gulf. The job there was very interesting; I won't bore you with details, but it was obviously going to take longer than the six months originally contracted. I came back for a short break in May, that would be May of last year, expecting to find some communication from Martin awaiting me. When I found nothing I posted off the button and brooch and remaining coins to your address in Hampstead. I reckoned he probably needed them to help in his research.'

'You were very trusting, Mr Carberry – Mike.'

'I knew Martin was all right.' It was amazing how that simple statement cheered me. After all the suspicions and doubts I had been floundering through in the past eighteen months, it was like a breath of clean, fresh air.

'What did you do after that?'

'I went back to the Gulf. Suffice it to say that the job stretched out, what with delays and unexpected complications, and I only returned a few weeks ago. I wrote a letter to Martin's Hampstead address as soon as I got back telling him I was back in the country and asking him to come over to discuss the whole thing. As I hadn't heard I wondered whether he had lost interest in the project. To be frank, his financial backing was not so important now; I made a killing in the Gulf, but I need those coins and bits and pieces back – they're our only means of identification so far. When I saw you in The Treasure Cave just now I thought Martin had answered my summons at long last.'

'And instead you've got just me.'

'I can't take it in that Martin's dead; and why have you come here if you know nothing about it? Or did you get my last letter?'

'I moved house after Martin's death; it looks as if more than one letter has got lost in the forwarding process. I can assure you that I didn't know of your existence until half an hour ago but I've got quite a story to tell you. Tell me first, does the name Pete Walmsley mean anything to you?'

His head snapped up and he looked at me warily.

'Pete Walmsley? I'd heard he was back again, in fact I think I saw him the other day. What has a nasty character like Pete Walmsley have to do with you?'

'Quite a lot.' And I told him everything; about the suspicions surrounding Martin's death; the threatening phone calls and my shadowing; about my commission in the Scillies and being followed here, and the frightening encounter with Pete Walmsley in the fog. He heard me out in silence, his eyes narrowing in concentration as he drummed his fingers on the arm of his chair.

'And what I can't understand,' I finished with, 'is how Martin got involved with someone like that and why they never cottoned on to your part in the whole business.'

'I've heard odds and ends of gossip about Walmsley since he left to live on the mainland, none of them very flattering. I believe he's got himself tied up with some London gang of dubious proclivities. He used to do some diving around here and I believe he was employed as a diver on one of the oil rigs at one time.'

'So Martin might have come across him in the course of his work and quite innocently mentioned it to him thinking that as an ex-local man he would be interested?'

'I think something like that must have happened; I don't suppose we shall ever know.'

'But he couldn't have told him about you.'

'I think Pete Walmsley's reaction must have made Martin suspicious and he clammed up before telling him any details. As I told you, Martin mentioned to me over the phone that he was being "got at". I imagine Walmsley and his associates tried to put pressure on him but it didn't work.'

'Martin wasn't frightened at all in those last few weeks

124

before his death,' I said thoughtfully, 'so they can't have been threatening him. He was just excited and strung up.'

'From what you've told me I reckon they were still hoping to persuade him to join forces with them in exploiting his knowledge. They'd actually followed him the night he got killed and gained possession of his briefcase?'

'It was found abandoned later, but I don't think it could have contained anything of importance to them or they wouldn't have started pestering me afterwards. It would be like Martin to keep what knowledge he had in his head and not write it down. I wonder what he had discovered?'

'And I wonder what happened to those coins etc?'

'They're probably still knocking about in some Post Office lost-property office and we may still be able to get our hands on them.' Excitement was rising and then I realised that I had, quite unintentionally, led them to their quarry. He saw the change of expression on my face.

'What's the matter?'

'They've probably followed me here. They've been waiting for me to make contact with someone, to do something with the supposed knowledge I'm thought to have and I've done just that, haven't I?' I looked round rather wildly as if expecting a gang to burst in at any moment and surround us.

'Steady on, you're not on your own any more. I should just like the chance to come up against Pete Walmsley – he might not like the results. If he or his friends try to interfere in my diving operations I shall take great delight in sorting them out.'

'You're actually diving again for the *Merchant Royal*?'

'We're just about to start. I have three helpers and we've got most of the necessary gear.'

'Can I come in with you, please?' I saw his look of embarrassment and I hurried on: 'I should like to help financially for Martin's sake. He left me money and a pen-

125

sion and I also do quite well from my work. I could afford to, and anyway, I should like a stake in it; there's big money involved and I don't want to be cheated out of my share.' As I thought, this statement had the effect I had hoped for.

'Cheated out of your share? Of course not, there is no question of that. With Martin gone you must certainly take his place. The other fellers will be tickled pink about this – a woman helping to support the venture.'

'And Rory will be frothing at the mouth with enthusiasm when he hears.'

'Rory? Who's Rory?'

'Rory Patterson . . . Then I stopped. I hadn't mentioned Rory Patterson to him. Somehow I had managed to tell my entire tale without bringing in Rory Patterson although he had been closely involved with everything that had happened, especially since I'd arrived here. What a field day a psychiatrist would have explaining this lapse. And I had some explaining to do to Mike Carberry. So I told him all about Rory Patterson, or rather, I thought out loud about Rory Patterson and the situation with him as far as I understood it and as I talked Mike Carberry mooched around the room and looked worried.

'I don't understand what this Rory Patterson really has to do with it,' he said when I had finally petered out. 'Okay, he was involved at the start through M. & K. and a suspected security leak. But that was all obvious nonsense and the file must have been closed a long while ago; why is he still involved?'

'I think he just got fascinated by the whole thing and wanted to follow it through, tie up the loose ends for the firm and satisfy his own curiosity. He's been tremendously helpful to me – I don't know what I would have done without him around.'

'It sounds to me as if he's trying to cash in on it himself.'

126

'Oh no; he was as much in the dark as me as to what it was all about until recently. He's really been acting as my protector – he nearly got killed the other day, I told you!' But that little niggle of suspicion about the real reasons for Rory Patterson's interest in me was worming diligently.

'You've got me and the lads to protect you now.' Mike Carberry was dismissive but I felt I had to take up the cudgels on Rory's behalf.

'He's become a good friend in the short time I've known him, I can't just cut him out. He's on the mainland at the moment trying to find out something about those pieces of crud that Martin gave me. He'll be back in a couple of days and I shall certainly tell him about all this. He'll be thrilled to get to the bottom of the mystery and I'm sure he can be very useful to us.'

Mike shrugged. 'You know him better than I, but the fewer people involved in this the better.'

'Rory *is* involved already. It's both of us or none at all.'

'You have got involved with him, haven't you? Don't be too trusting, Bethany, this is a nasty old world.'

'Well, I've trusted you, haven't I? And I don't really know anything about you.'

'And I've confided to you all I know about a little matter involving a vast fortune. It works both ways. There's nothing much to know about me; I'm a simple fellow. Here, I sleep and work . . .'

He gestured expansively around the room and I was moved to ask: 'What about your wife? Your family . . ?'

'I'm not married. I've never felt the need. I'm a bit of a rolling stone which would be hard on a wife, and I've never been short of female companionship.' He grinned, looking more than ever like a latter-day Viking and I had to admit to myself that he was the most macho-looking man I had ever seen. I could well imagine he had no trouble pulling the birds. But he wasn't my type, I told

127

myself firmly. I pounced on something else he had said when he had first greeted me and which had been puzzling me ever since.

'You said you recognised me from the photos. What photos?'

'The photos Martin took on your honeymoon.'

'But they didn't come out. The film was a failure.'

'It wasn't, you know.' He rummaged in a drawer of the table and produced a folder of photos.

'But I don't understand, Martin said the film had jammed and they were all a write-off.'

'This may have been the reason why.' He sorted through the photos and held some towards me. There were a couple of exposures showing a group of rocks sticking up out of a turbulent sea that could have been anywhere, some others showing close-ups of what I took to be lumps of crud and a few more with rather blurred pictures of coins and pieces of metal.

'I was so disappointed that we had no photos, no pictorial record of our holiday,' I whispered; 'why couldn't he have shown me – told me all about it?'

'He would have shown them to you eventually, wouldn't he? But he was prevented by his death.' He handed me the rest of the photos. There were happy ones of Martin and I, sunburnt and relaxed, laughing into the camera, views of different parts of the islands, close-ups of flowers and birds; all the usual subjects one would expect from a holiday spent in glorious surroundings with glorious weather. I felt the tears starting to my eyes as I faced Martin; a happy, carefree Martin, across the celluloid with the memory of nineteen anguished months between us, and I turned away and blundered over to the window.

'Don't mind too much, Bethany. Martin was a deep one.'

He was indeed. I hadn't really known him, had I? Just as Rory Patterson had suggested; and I didn't know Rory either. Perhaps I was one of those shallow people who would always be taken in by superficial values and was incapable of having a deep, meaningful relationship with anyone. But no, that wasn't true: Martin and I had had something going for us; nothing that happened now could erase those eighteen months of marriage.

'I'm sorry, it just caught me on the raw.' I turned back to face Mike Carberry who watched me with sympathy.

'I reckon us men don't always get our sense of values right as regards the fair sex, but don't have any doubts about Martin. He thought the world of you, I realised that every time we met. How are you managing without him?'

'At first I thought it was impossible that life could go on without him, but it did. I suppose I've come slowly to accept it. I had my painting and I concentrated on that, though this awful fear that Martin had got involved with something criminal and this sense of being hounded didn't help. Do you know, at one point I thought I was going mad, and I'm sure the police thought so too. Rory Patterson thought they may have actually been muzzled.'

'Did he now? I'd like too know a lot more about your Rory Patterson. I reckon he could do with some investigation.'

'Well, he'll be back in a few days so you'll be able to have it out with him. In the meanwhile, what about our treasure hunt?'

'You really mean it? You're coming in with us?'

'You bet. You try and keep me out now, and I'll join forces with Mr Walmsley and his friends.'

'That I cannot allow, so I guess I'm lumbered with you for better or worse.'

'There are more gracious ways of expressing it.'

He laughed and bounded to his feet again. 'How about

a trip tomorrow to the Western Rocks and the Bishop Rock?'

'To dive?' I couldn't keep the excitement and apprehension out of my voice.

'Heaven forbid! You will certainly not be diving, not tomorrow or at any other time. As I told you, it is a long, arduous training, but I'll take you out there to see what it is like. We'll even avoid Crim, in case our friends are around. We will make an innocent trip to see the seals and do a little birdwatching; I'll show you the puffins on Annet.'

'And do you indulge in a lot of bird-watching?' I asked innocently.

'Frequently, but not always of the feathered persuasion.'

'I asked for that, I suppose. I hope my presence won't inhibit your activities.'

'I'll survive, After all, I've got you to fall back on.' I hurriedly put the length of the room between us.

'Don't get any ideas like that, Mr Carberry. I mean our association to be a purely business one.'

'Fair enough. I should only try and make you at your invitation.'

'Which you can take from me will not be forthcoming. Do you often get turned down?'

'It has happened. Don't worry, Bethany, you're quite safe with me.'

'I'm glad to hear it. Now tell me more about your diving experiences and your partners in this venture.'

They were fascinating, the tales he had to relate, and I came away with my head spinning with facts about Merchant Shipping Acts, salvers rights, the Receiver of Wrecks and the restrictions on the length of dives in deep water. Needless to say I did not make Halangy Down that morning. I slipped back to Porthcressa Bay and spent the rest of the day swimming and lazing in the sun, my painting forgotten.

Mike Carberry was waiting for me the next morning when I arrived on the quay. He was pottering around in a small motorboat.

'Is this your diving support vessel?' I asked after we had exchanged greetings, unable to keep the disappointment out of my voice.

'Hardly. Today we are just innocent trippers. I'm glad you've brought your camera with you.'

I couldn't help feeling superior as he started the engine and we sped out of the harbour ahead of all the launches that still wallowed at the quayside collecting passengers.

'I'm going to make a small detour,' he shouted above the noise of the engine; 'there's something I want you to see. With any luck they're still around.'

He set course for Samson and when we were about half-way there he throttled back the engine and we chugged slowly in a wide circle.

'Look!'

'What?' As I didn't know what I was supposed to be able to see, I found his command difficult to follow.

'Over there – look!'

Then I saw what he was pointing at. Several large fins cutting through the water some way ahead.

'Sharks!'

'Dolphins.' He laughed at my horror. 'There's been a school of them hanging around here for several days.'

He watched the rolling bodies catching the light as they heaved through the deep blue water and then lost sight of them.

'I don't think they're going to perform any more today.'

Mike swung the boat round and we picked up speed,

131

heading south-west towards the tip of St Agnes and Annet.

It was a warm day with a powerful sun filtering through a heat haze. I stripped down to my swimsuit and shorts under the appreciative eye of Mike and watched as Annet loomed nearer. Gulls wheeled overhead and a string of shags colonised a low-lying shelf of rocks. Above them a solitary cormorant posed on the tip of the outcrop, drying his half-extended wings and looked like a sacrificial phoenix about to rise from the flames. The whole of Annet glowed as we approached; its mantle of thrift, now in full bloom, smoked pinkly in the hazy sunshine. Mike cut the engine and we drifted close.

'You're not allowed to land at this time of year; the whole island is a bird sanctuary in the breeding season. Have you seen the puffins before?'

'Only a fleeting glimpse.' We saw them then; a small group which whirred past us and settled on the water nearby. I was amazed all over again at how small they actually were.

'They're all head and beak and what absurd little wings.'

'Strong enough to carry them miles across the ocean.'

'Yes, that's true. It just shows how appearances can be deceptive.'

They bobbed ahead of us, their striped beaks giving them the comical expression of sad clowns and I managed to get several good shots of them before they flew off again. Mike re-started the engine and we moved away in the direction of the Western Rocks.

The weather was extraordinary. It was very hot and the invisible sun, hidden by a layer of haze that was surely getting thicker by the minute, burned into my exposed arms and legs. It was very calm, with not the hint of a swell.

'It's getting foggier, isn't it?' I asked Mike as he tugged at his beard with one hand whilst guiding us deftly between patches of grey and black rock.

'Yes, it is.' He squinted up at the sky. 'We may have to turn back. These patches of fog are very local but you can never be sure how far they extend. You should be wearing a sunhat, you know. You can get very burnt under these conditions; I'm used to it.' He eased the speed and we nosed slowly forward. It was an eerie experience. I felt as if we were enclosed in a little hot bubble drifting aimlessly in outer space. It was definitely foggy now and the clumps of rock we passed were blurs on the edge of vision.

A small fishing boat loomed up on our starboard. It was manned by one ancient-looking man amidst a welter of lobster and crab pots. The smell as we got upwind was indescribable; it reminded me of my journey back from Bryher. I could hear his radio telephone bleating into the silence and Mike hailed him and they had a shouted exchange.

'I'm turning back. Sorry to disappoint you, Bethany, but it's getting worse. If we miss the Bishop Rock – and it's easy to do in this weather – the next stop's America.'

'You're the skipper. And I'm not dressed for a long sea voyage.'

He grinned and swung the boat round and I waved to the fisherman before he was swallowed up from sight.

We nosed slowly through the glassy sea and I leant back against the gunwhale and closed my eyes. I had every confidence in Mike Carberry's navigational skills; he knew these waters like the back of his hand, but I didn't want to distract him with idle chatter. I think I must have actually dozed. The masked sunlight beat against my eyelids and I slipped off my sandals and stretched my legs out across the centre thwart.

How long I relaxed in this semi-conscious state I don't

133

know, but a sudden exclamation from Mike jerked me back to reality. At the same time I heard it – the staccato roar of a powerful engine homing in on us and getting louder by the second.

'There's a bloody maniac out there!' Mike tightened his hold on the wheel and strained to see through the fog. The sound was all around us; quite terrifying because one couldn't tell from which direction the craft was approaching.

'What the hell is he up to?'

Just as I thought we were going to be swallowed up as if by an avalanche I saw the shape emerging from the mist. Large, jutting bows cut through the water like a scythe as it headed straight towards us. I let out a shout and Mike wrenched at the wheel but we were on a collision course. There was a sickening crash as the raked bows caught us amidships and I was thrown backwards, over the side and down into the viridian depths.

The water was icy. I swallowed a good deal and fought my way to the surface gasping and spluttering. I tore my hair away from my eyes and trod water. There was no sign of Mike Carberry or his boat. A long swell of water hit my head and shoulders and I went under again. When I surfaced the alien boat was bearing down on me. It was going to run me down. I bobbed helplessly in the water like a cork expecting to be smashed but at the last moment its engine was cut and it swept sideways past me. A man leaned over the stern and grabbed me as I was swamped by the wash. I caught a heart-stopping glimpse of red hair as the water closed over my head and I struggled feebly as strong arms plucked me out of the sea and hauled me on board.

Chapter Seven

I collapsed in the bottom of the boat choking and retching, sure that I was going to be sick. I just wanted to close my eyes and float off into oblivion but there was surely something I had to do first. I clawed my way up onto my hands and knees, my head reeling, my hair a wet curtain clinging to my face and neck. I was kneeling on bottom boards that shifted slightly in an oily bilge and an expanse of sharp, white fibreglass reared up beside me. Braced against this was a pair of jean-clad legs wearing filthy plimsolls. My eyes travelled upwards and as awareness returned of what had happened and where I was, I was pulled up to face the owner of those legs. Pete Walmsley pinned me against the side of the boat and leered at me with pale, gooseberry eyes.

'Well, sweetheart! This is where you start singing.'

'Mike Carberry! What's happened to Mike Carberry?'

'Don't you worry your head about him, the devil looks after his own.' I looked round wildly; at the empty sea and the fog rolling by. There was a roar as the engine sprang to life again and the large powerboat responded to the wheel and gained way.

'You can't leave him! He's out there somewhere!'

Pete Walmsley tightened his grip on me. 'You tell us

what we want to know and maybe we'll go back and look for him.' His companion at the wheel, a dark, greasy youth opened the throttle and the boat sprang forward, surging away from the spot where Mike and his boat had disappeared. I struggled desperately, horror at Mike's fate completely overshadowing my own predicament.

'You're murderers! You killed my husband and now you've killed Mike Carberry!'

'We didn't kill your husband; that was an unfortunate accident. As for Mike Carberry; to think he was involved in this all the time and we didn't realise it. I knew if we were patient you'd lead us to your friends.'

'You don't understand,' I cried bitterly, 'I didn't know of Mike Carberry's existence until yesterday. Damn you and your treasure hunt – no ship is worth two mens' lives!'

'So they found it!'

'Found what? You tell me.'

'A certain Dutch East Indiaman called the *Maria Johanna*?'

'If you know all about it why have you been persecuting me?'

His answer was to jerk my arm painfully and snarl: 'Well?'

'They think they have found it.' Then as realisation sank in, 'They thought they *had* found it.' I choked and had another coughing fit. He shook me impatiently.

'Where?'

'I don't know, out there somewhere.' I gestured towards what I thought was the direction of the Western Rocks.

'Don't play with me, sweetie.' His fingers dug painfully into my shoulders and I tried not to cringe. 'Just exactly where?'

'You've made a mistake.' I even managed a little sarcastic laugh. '*I* don't know except that it was somewhere near the Western Rocks. You've just killed the only man who had some idea of the position.'

'What do you mean?'

'Mike Carberry has dived out there for several years and twice he has made finds that indicated he might have found the *Maria Johanna* but he was unable to pinpoint the exact location. He was just about to start diving operations for the third time.'

'And you don't know where?'

'Of course not, only that it was somewhere amongst the Western Rocks – that's the area containing most of the wrecks, isn't it? Even if he had mentioned a name it would have meant nothing to me; I'm a stranger to these parts.'

I don't know why I lied so strenuously. I felt a complete revulsion against the whole world of wrecks, diving and treasure and I wanted no more to do with it; but all the same I didn't mention the *Merchant Royal* or the Crim Rocks, considerably north of the Bishop and Western Rocks.

'And where has Patterson gone?'

That shook me anew. If only Rory were here now, but he was better out of it.

'You frightened him away, didn't you?'

'Mrs Carr, you're wearing my patience.'

'You know who he is, so therefore I presume you know *what* he is. He is an investigator and he has gone back to the mainland to investigate you and your bunch of hoodlums!'

He got a hold on my wet, slippery hair and jerked my head back. 'It would pay you to be nice to me, darling.'

'I'd rather humour a boa-constrictor! You won't get away with this you know, running down an innocent craft and murdering half the occupants!' As I hissed at him I wondered whether I would be allowed to live and lay evidence against him. I needn't have worried.

'A collision in thick fog, the fault of no-one? And frantic efforts to rescue the crew resulting in the saving of one of them? What a shame we were unable to pick up the man.'

'It's your word against mine.'

'The ravings of an hysterical woman, distraught with grief? I don't think the police would believe you, you know, especially if they investigated your background. You have a recent history of persecution mania and psychosis – remember?'

I felt completely helpless. It was quite true, no-one would believe me. I sunk onto the coaming and he let me go, reading the despair on my face. 'What more do you want of me?' I whispered. 'I've told you all I know.'

'I'm not so sure about that'. His eyes narrowed unpleasantly. 'The boss wants to see you. No doubt he'll be able to sort out fact from fiction.'

'You're taking me back to St Mary's?'

'No, St Agnes. We must report this tragic accident – perhaps we'll offer to go back and help search, eh, Gary?'

The youth at the wheel sniggered and made a quick manoeuvre that resulted in the boat rolling sideways. I fell against Pete Walmsley and shuddered as he grabbed my shoulders once more.

'First,' he continued, 'we're going to take you somewhere nice and quiet where the boss won't be interrupted.'

I was beyond being scared. I didn't care what happened to me any more. I slumped against the side and stared bleakly at the water swirling past. The mist was clearing. Even as I registered this fact we skimmed through the edge of the haze and emerged into full sunlight. It was unbelievable. One moment we had been in a muffled, shuttered world; the next we were out on a blue sea under a blue sky with unlimited visibility, the fog an impossible memory. Ahead of us to starboard was St Agnes, the white tower of the disused lighthouse gleaming in the sunshine.

Where were we going to land? Surely not at the quay at Porth Conger which the inter-island launches used? But no, we headed in towards the harbour of Periglis on the western shore, where the old jetties and abandoned life-boat slip lay under the shadow of the squat, square church. The curve of the beach was stony with a tangle of weeds above the tide-line, and it recalled fleetingly the many little fishing hamlets of my native East Anglian coast. On the right of the church as we approached was a camping site, the blue, yellow and orange tents perched almost on the beach itself on a grassy plateau that backed the shore. There were people about; families with child-ren, and fishermen and boatmen.

This gave me hope. My captors couldn't frog-march me to their assignation point past all these people without running the risk of me advertising my plight to all and sundry, which I fully intended doing. As the engine was throttled back and we headed towards the jetty I searched the shore intently, seeking my chance.

'Now, darling, are you going to behave or do we have to knock you out and carry you ashore?'

'You'd have a job explaining away an unconcious body.'

'I think it would lend realism to our sad tale of a colli-sion in the fog. Those good men,' he gestured sarcastic-ally towards the shore, 'will rush off to sea to start a search and we will be left in peace to get you away.'

'You've thought of everything.' I watched stonily as we came to rest against the jetty. Nobody paid us any atten-tion. Pete Walmsley propelled me off the boat closely followed by the youth called Gary. He twisted one of my arms up behind my back and held it in a grip like a vice

139

while he wrapped his free arm around my shoulders and clamped me against him. To the casual onlooker we must have looked like a courting couple overcome by passion in the midday sun. I tried to struggle and he jabbed one of my bare feet with a vicious movement of a plimsolled heel.

'Come on, sweetie, move.'

I tried to hang back, to drag on him like a dead weight but he just tweaked my captured arm till I gasped with pain and was forced to fall in with his stride.

Two men who had been working on their lobster pots near a black, derelict-looking hut, straightened up and moved towards us. I opened my mouth to shout and my head was jerked down onto Pete Walmsley's shoulder and he hissed into my ear: 'You try anything and it will be the worse for you.'

The men hailed us. They wanted to know what the weather conditions were like beyond Smith Sound and whether it was still foggy. Pete Walmsley was forced to relax his hold and I edged imperceptibly away. He also had to tell his tale of the collision. He laid it on thick. Listening, I could almost believe his version; it *had* been an accident, he *had* searched desperately for survivors, he *had* come to St Agnes to summon help. It was in my interests to play along with him, to let him think I had given up, so I slumped despondently against a pile of pallets and hung my head.

His story brought the reaction he had anticipated. There were exclamations of horror and sympathy and my captors were eased back along the jetty to a barrage of questions. Surely now I could make a dash for freedom? Even as I straightened up Pete Walmsley seemed to read my mind and turned back to me with an angry movement.

'Look!' I shouted, gesticulating wildly out to sea, 'There's Mike Carberry. He's safe – his boat didn't sink!'

140

All heads swung round to watch my pointing finger and I seized my opportunity and shot up the path. As I tore over the uneven ground, my bare feet taking a beating from the rocks and rough grass, I risked a glance backwards. Amazingly, the four men were still looking out to sea and exchanging exclamations. I couldn't believe my luck. I was sure Pete Walmsley wouldn't let me get far. I swung to the right and raced towards the campsite hoping to enlist help. The adults I thought I had seen from the boat all seemed to have disappeared, but a knot of children ceased their game and looked at me curiously. I made a quick decision.

'Please can you help me?' I gasped for breath and must have looked pretty desperate, and they circled around me like a pack of inquisitive young animals. 'I'm involved in a game of Survival and I have to get away.'

'Is it for telly?' The speaker was a boy of about eleven and he drank in my appearance with avid eyes.

'It's a sort of rehearsal, but it's very important that I get away from those men over there at the end of the jetty. Where can I hide?'

There was a hasty confabulation amongst the children and various suggestions were cried down whilst I hovered in an agony of impatience, aware that Pete Walmsley had broken away from the others and was making his way back along the jetty.

'Hide in the church, you'll be safe in there.'

'But surely they'll find me?'

'We'll tell them you've gone along the path to Higher Town, it runs past the church.'

They shepherded me up the slope towards the church and as we ran the young boy who appeared to be their spokesman, and was the only one who seemed to appreciate my panic, threw questions at me.

'Is it the ginger-haired man?'

'Yes, and the young dark man. They really mustn't find me, it's most important.'

'Don't worry, we'll head them off.'

We had reached the back of the sheds where the path led upwards past farm buildings and we were out of sight of those on the waterfront. There was a gate to the right leading into the churchyard; a small, quiet oasis of cropped grass, fuchsias, veronica and escallonia bushes, humming with bees. I blundered towards the porch, shattering the peace, and my band of youthful helpers dispersed. Once inside I was brought to an abrupt halt by the east window.

The church itself was small with a plain interior of stark pews and pannelled walls but the stained glass window was beautiful. A simple gold cross hovered above billows of turquoise glass, each one a slightly different shade from its neighbours, and above a few gold stars broke the expanse of blue glass sky; an evocative momento of the Atlantic lapping the nearby shore. It looked modern and was quite breathtaking, and for a few seconds I forgot my real purpose in being in the church. Then I remembered and looked around for somewhere to hide. There was not much cover and I ended up crouched against the pannelling at the back where I could still keep an eye on the east window and the door.

I wondered what was happening outside. Had Pete Walmsley been lured away or was he likely to come charging in at any moment? I shuddered and wriggled my scratched, burning feet. I was feeling cold. My bikini and shorts had more or less dried on me but I felt decidedly bare in the chill, dim, interior. Gradually the peaceful atmosphere seeped into me and calmed me down. I remembered that I had not been to church for a long time. I had denied my upbringing and turned away, but now I felt ashamed. Crouched on the floor I clutched the end of

142

a pew and tried to pray. I prayed for Mike Carberry, so newly-found a friend and so suddenly lost, and I prayed for all the myriads of men who had lost their lives in these waters; many named on remembrance tablets like the one in this church, many more, unknown, unnamed, who had found watery graves far from their homes and country.

I don't know how long I knelt there but I was suddenly aware of a noise outside. Someone was approaching the door. I ducked down behind the pew, unable now to see but hopeful that I was out of sight. I heard the latch click and the door swing open and a shaft of light fell across the floor in front of me.

'Bethany? Bethany, are you there?' I froze as the whisper echoed round the panelled walls. There was a silence for a few seconds then I heard footsteps as the speaker moved closer across the aisle that separated the nave from the chancel. There was a thud as if he had stubbed his toe against some unseen object followed by a muffled curse. I couldn't believe my ears, but still I huddled behind the pew afraid I was hallucinating.

'Bethany? Where are you?' This time I definitely recognised the voice, unbelievable though it was, and I bobbed up into view. Mike Carberry, clad only in a singlet and shorts, was staring round the church in a puzzled manner. He did not see me at first.

'Mike, I thought you were drowned!'

I threw myself down the nave towards him and he caught me and hugged me to him. He was still decidedly damp.

'Bethany, thank God! They told me you were here. Are you all right?'

'Yes, but what happened to you? There was no sign of you or your boat and I thought you were dead!' My voice cracked alarmingly.

'I'm not got rid of so easily.' He stroked my hair. 'I was

picked up by that fisherman and we followed you back here at a discreet distance. My own boat went to the bottom.'

'Oh Mike! So you really were out there when I tried to create a diversion – no wonder they were so startled that they let me get away.' I told him all that had happened to me and he filled in his part in the drama. We were still talking in whispers as if afraid of being overheard and I started to shiver, reaction setting in.

'Bethany, you're cold.'

'I haven't got much on. Nor have you, come to that.'

'Come on, let's get out of here.'

'Where are we going? Pete Walmsley . . ?'

'It would give me great pleasure to catch up with Pete Walmsley but I'm getting you out of the way first. I'll deal with him later.'

'Where has he gone?'

'He's over the other side of the island by now, I should think. Your young friends have led him a fine dance.'

'They thought it was all part of some game.'

'Well, thank goodness they were old enough to appreciate your feminine charms and come out on your side. Come on.'

I stumbled after him as he led the way back towards the jetty; then he saw my bare feet and stopped, horrified.

'Your feet! My poor Bethany, I hadn't realised you'd lost your shoes. All your stuff went down with the boat I suppose?'

'My camera and my rucksack. Thank heavens I hadn't got my painting gear with me.'

'You can't walk like that – your poor feet are bleeding.' And despite my protestations he swung me up in his arms. 'The fisherman who picked me up is going to take us back to St Mary's.'

'Mike, aren't you going to report them? The police, or should it be coastguard . . ?'

'No.' Then he glanced down and saw the look on my face. 'It wouldn't achieve much purpose and I don't want anyone investigating our affairs at the moment.'

'But if Pete Walmsley and his friends were arrested, it would get them out of our hair.'

'Small hope of that. It's their word against ours and if they insist on their version there's no way we can prove them wrong. We've both got out of it alive, be thankful.'

'But Mike, your boat . . .'

'I may be able to salvage it, don't worry. At least we know what we're up against now. I don't want any further news of our discovery leaking out around the islands.'

'They haven't caught up with us. They think it's the *Maria Johanna* and I told them it was somewhere on the Western Rocks.'

'Good girl, but we're going to have a job keeping our diving operations secret.'

'Mike, you're the one in danger now. They know that you can lead them to it.'

'Would that I could. But we've got the field narrowed down to quite a small area now. It must be somewhere on the northern tip of the Crim group. When's your friend coming back?'

'Rory Patterson? In a couple of days I think.'

'Perhaps he can give some help with the legal side.'

I pondered on this as Mike strode down to the jetty with me held tightly in his hairy arms. Had Rory had legal training? I had told Walmsley he was an investigator and Rory himself had told me he was involved in security and industrial sabotage. Did this mean he was, or had at some time actually practised as a lawyer? I really knew so little about Rory Patterson and his background.

I remember very little of the journey back to St Mary's.

Suffice it to say that my relief at being rescued overcame my olfactory scruples to the extent that I gratefully accepted a sweater from the fisherman and wore my borrowed garment with no compunction. Back at the cottage I slunk quietly to my room avoiding the eagle eye of Mrs Pethick, and spent a long while soaking in a hot bath.

The next morning Mike Carberry phoned me to see if I had recovered from my ordeal. After I had put the phone down, Mrs Pethick asked if I was going out that day.

'No, I'm going to paint locally. I'll have an evening meal, please. By the way, have there been any messages for me?'

'No, were you expecting one?'

'Mr Patterson has gone back to the mainland for a few days on business; he may possibly phone through.'

Rory Patterson had been gone three days, and I had received no communication from him. I was rather piqued.

'My daughter's coming over at the end of next week, Mrs Carr, I hope you've remembered?'

'Yes, I'm going back next Thursday to London and I'll return a fortnight later, if that is all right with you?'

'Yes, my daughter can never manage more than about twelve days at a time; the rooms will be available again at the beginning of July.'

When Mrs Pethick had gone I sat down and planned my itinerary for the weekend.

I hired a bicycle and spent the Saturday and Sunday riding round St Mary's. I gave the harbour and quay a wide berth and went inland and near Watermill I found Russian comfrey, yellow bartsia and bog stitchwort which were welcome additions to my sketchbook. I also went to Pelistry Bay and at low water walked across the bar to Toll's Island. Here I picnicked in splendid solitude amongst the pungent bracken fronds.

Rory Patterson did not phone me and I wondered whether I might receive a letter on Monday. The islands are cut off from the mainland on Sunday. The *Scillonian* does not sail and the helicopters are grounded, so I knew he could not return until early next week. He managed to surprise me though. I overslept on the Monday morning and was pottering around the studio in dressing-gown and bare feet, coffee mug in hand, when there was a knock below on the front door and Mrs Pethick yelled up the stairs: 'Your Mr Patterson is back.'

I tightened my tie belt, pushed my fingers through my curtain of unbrushed hair, caught sight of myself in the mirror and groaned. He bounced up the stairs and was through the door before I could reply to Mrs Pethick. He seemed larger than life, full of pent-up energy and I felt at a distinct disadvantage.

'When did you get back?' I squinted at him through strands of hair and gesticulated with my coffee mug.

'Just now. Is that for me?'

'No, do you want some?'

'Of course, why do you think I've come? I'm suffering withdrawal symptoms from lack of caffeine.'

I wandered over to the gas-ring and busied myself with kettle and coffee jar but he came after me and put his hands on my shoulders and swung me round to face him.

'You don't seem very pleased to see me.'

'You took me by surprise. Do you mean you've actually come over this morning?'

'By the first flight. It's not exactly the crack of dawn, you know. Anyway, how are you?'

'I'm fine,' I muttered crossly. 'Did you get all your business deals sorted out?'

'Business deals? I had some business to attend to and I've cleared that up; but I'm afraid I had very little joy with our treasure trove.'

'Oh, don't bother about that,' I said airily; 'it pales into insignificance beside my awesome discoveries.'

'Your discoveries? What have you been up to? Don't tell me you've found our wreck laden down with treasure just waiting to be plucked out of the sea?' He grinned as he stirred his coffee and I longed to strike that complacent smile off his face.

'As a matter of fact, you could say yes, I have done just that, with the help of friends, of course.'

'Friends? What are you talking about? You haven't been pressurised by Walmsley and his gang, have you?'

He narrowed his eyes and there was something about his tone of voice that needled me.

'I'm talking about my new business associates. Such a lot has happened since you've been away.'

'Bethany, what are you on about? Are you sure you're all right? You seem very odd.'

'I've only been half-drowned and kidnapped amongst other things. I've recovered from this but at the moment I think that I'm suffering from being discovered "*en déshabillé*".'

His lips twitched. 'Bethany, you look absolutely adorable, though I know you won't believe me. Go and get dressed and we'll start again. I'll wait here and commune with Percy.'

Percy was wedged in one of the armchairs and Rory walked over and tweaked one of his ears. 'Hello, ratbag, how's the old avoirdupois?' If he had been a dog Percy would have thumped his tail. As it was he managed to convey that he was absurdly pleased and that he had just been paid the ultimate in compliments.

'That cat's reaction to you is quite disgusting,' I said

darkly as I went towards the door. 'Do make yourself some more coffee.'

Rory indicated that he had every intention of doing so and I ran down to my bedroom wondering why nearly every meeting with him seemed to end with me seething with exasperation.

I dressed quickly and when I returned he was sprawled on the studio couch still drinking coffee, his pipe sizzling and filling the room with billows of smoke. I pointedly crossed to the window and flung it open. I noticed that he'd been through my sketches. They were strewn higgle-dy-piggledy across the desk and he'd made no attempt to conceal his search.

'You don't mind . . ?' He saw me looking at them.

'They did happen to be in order.'

'You've been busy. How is it going?'

'Very well as far as I've got. Unfortunately my camera with a half-exposed film containing a lot of flower shots that I was going to work from later is lying at the bottom of the ocean at this moment. Off Annet to be precise.'

With maddening slowness he tapped out his pipe and fiddled with dottle and matches. Then he leaned back and drawled: 'I presume you are going to tell me what this is all about. You're not just dropping these little nuggets of tantalising information as conversation fillers?'

So I told him all that had happened since he'd been away. About my first accidental meeting with Mike Carberry and all that had followed it. It occurred to me as I talked that this was the second time I had gone to great trouble to explain one man to the other. He heard me out in silence, only the gleam in his eyes betraying his growing excitement. When I had finished he bounced to his feet and grabbed my hands.

'What are we waiting for? Take me to meet your new friend.'

'He's probably out in his boat at the moment. Aren't you at all concerned that I was nearly drowned?'

'You weren't born to drown, Bethany, you've got a mermaid's tail. Don't worry, when I catch up with friend Walmsley I've got two scores to settle.'

'What have you been up to? Stands London where it did?'

'Alas, poor city; without your company it palled. I'm not sorry to be back.'

'And you weren't followed, mugged or the object of any murderous attacks?'

'Let's say, I took great care not to get myself into any situation where I laid myself open to such possibilities.'

'You talk as if all that has happened to me has been my own fault.'

'Some would say you were accident-prone. Now be a good girl and put me in touch with your Mike Carberry.'

'Put you in touch? You don't think I'm letting you two get together when I'm not around, do you? I'll arrange for us *all* to meet. I'm very much part of this, you know; I'm taking up Martin's stake in this treasure hunt. It is a costly business mounting a diving project.'

'Then I'm sure my support will be needed too – I'm not destitute.'

I managed to get Mike Carberry on the phone and we arranged that I and Rory and he and his three colleagues would all get together at his place that evening. He told me that he had had no luck so far in salvaging his motorboat, but in view of what had happened he was keeping a close eye on his other boat.

'Where is it, Mike, you haven't told me?'

'It's moored right out in the harbour in full view of everyone.'

'Then surely no-one could damage it without running the risk of being seen?'

'I hope not, but it has its disadvantages. We can't slip in and out without advertising our actions to everyone on the island. That is one of the things we have to discuss tonight.'

He rang off and I returned upstairs to Rory Patterson who was hovering near the window looking preoccupied. I told him the arrangements and he nodded abstractedly.

'I expect you've got plenty to do today, I'll see you this evening.' He couldn't conceal his impatience to get away and he clattered down the stairs and collected his luggage which he had dumped in the porch. I was absurdly hurt. I had been annoyed at the way he had constantly seemed to be breathing down my neck before but I had got used to having him around. Now he had apparently decided that I was no longer in any danger and had lost interest in keeping me company.

Again the little core of suspicion that was slowly growing inside me put out warning signals. Rory Patterson had not been interested in me personally, but only in what I represented, in what I could lead him to. I should be very interested to hear him explain his motives and part in the business to Mike Carberry when we met later.

I discovered why he had not wanted me around and what he had been up to during that day when he collected me from the cottage at eight o'clock.

'Well, I've been checking up on your Mike Carberry and he appears to be completely *bona fide*.'

'You've been doing *what*?'

'Checking up on Mike Carberry and his colleagues. He's well liked by the locals and envied in a good-natured way for the little packet he's just made in the Middle East.'

'You've got a damn cheek, poking and prying into

other people's business! I hope your enquiries were discreet and he doesn't get to hear of it.'

'I was the soul of discretion. You really are too trusting, you know, Bethany.'

'Yes, I am beginning to think I am.'

'What do you mean by that remark?' His brown eyes widened to suggest aggrieved innocence, but I was aware that he was not as relaxed as he would have me think. Beneath his nonchalance he waited, poised for my answer.

'I think that Mike Carberry is an open book compared to you.' I might have known I couldn't inveigle him into any admission he did not choose to make. He slipped a red herring into the conversation.

'I hear that he is an extremely personable man and has half the female population on its knees.'

'He's the most handsome man I have ever met.' I returned his gaze defiantly. Let him make what he could of that.

'Perhaps that's why Martin took great care to keep you apart.'

I refused to rise to that, I snatched up my handbag and a jacket. 'Come on, we'll be late.'

It had been another hot, sunny day but now there was a freshness in the air and the sky was streaked with mackerel cloud. The water in Town Bay had an almost yellowish tinge and sounds seemed to carry even further than usual. A dog barking on Porthmellon Beach could be heard echoing all over Hugh Town. Seagulls sat in rows on the grey slate roofs and scolded as we passed. Rory strode along, hands in pockets, his head lowered in concentration, his brown hair sticking up in great dishevelment. I trotted by his side and wondered what would be the outcome of this meeting.

I needn't have worried. The two men seemed to take to

152

each other after an initial wariness. Mike's three partners were already there, seated round the table in the upstairs room that I had been in before. This room was Mike's office but I hadn't realised that the building was so large. It was a positive rabbit-warren with numerous other rooms, including Mike's living and sleeping quarters, rambling over the downstairs boatshed.

Two of the men were brothers, Tom and Bill Shepherd, whom I later discovered were distant cousins of Mike. They were completely unalike; Bill being tall and lanky with straight, sun-bleached hair; whilst Tom was shorter and more thickset with mousey, crinkly hair. The other man was considerably older, nearer forty and was the antithesis of Mike as far as colouring was concerned. He had black, curly hair touched with grey and a black, bristling beard and moustache and dark, deep-set eyes. His name was Magnus.

After introductions all round Mike waved us to seats and produced cans of beer from a little fridge tucked away in a corner.

'Bethany, dear . . ? There's whisky if you prefer.'

'Beer's fine, thanks.' I accepted a can, secretly gratified at the fleeting annoyance on Rory's face at Mike's endearment.

'Has Bethany brought you up to date with everything?' enquired Mike of Rory.

'As I understand it, instead of the valuable Dutch East Indiaman you thought you had found, you now have reason to believe it could be an even more valuable, older wreck, a British ship called the *Merchant Royal*. However, you have no positive identification either of the wreck or the location. Is that correct?'

'That just about sums it up. What we do now is to make a methodical search of the area with the magnetometer. Look, we've marked it out on this chart of Crim.' We pored over the chart spread out on the table. It went into great navigational detail and Mike had divided it into sections with pencil lines.

'Excuse my ignorance,' I said, 'but what *is* a magnetometer?' Magnus answered me. 'It's a sensitive electronic instrument which measures the earth's magnetic field and shows up anything that alters it, such as ferrous remains like cannon or anchors. We drag the "fish" behind the boat and the recorder on board plots a graph. Bronze or gold and silver coins don't effect it, only iron of course.'

'So what happens?'

'We dive where it blips,' said Tom succinctly.

'Unfortunately, it's not as simple as that,' said Mike. 'If a later, iron ship has gone down in the area it completely buggers up the works, if you'll excuse the expression.'

'And does that often happen?'

'There's wreck upon wreck out there. Every country has produced its own toll of shipwrecks. Most have long since split up and dispersed without trace, but logically speaking, if they remained intact you'd have a column of ships one on top of each other going back to your Viking longboat and Phoenician galley.'

'How romantic,' I breathed, and was rewarded with a derogatory grunt from Rory.

He pointed with the stem of his pipe at the chart. 'So you methodically comb the area you've marked out and hope to come up with something. How long will that take?'

'It's impossible to say. We could find something on the first dive. It could take weeks, months . . .'

'You're not going to be able to keep it secret, are you?' I said. 'Can nothing be done to stop other teams from having a go?'

'No, that's the trouble. Until we get a positive identification and claim Salver and Possession it's a free for all. We must work on that. Did you find anything out about those two pieces of crud you took to the mainland?' he asked Rory.

'Not much. It was incredibly difficult to break them up.'

'They use explosives,' I said smugly.

'Really?' His eyebrows shot up. 'No wonder I had trouble with a hand drill. There was a small, hammered silver coin, worn smooth and blank, some iron shot and part of an iron link which presumably came from a chain originally.'

'We need those artefacts that I posted to Martin,' said Mike tugging at his beard. 'They could help to date it, if nothing else.'

'They must still be in Post Office custody somewhere,' I said. 'As Martin's next-of-kin I can lawfully claim them. I'm going back to London on Thursday; I'll try and chase them up.'

The talk moved on to diving procedures and touched amongst other things, on the relative advantages of 'dry suits' over 'wet suits'. It was all highly technical and I must admit that a lot of it went over my head, but annoyingly Rory Patterson seemed *au fait* with it all. He had done his homework well. I sipped my beer and listened carefully, determined not to be left out completely. It was nearly midnight before the discussion finally broke up. My head was reeling from the facts it had tried to assimilate and the close atmosphere, not helped by the smoke-screen from Rory's pipe.

'How are you travelling across to the mainland?' asked Mike as I zipped up my jacket.

'I think by helicopter. It's so much quicker; I can do the journey in one day without having to travel overnight.'

'There's a big wet coming.' This was from Tom who stood by the open door apparently sniffing the night air.

155

'The weather's going to change?'

'There's a lot of weather coming this way in the next few days. You'd be better off flying unless you're a good sailor.'

'Thanks for the warning. I hope I can get a flight at such short notice.'

'I'll see you get fixed up,' said Rory, stretching as he got to his feet.

'Don't tell me you know a little man in the BA hierarchy?'

'I have some useful contacts.' He winked at the others as he escorted me down the stairs and goodnights echoed across the yard.

It was cold outside and I shivered and turned up my collar. The moon sailed erratically through silver-threaded clouds, and out at sea lights winked from moored yachts. It must have been high tide; you could hear the water hissing and sucking nearby as we walked back along The Strand. There was no-one about and only a few upstairs windows showed lights. Rory put his arm round me and I leaned against him, glad of his support.

'What are you going to do whilst I'm away?' I asked as we turned up Garrison Lane.

'I expect I shall survive your absence somehow. I intend going out with *Sea Wolf*.' *Sea Wolf* was the name of Mike's boat.

'I should have thought you would be a liability in a boat.'

'I know the divers are the star turn, but extra crew on the support vessel is always welcome. I'm sure I can make myself useful.'

'Mind you don't fall in,' I said sleepily.

'I'll assume that remark is the result of a sleep-befuddled brain and ignore it. It's past your bedtime, you're not making sense.'

'It was a perfectly sensible remark. After all, Mike and I fell in, didn't we?'

'I see what you mean. I'll take your oblique warning to heart and be careful.'

By the time we had climbed the last of the hill and turned into Sallyport the moon had disappeared completely. There were no stars in the sky, only a faint lightening of the black dome above our heads where the moon should have been. The wind snaked through the echiums and palms hanging over the wall, carrying with it the mournful tolling from Spanish Ledge.

I was not sorry to get inside; to the light and warmth and the comforting presence of Percy. My dreams that night were a confused jumble of ships, both ancient and modern, treasure trove, bearded men and a smoke-filled room. I didn't hear the rain beating down on the roof as the first squall reached us.

Chapter Eight

I was busy during the next couple of days sorting out my work. Mrs Pethick had agreed to store some of my belongings until I returned, and Rory had managed to book me on an early flight on the Thursday morning. It rained a lot; heavy showers that came without warning, and even when the rain stopped the cloud cover did not thin. The islands were shrouded in a heavy pall of cloud and a dark, sullen sea separated us from the off-islands which were just uninviting blots on the horizon. I could imagine that if one were a permanent resident, there would be times when one felt quite claustrophobic; a little island community cut off and afloat in the vast Atlantic.

Rory Patterson had asked me to have dinner with him at the Star Castle Hotel on my last evening. He had booked in there again on his return and I wondered idly who was footing the bill. He came to collect me earlier than I expected and shook his head at my thin dress.

'Put on something warm and your kagool. We're going to do the Garrison Walk.'

'Are we?' I looked askance but bit back any further comment.

'We haven't done it yet and this is just the evening for it.'

'The Garrison Walk should be done on a fine, balmy evening when the full glory of the sunset can be appreciated.'

'A quick, bracing walk will do you good. Chase all the cobwebs away before your incarceration in murky London.'

I sighed and reluctantly changed my thin sandals for heavier shoes. Actually, I would be glad to get some fresh air and the walk under these conditions would not be so painfully full of memories. Dodging the rainstorms and braving the strengthening wind would take one's mind off sunsets and all the moon in June business.

We got onto the Garrison Path by the access route from Sallyport, and I clung to Rory's hand as we went through the tunnel, reliving my horrible encounter with Pete Walmsley in the fog. There was no fog tonight, only a grey, louring sky and a rain-spattered wind. We made it round the Hugh without getting soaked, and needless to say we did not meet many people. We arrived at the castle breathless and windswept.

'You've acquired a healthy glow,' said Rory, watching me untie my scarf and shake my hair free as we went through the archway.

'And an appetite to match.'

'Good, then let's hope you do justice to the food.'

The dining room was a pleasant, panelled room, discreetly lit, and the service and food were excellent. I drank too much. That is the only excuse I can find for what happened afterwards.

Rory persuaded me to try a steak dish and with it we had a red wine which was more potent than I realised. After three glasses I was decidedly mellow. I don't think I had ever felt so relaxed in his company before, and I agreed with everything he said which must have surprised him. He seemed to be particularly agreeable that evening and

159

suddenly the prospect of leaving the Scillies and going back to London was not such an attractive proposition. I wanted to stay here with Rory and be wined and dined and made much of. I think I said as much to him, fumbling to explain how I felt in my semi-inebriated state. His eyes crinkled up with laughter but he was very gentle with me.

'You won't feel the same in the morning. It's time we went – you've got an early start.'

We were not so lucky on the way back. We had hardly left the shelter of the castle when the rain started and in a few minutes we were drenched to the skin. It was an absolute cloudburst. We tried to shelter under the Gatehouse but it provided no cover from the driving rain and we ran on down Garrison Hill with the water cascading round our ankles as the whole path turned into a surging stream. By the time we reached the cottage my feet were squelching in sodden shoes and my hair was plastered against my face and dripping down my neck in rats' tails. The wet and cold should have sobered me up. Instead it had the opposite effect and I felt reckless and light-headed.

Rory took my key and opened the door and we clattered up the stairs. As we reached the top I tripped and he grabbed me to stop me falling. I swayed against him and then I was in his arms. He held me tightly, his lips brushing the top of my head, and suddenly all the pent-up longing inside me was released and I clung to him shuddering with emotion, waiting for the kiss that was to come. Instead he released me and stepped back.

'It's getting late, Bethany, I had better go.'

'No, I want you to stay. Please, Rory, don't leave me.'

My voice must have risen for he shushed me and laying his fingers on my mouth he whisked me inside the door. As his hand went up to the light switch I grabbed it and pressed myself against him. 'Hold me Rory, please.' For a

160

few seconds he held me tightly enfolded in his arms and I could feel his heart beating against mine; then he gave a sort of groan and pushed me away, snapping down the light switch.

'Perhaps black coffee would be a good idea.' He drew the curtains and walked over to the gas-ring.

'I don't want coffee, I'm perfectly sober. I'm asking you to stay, Rory, do you understand? I want you to stay all night.'

He shook his head like someone who has been pole-axed. 'You don't know what you're saying Bethany.'

'I do, I do. You think I'm drunk, don't you?'

'I don't think you're drunk but I think it's the wine talking.' He neatly side-stepped out of reach as I looked like hurling myself at him again. That got to me.

'You're rejecting me.'

'I'm trying not to take advantage of you. You don't really mean it, you'll feel differently in the morning.'

Suddenly the euphoria left me. I was stone-cold sober. Cold physically and sick cold deep down inside. I started to cry soundlessly, the tears running down my cheeks.

'Go away, Rory, I hate you. I always have, you know.'

'Oh, my God, Bethany . . !'

He started towards me but I cried at him: 'Don't touch me! Go away!'

He rammed his hands in his pockets. 'I think I had better.'

He looked haunted, his expression positively wretched, and he turned blindly and blundered out of the door.

I remained standing a long while after he had gone, hugging myself tightly to try and stop shivering, whilst the tears flowed unchecked and I stared at the open door.

*　　　*　　　*

Fortunately I was too busy the next morning to dwell overmuch on what had happened the night before. That would come later when I had time to spare. As it was I slept heavily and woke later than I had intended and had a mad rush to get myself to the airport in time to check in for my flight. The rain had cleared overnight and a watery sun was making efforts to gain command of the day but I did not think it would stay fine for long.

As I walked across the tarmac towards the helicopter, which stood poised for take-off, its rotor gyrating deafeningly like an enormous whistling kettle coming to the boil, I turned for a last look at the island. The reception buildings and the backing pines stood stark against a pale sky but the middle distance was shrouded in mist and the sea was invisible. It was my first flight in a helicopter and I had been looking forward to stupendous views but the weather was not cooperating. The islands fell away in a series of grey smudges and then we were flying over a grey sea.

The flight lasted a mere twenty minutes and there was no hold-up at the Penzance terminal. My luggage was checked out, I made the short journey to the station by airport minibus and I was on the train bound for Paddington by half-past nine. The day stretched in front of me. I tried to read but I couldn't concentrate; thoughts of Rory Patterson and my behaviour of last night kept intruding.

In the cold light of day I could only feel relief that he hadn't taken me up on my offer. My cheeks burned as I remembered how I had thrown myself at him shamelessly. Whatever had come over me? He had rejected me – politely, gently, but definitely – and I wondered how I would ever face him again. Damn Rory Patterson, I thought angrily; I'm going to forget him for the next two weeks. Let him think I was drunk; let him

162

amuse himself at the thought that he could have had an easy conquest; what did I care?

As the train sped across England over countryside gently steaming in the sunshine I carefully blotted out any thought of Rory Patterson and concentrated on checking which flowers I still had to paint on my return.

The flat had been broken into. I let myself into the tiny entrance hall, waded through the letters and circulars on the mat, dumped my bags on the floor, and wondered why I had left the drawer of the hall table pulled right out. Then I opened the door to the living room. Here chaos greeted me. Everything movable had been moved; the books from the bookcase thrown on the floor, cupboards emptied out, their contents scattered the length of the room, cushions stripped from the chairs, my record collection tossed onto the table; even the pictures had been wrenched off the walls. I gave a choking cry and hurried to the bedroom. Here the tale was the same. It was as if a giant hand had wantonly snatched everything up and let it fall. The bathroom and my tiny kitchen had had the same treatment and in the studio my canvases lay in a drunken heap and tubes of paints and brushes littered the floor.

I stared at the mess and felt a scream starting in my throat. Oh no, the nightmare couldn't be starting all over again, it didn't make sense; but maybe this time it had been a genuine burglary. I pulled myself together and checked the contents of the flat. As far as I could see nothing had been taken, just a thorough search made. But why? The action had moved with me to the Scillies; why was someone still interested in what my flat might contain? Then common sense took over and I carefully examined the mess again. I noticed what I had at first missed; there was a thin film of dust everywhere, covering every surface and filming my scattered belongings stewn on the floor. This ransacking had been carried out a long while ago, probably within hours of my leaving the flat. Pete Walmsley's gang were almost certainly responsible and they had found nothing because there was nothing to find.

Now that the first shock had worn off I felt anger curling through me. Anger at the destructive mind behind this search. Someone had delighted in the vandalism. And I had to clear up the mess. There was no point in informing the police, but I needed help and someone to share my discovery with. I phoned my friend Lisa and miraculously she was at home and not doing anything that evening. I told her there was something that I wanted her to see and she agreed to come over immediately. While I waited for her to get from Chelsea to North Finchley, I went through my post. One letter immediately caught my eye; it had a Scilly postmark and had been forwarded from my old Hampstead address. I tore it open. It was the letter that Mike Carberry had written to Martin on his return from the Gulf; the one he had told me about. By a stroke of luck it had arrived after the flat had been ransacked. I wondered what had happened to the original coins that Martin had brought back for identification. I had not come across them when going through his things. Maybe they were still languishing in some filing cabinet at M. & K. Maybe that was what had put Rory Patterson onto me.

Lisa made the journey in less time than I had thought possible. She arrived on the doorstep looking stunning in a purple and grey creation, a Gucci bag slung over her shoulder, her hair sculpted close to her head in curved spikes of a colour that verged on magenta.

'Bethany, are you all right? You sounded very odd on the phone. How long have you been back?'

'I've just got back. Thanks for answering my SOS so quickly. You look terrific.'

164

'What has happened?'

For answer I took her arm and led her into the living room.

'My God! No wonder you sounded odd. What has been taken? Have you rung the police?'

'Nothing's been taken, just a thorough search made.'

'But this is what happened before in the Hampstead flat. Are you still being persecuted? Are the police doing anything?'

'I haven't told the police. I have no intention of doing so. As for my persecution mania, it was for real but I now know what it is all about.'

'I must say you don't seem all that perturbed about this,' she gestured round the flat, 'and you're different somehow.'

'Different? In what way?'

'You don't seem to be haunted any more. You're alive again and living in the same world as everyone else. Your stay in the Scillies must have done you good after all. Now tell Auntie Lisa all about it.'

'There is so much to tell, but first, Lisa, you must promise not to breathe a word of it to anyone. This is in strictest confidence and it's not just my secret, other people are involved.'

'Cross my heart and hope to die!' She rolled her eyes, screwed up her face and clutched her bosom, and suddenly the years fell away and we were a pair of grubby schoolgirls again, giggling conspiratorily behind the rows of pegs in the changing rooms as we exchanged outrageous secrets. I gave her a brief resumé of the facts whilst she stared at me wide-eyed.

'Bethany, you're having me on! Buried treasure, shipwrecks, an evil gang! You can't be serious?'

'I am. I told you, Lisa, this is for real. So much has happened, you wouldn't believe.'

165

'I can't wait to hear, but not right now. What are you going to do about this?' She indicated the mess.

'I was hoping you would help me clear it up.'

'I will, but not this evening. You must be whacked after your journey. Have you eaten? Have you got any food in?'

'No, to both your questions.'

'Then you had better come back with me. I'll rustle up a meal and you can stay overnight and we'll come back here in the morning and tackle this.'

'Are you sure? I mean are you . . ?'

'I'm living a life of impeccable purity. In other words there's no-one living with me at the moment and yes, I can spare the time. Fortunately I knocked off my latest masterpiece yesterday and it's all under wraps now.'

I gratefully accepted her offer and was glad to turn my back on the chaos and follow her out to her car. It was an Audi Coupé F1. 'My, this is putting on the style. How long have you had this?'

'Nearly two months. Surely I told you about it?'

I couldn't remember that she had and even accepting her high-living standards, I didn't think her salary stretched to a model such as this.

'I can read you like a book, Bethany. You're wondering if I'm a kept woman.' She grinned wickedly at me as she unlocked the door and tossed my case onto the back seat.

'Lisa, the thought never crossed my mind,' I said in confusion,and she laughed.

'Actually, to be perfectly honest, my Great Aunt Abigail would have said I was living on immoral earnings. It was a gift from an admirer.'

'A parting gift?'

'How quick you are. Yes, a parting gift. You see how simple my way of life is; no complications like court orders or alimony.'

166

'I suppose you know what you are doing.'

'I believe I have shocked you.' She slid the car into gear and we purred off towards Finchley Road.

'I gave up being shocked at anything you did years ago.'

I relaxed as she handled the car deftly and brought us swiftly through the intermittent traffic of a summer evening to Bayswater and on through Kensington into Chelsea.

Lisa lived in a luxurious apartment off Cheyne Walk. It was large and airy and stuffed with an assortment of belongings ranging from very avant-garde pieces of furniture to some choice antiques and odds and ends she had collected on her travels. It should have clashed and grated on the nerves but somehow it all hung together and made the perfect setting for the extraordinary person who is my friend Lisa.

Whilst I washed and tidied up and unpacked my night-things in the spare bedroom, Lisa busied herself in the kitchen making an omelette. She is a good cook though inclined to be heavy-handed with the garlic and herbs. The omelette was a small masterpiece in its way and she also managed to conjure up a green salad and rolls and cheese. She produced a bottle of red wine which she expertly uncorked and poured into large tumblers.

'What are we celebrating?'

'Your return and this exciting tale you're going to tell me more of when we've eaten.' I suddenly realised I was ravenous; I had only had a snack on the train and the cooking smells released my appetite with a vengeance. I tucked in and as we ate Lisa brought me up to date with her latest activities.

'Have some more wine, we can't waste it.' She poured the rest of the wine into my glass.

'Why not, I can't disgrace myself here.'

'You're never going to tell me you got drunk?'

'Not drunk exactly, but I certainly had too much. It may seem amusing now but it wasn't funny at the time.'

'Why, what happened? Don't tell me someone tanked you up and made a pass?'

'It's worse than that. I threw myself at someone and got severely rebuffed for my pains.'

'Bethany, that does seem out of character; and who was this paragon who turned you down? Thank heavens he did for your sake.'

'It was one of the men I've got involved with over there. Do you notice I say *one* of the men? There are several dishy men swimming in my orbit at the moment. How does that take you?'

'I am astounded and envious. The action all seems with you at the moment. Do tell me more.'

'His name is Rory Patterson.' Suddenly I did not want to go on. What had been going to be an amusing anecdote to entertain Lisa was too painful to relate. Then I saw her face.

'You *know* him?'

'I know a Rory Patterson, or rather I know of him. He used to be connected with M. & K. Tall, thin, lots of untidy dark hair, a laconic manner?'

'That sounds like my Rory Patterson. How on earth do you know him?'

'I don't know him personally, just by reputation.'

'And has he a bad reputation? I mean, was I lucky to escape with my virtue intact?'

'Oh, I don't think you were in any danger in that respect.' She looked at me thoughtfully and then spoke slowly as if picking her words with care, 'Do you remember the Donnelly case?'

'The Donnelly case? No, I don't think so – wait a moment, the name rings a bell. How long ago was it?'

'It must be all of four years. It involved Ned Donnelly, the photographer.'

'I do remember vaguely. Wasn't it some rather unsavoury case involving sex with a minor, homosexual sex?'

'Yes. It created quite a scandal at the time and it ruined Ned Donnelly. He was a brilliant photographer with a brilliant future in front of him. After that he was finished.'

'I remember seeing some of his work. He was very good. I don't really remember any of the details, what happened?'

'He got involved with this boy. Quite innocently on his part. I honestly think he had no idea this boy was under age. He was a vicious little tyke, old beyond his years and he set out to break Ned Donnelly, which he did.'

'But surely he was acquitted?'

'Eventually, but there was so much mud raked up, a great deal of it stuck. He was a self-confessed homo and the gutter-press got its knife into him. He never produced any more work in this country after that. I believe he went to live in Australia and I seem to remember hearing that he has since died.'

'But what has all this got to do with Rory Patterson?'

'Rory Patterson was a friend of his. Donnelly lived with him after the trial, before he went to Australia.'

'Are you saying that Rory Patterson is gay?'

'I'm not making any such imputation. All I'm saying is that even in this day and age homos and heteros don't usually live together.'

I felt as if my world had turned upside-down and my distress must have shown.

'My God, Bethany, you haven't fallen for him, have you?'

'Don't be ridiculous. I'm still in love with Martin.'

'That's a pity. But seriously, how have you got involved with him? What has he to do with your treasure hunt?'

So I told her everything, going back to my first sight of Rory Patterson in the boardroom of M. & K. and all the

169

subsequent happenings. She was practically bursting with suppressed excitement by the time I had finished.

'The whole thing is quite fantastic; it reads like something out of a far-fetched thriller. Are you sure you haven't imagined it all?'

'No, I can assure you that it's true. But it's not all excitement and jubilation. The stakes are so high that this gang won't stop at murder to get their hands on it.'

'Martin? My poor Bethany . . .'

'I'm convinced now that Martin's death *was* an accident, though of course they were responsible, but they deliberately tried to eliminate Mike Carberry when they ran down his boat.'

'You did get yourself mixed up in something, didn't you? Thank goodness you're home.'

'But I'm going back; don't you understand? I'm helping to back this treasure hunt financially. I've got a stake in it and I shall get a share in the profits.'

'You really think they'll find this ship?'

'I think they've got a very good chance. I just hope that Pete Walmsley's gang don't get there first. It's rapidly developing into open warfare.'

'Bethany, you're amazing. You've got caught up in gang warfare, kidnapping, attempted murder, you name it, and you sit there as calm as you please, not batting an eyelid.'

'I've had my moments, I can assure you. All I can think about now is what you've told me about Rory Patterson. I just can't believe it.'

She shrugged. 'Leaving that aside, there's something else I think you ought to know.' I looked at her questioningly and she continued: 'He's not employed by M. & K. any longer. I've just remembered, he resigned about a year ago. I believe he's supposed to have come into some money and there was a rumour about his writing a book.'

I stared at her in astonishment. 'But he told me he was investigating on behalf of M. & K. At least that was the impression he gave me.'

'Quite. I think you ought to ask yourself whether this treasure hunt is not a three-pronged affair.'

'You mean Rory Patterson has been after the secret for his own ill-gotten gain? That's ridiculous!'

'You know him better than I, but he seems to have been keeping a very low profile about his motives. And from what you say he's clung to you like a leech.'

'I thought he was concerned about my safety, that he was protecting me.'

'For one of his suspected inclinations he seems to have carried his interest in you rather to extremes. How did he behave?'

'We spent most of the time we were in each other's company engaged in verbal sparring. We had got it down to a fine art. I still can't believe he's one of those. He smokes a pipe.'

'That is the ultimate in *non sequiturs*. They're not all tat and camp you know. Anyway, I may be wrong about him. Was he very excitable?'

'*You* described him as laconic. Most of the time he is so laid-back he's practically horizontal.'

'Oh well, don't let it worry you. Now you know the facts you can act accordingly.'

Our talk moved on to other topics and Rory Patterson was not mentioned again, but I could not forget what I had learned about him and after I had gone to bed that night I lay awake a long while thinking about it. And the fact that he might have been using me for his own ends didn't bother me half as much as the thought that he might be gay. How could anyone so tender, so humorous, so infuriating, so callous and . . . yes, so attractive, be gay? But why not? I knew perfectly well that it was possible for

171

a woman to have a very good friendship with a man of that persuasion; it happened frequently. Why then, did I feel so desolate, so let-down? I eventually got to sleep in the small hours; and as I drifted off I remembered Lisa's words about him writing a book. That would bear investigation.

The next day Lisa took me back to Finchley and we spent the day cleaning up the flat. It was an onerous task but Lisa insisted that it could have been worse.

'In this instance it was a case of somebody looking for something. They didn't find it and they didn't put things back afterwards but they didn't indulge in wanton destruction either. You've got off lightly.'

'Well, thanks for that small comfort. You said something last night about Rory Patterson writing a book – would you care to elucidate further?'

'You're still worrying about him? All I know is that I was told that he had left the action with the intention of writing a book.'

'Fiction? A novel?'

'I've no idea, but I shouldn't think so. He has quite a few strings to his bow you know. He's got a degree in sociology and economics and he's studied law.'

'You seem to know a lot about him,' I said accusingly.

'Look, I studied the Donnelly case closely at the time and its aftermath. I am a journalist, aren't I?'

'You mean you actually wrote it up?'

'I don't report on scandals,' she said coldly, 'there are others to do that job. But I was commissioned at the time to do a series of articles on the effect a trial can have on a family or local community even if the accused is acquitted. As you can imagine, the Donnelly case was a perfect one to follow up for my investigation.'

Later, when we had almost finished and the flat was more or less back to normal, Lisa brought up my obsession with Rory Patterson again. 'I've been thinking,' she announced, putting the last of my shoes back in the cupboard and closing the door, 'I'm due for some holiday and I could do with a break. I think I'll come over to the Scillies after you've returned.'

'To stay with me?'

'Can you accommodate me in your rooms?'

'There's a studio couch you could use and I expect I could arrange it with Mrs Pethick, my landlady. But it wouldn't be quite what you're used to.'

'Nonsense, I'm quite good at roughing it if needs be.'

'I wasn't meaning that. The whole idea – the Scillies – they're just not your scene at all. I mean there's nothing to do, no night-life or anything like that.'

'Just to acquire a suntan like yours would be worth it. You look as if you'd spent a month in the Bahamas. Besides, you've made me so curious about the whole thing that I really must see for myself. Your Mike Carberry sounds like God's gift to women. Do you think we'd hit it off if we met?'

'I think the results might be interesting,' I said cautiously, 'but are you sure you won't be bored?'

'Of course not; and I think you need another woman to help look after your interests. You seem to be very up-tight about Rory Patterson.'

'I'm *not* up-tight about Rory Patterson, he means absolutely nothing to me.'

'I shall assess the situation with my own eyes. You don't seem very enthusiastic about my suggestion.'

'Yes I am, it will be fun having you. I was just dubious about whether you would really enjoy it. When will you come?'

'In about three weeks. That will give me time to get my

current assignments sorted out and you will have settled in again by then.'

'So long as you don't intend to write up this story.'

'Of course not, as if I would break your confidence!'

So we left it that she would join me on St Mary's in the second week of July. But I wasn't sure that she really meant it and was quite prepared to hear nothing more on the subject.

I spent the next few days collating my paintings and meeting with my publishers. I also fitted in a flying visit to Suffolk to see my family and reassure them that I was alive and well. The next task before I returned was to try and trace the missing artefacts that Mike Carberry had posted to Martin. The local Post Office was very helpful and it eventually turned out that the packet had been forwarded from the old flat in Hampstead to the Finchley address. As no-one had been there to receive it and sign for it it had been taken back to the local office and a note left in the door telling the addressee to call and collect it. For some reason I had not received this note and as the package had not been claimed it had been sent to the Returned Letter Branch at Portsmouth to be held for about a year during which time efforts would be made to trace the sender. At the end of this period if still not claimed the contents would be put up for public auction.

This information had me dashing down to Portsmouth. It must be quite a year and I wondered if it was too late. Fortunately the next auction was not due for another week, and armed with Martin's death certificate and the certificate of probate, I was able to claim the packet. It had been opened but the Post Office had been unable to trace Mike Carberry, presumably because he had been out of the country at the time.

174

The contents were to me disappointing; a misshapen, blackened metal button which I took to be of brass or some inferior metal, and a gold brooch, the pin broken and the stone out of the centre missing.

The next step was a visit to the V. & A. By this time I was getting quite expert at evasive action and I managed to avoid the question of how they came into my possession. The evidence was inconclusive; the button was probably off a naval uniform, impossible to date within a couple of hundred years, and the brooch was seventeenth century and had originally been a nice piece of jewellery. Armed with this knowledge, which I did not think would be of much help to Mike Carberry and his team, I prepared for my return to the Scillies. Before I left London I saw my solicitor about investing money in the hunt for the wreck.

The weather had been miserable over the last two weeks. What had started out as a record summer weatherwise had deteriorated into a typical English summer, with frequent showers and below average temperatures. I had watched the weather forecasts for the south-west and the weather was even worse in that area; continual rain and strong winds. The Scillies were actually mentioned at one point after a particularly nasty storm. I wondered whether these conditions were hampering the search for the *Merchant Royal*, and if the team had had any luck with their diving operations.

I had not communicated with anyone on St Mary's. I had nothing to say to Rory Patterson, and my information for Mike Carberry about the artefacts could wait until my return, but I did ring Mrs Pethick and let her know on which flight I was booked to check that the rooms were available again. I was not sorry to leave London; the Finchley flat seemed a dismal place and I was not looking forward to living there again when my assignment was over. My publishers had been pleased with the work I had produced so far and I was itching to get painting again.

The morning I left I woke up to sunshine and blue skies. I travelled down to Penzance on the ten-fifteen train from Paddington, and as we sped westwards the temperature rose considerably. It was a perfect day for flying. We soared above hyacinth seas and at one point passed over the *Scillonian* – a toy ship ploughing her way towards the mainland. I had a panoramic view of the islands as we approached St Mary's; green and gold isles nestling on a shelf of ocean that ran the gamut of blues from aquarmarine and turquoise through to peacock and indigo. We swept over St Martin's with its red and white daymark and the white scimitar of beach curving round St Martin's Flats, and then we were plummeting down towards the airport.

Rory Patterson was there to meet me. As I hurried down the steps, the wind whipping my skirts about and playing havoc with my long hair, he materialised from the reception building and loped towards me. The wind did nothing for his hair-style either. He grabbed me eagerly and for one startled moment I thought he was going to kiss me. I hurriedly disengaged myself from his grasp.

'What are you doing here?'

'That's a nice greeting. I've come to meet you. Mrs Pethick told me which flight you were arriving on. Have you any more luggage?'

'Yes, a case.'

Whilst he gained possession of my case I watched him furtively. He looked as disreputable as ever in faded old jeans and a dark shirt rolled up above his elbows displaying sinewy, brown arms. I decided that the reason his hair always looked so dishevelled was because it was absolutely dead straight and grew out of his scalp at random following no style or cut. At that moment the wind was blowing it about in peaked wedges and a dark swag was plastered over one eyebrow.

As he swung me up into the back of the Volkswagon van that was to take us into Hugh Town he rolled his eyes and asked sarcastically: 'Are you sure you'll know me again?'

'I was just wondering why you always managed to look as if you've slept in your clothes. Perhaps you do. You must cause great distress to the management of Star Castle.'

'I can see you're in top form. How did the holiday go?'

'It wasn't a holiday, I've been very busy. What's been happening over here? Have you found the *Merchant Royal* yet?'

'Sssh! My dear girl, you must control your tongue, who knows what ears are flapping. The weather's been atrocious since you've been away. There's only been a couple of days when we've been able to dive at all.'

'*We*? Don't tell me *you're* exploring the ocean bed?'

'I was speaking figuratively. It's been most frustrating, but it looks as if you've brought good weather back with you.'

Back in Sallyport, Rory paid off the driver and I hurried up the steps to the cottage to be greeted effusively by Mrs Pethick. The questions and remarks came thick and fast and Rory egged her on. Percy pounced on us with a thrilling purr and wound himself in and out of our legs producing a great display of affection which I think was motivated more by Rory's presence than mine.

'That cat's missed you,' said Mrs Pethick; 'he don't like the children. I've got a nice meal all ready for you in the oven. Perhaps Mr Patterson would like to share it?'

177

'Mr Patterson is a very busy man,' I said firmly.

'I am?' said Rory favouring me with an innocent stare. 'Mrs Pethick, that's very handsome of you and I shall be pleased to take you up on your offer.'

Later, up in the studio away from the eagle eye of Mrs Pethick, I felt more able to relax; but I couldn't forget what Lisa had told me about him and I just couldn't equate it with the very masculine figure sprawled out in the chair near me. We had exchanged news but I had been very off-hand and wary and I hoped he would take the hint and leave. Instead he lunged out of the chair and crouched by mine, capturing my hands in his.

'What's the matter, Bethany, what's happened?'

'Happened? What do you mean?' I shrank back from him but he yanked me to my feet and forced me to meet his eyes.

'Something is up. You've been behaving most peculiarly since you've been back. What's bothering you?'

'Nothing is bothering me,' I said, trying to break away unsuccessfully. 'I've just discovered that you wheedled your way into my confidence with a pack of lies, and I don't care to be used.'

'Used? Now what are you talking about?' He looked genuinely astonished.

'You don't work for M. & K.,' I said accusingly, 'you resigned from there over a year ago.'

'Oh-ho, so that's how the land lies? And where did you dig up that piece of information?' He let go of me abruptly and ramming his hands in his pockets, he paced the floor.

'I haven't been prying into your affairs. I just happened to mention your name to a friend and she told me.'

'And who is this friend?'

'Lisa Shaw.' I was annoyed that somehow he had got me on the defensive.

'Lisa Shaw? Of "The Monday Spot" fame?'

'You know her?'

'I should think most people have heard of *that* Lisa Shaw; the thinking man's answer to Jean Rook.'

'She gets her facts right.'

'True. I admit it, Bethany, I'm not on the staff of M. & K. any longer, but I still do a little free-lance work for them. I was tying up a loose end.'

'You'll have to do better than that.'

'Suppose I told you that I'd fallen for your "*beaux yeux*" and that was the reason I followed this up?'

'Don't be ridiculous,' I snapped, unhappy in my new-found knowledge. 'Why did you leave M. & K.?'

'I inherited some money, enough to enable me to give up work, temporarily anyway, and concentrate on something I have always wanted to try my hand at – writing a book.'

'A novel?'

'Yes. Actually two books. A novel and also a tribute to a very dear friend.'

'Ned Donnelly?' It was out before I could stop myself.

'So now we're getting to the nitty-gritty. Yes, Ned Donnelly.' He fixed me with a cold, blank stare. 'He was a fine person; he never corrupted anyone. He was very talented and a dear friend. The world lost a very gifted photographer when he died. I am getting together a selection of his work, some of it, the Australian stuff, never published before and I am writing a text to go with it.'

'You lived together?'

'He lived with me for six months before he went to Australia. Come on, Bethany, why don't you ask me the question you're longing to ask?' His voice was icy and I flinched away from the look in his eyes.

'How you live your life is no business of mine.'

'Isn't it? I think you're so overcome with morbid curiosity about my sexual predilections that you can hardly con-

179

tain yourself. It's all hanging out.'

'I tell you, I don't care!'

'Really? Well, I'm not going to satisfy you. There's only one way in which I could prove to you that I'm not queer . . ' He gave me such a deliberate lecherous look and his eyes flickered round the room and alightened on the studio couch so that I was in no doubt what he meant. '. . . But I'm not going to.'

'No, we know you don't fancy me, don't we?'

I immediately wished it unsaid. He came after me with such ferocity that I was scared. I backed away, tripped over Percy and ended up in a heap on the floor. He stood over me, breathing heavily and fighting for control, whilst I glared at him through a curtain of hair. Then his mouth twitched and he started to grin. I continued to glare but when the grin became a chuckle I saw the funny side of it too and joined in the laughter.

'Get up.' He pulled me to my feet. 'Are you all right?'

I nodded weakly. Percy had taken cover under the coffee table and from there he peered out, his tail lashing from side to side. 'Percy . . ?'

'Damn Percy, his dignity is ruffled, that's all.'

'I suppose you could say mine is too. Rory . . . '

'Don't push me, Bethany,' he cut in. 'I suggest we change the subject.'

'Certainly, what would you like to talk about, cabbages and kings?' He wasn't amused.

'I think your Lisa is a stirrer. It's a pity she couldn't mind her own business.' His hand was on the door knob and I knew he was going, but I got the last word.

'You'll be able to tell her so to her face. She's coming to stay.'

I wasn't sure if he heard me, he was already clattering down the stairs, then I heard the front door slam. I shrugged and started my unpacking.

Chapter Nine

The next day *Sea Wolf*, with a full complement of divers plus Rory Patterson, went out to Crim. I phoned Mike early that morning and caught him just before he left. He was delighted to hear from me and after we had brought each other up to date with our news we discussed the legal side of our venture.

'Come round tonight after we get back, after eight, say, and we'll draw up a proper contract and make things official.'

'Shouldn't we have a lawyer to do that?'

'Surely we can leave all that to Rory Patterson, he's our legal eagle.' That stymied me and I didn't answer. 'Are you still there, Bethany? I presumed you'd be happy for Patterson to deal with it, after all he is your protégé.'

'Rory Patterson is no-one's protégé but his own. I suppose it will be all right if you and your partners are quite happy. Have a good day diving – I shall expect a bronze cannon at least.'

I went across to St Agnes and spent the morning and part of the afternoon on Gugh, the island which is joined to the east coast of St Agnes by a sand bar except at high tide. Here I found mullein and two other prized plants – viper's bugloss which is found only on Gugh, and wild thyme which shares its distribution in these islands between Gugh and Great Ganilly, one of the Eastern Islands. I was pleased with my day's work, not least because I had had a day to myself with no distractions; no-one following me or threatening me or breathing down my neck. The action now was all with Mike Carberry and his team out on Crim. How true this observation was I found out later that evening.

Even in the short while I had been away I noticed a difference in the gardens. Mesembryanthemums and geraniums still creamed down the walls but now the aenomiums were coming into their own, the fleshy succulent 'roses' throwing out clusters of vivid yellow flowers, and everywhere the agapanthus lilies were budding up, slits of heavenly blue showing through the tightly packed buds. As I walked down into town to keep my evening appoinment I passed an exotic catalpa wafting its strings of cream bells over a garden wall and I almost expected to hear it tinkling in the breeze. The air was limpid and little feather curls of cloud drifted high across the gold-washed sky.

I ran up the steps to Mike Carberry's place and knocked on the door. There was a long pause before the door swung open and there stood Mike. I just had time to register that he had a beautiful black eye like a panda when he swept me into his arms and gave me a smacking kiss. As kisses go it was quite something; tickling beards are unimportant when the lips behind them are so expert. I was practically sagging at the knees by the time he released me.

'Bethany, how are you?'

'I'm fine, Mike, but what's happened to you? Your eye . . ?' Then I realised that the man sitting at the table had swung round and was an interested spectator of our little love-scene. It was Rory Patterson and he looked

182

decidedly battered; an ugly bruise and graze high up on one cheekbone and scraped knuckles. My startled gaze took in the other occupants of the room. Tom Shepherd also had a black eye and a split lip, and his brother Bill had a gashed eyebrow and a bandaged arm. Magnus was propped in a chair and against his pallor the bruises stood out as livid marks.

'My, oh my! What have you been up to?'

They all looked rather sheepish and I advanced further into the room. 'Don't tell me – I should see the other side. What on earth happened?'

'We had a little fracas.' This was from Rory Patterson as he staggered to his feet.

'That must be the understatement of the year. Do you care to elucidate further?'

'Our friend Pete Walmsley and his side-kicks are making a nuisance of themselves,' said Mike. 'They followed us out to Crim and interfered with our diving operations.'

'They cut our mooring lines and our markers,' said Bill grimly, 'and they dived with us.'

'We chased them back to Perigles,' said Magnus grinning and then flinching as he shifted his weight, 'and decided to teach them a lesson.'

'So you had a fight,' I said eyeing them all suspiciously. 'They might have been armed.'

'One of them pulled a knife,' Bill indicated his bandaged arm, 'but I managed to get it off him.'

'But you might have been badly hurt, all of you.'

'Magnus came off worst,' said Mike; 'he got two cracked ribs.' Then as he saw my expression, 'Don't worry, he's been strapped up. Officially he slipped on a wet deck and collided with the lifting gear.'

'You mean you followed them back to St Agnes and had a fight on the jetty in full view of everyone? So much for this venture being a secret.'

183

'There was no-one around and we didn't go ashore,' said Rory, looking remarkably complacent.

'You mean you actually boarded *them*? Suppose they go to the police?'

'I don't think they'll do that. Do sit down, Bethany, you're making me nervous.'

I sat down and eyed them all sceptically. 'Do you know, I think you all enjoyed it. You're like a pack of schoolboys, you ought to be ashamed of yourselves. Suppose they had got guns?'

'They wouldn't have used them in the circumstances.'

'Well, you all seem remarkably pleased with yourselves.'

'That's because, Bethany my dear, we've actually had some luck today. Look!' and Mike gestured to the table. 'I've found you your cannon. Actually it's a piece of one, and iron, not bronze, and there's a few coins to be going on with.'

I looked at the things on the table. It was amazing I hadn't noticed them before. 'You've found the site!'

'I think we have. Or at least, we've pinpointed the area where we think it went down. The cargo will have scattered over quite a distance. But we've got a defined location now in which to dive. There's a lot more stuff down there.'

I looked at the coins. Most of them were silver but one or two were gold and I asked the leading question: 'These came from the *Merchant Royal*?'

'No, we can't prove that.' Magnus leaned over the table and ran his fingers through the coins. 'We've got ducatoons, Spanish pistoles, rijders, thalers, one rose noble and three gold ducats. All old, dating from around the sevententh century, but that's as far as it goes.'

'But if the money the *Merchant Royal* was carrying came from Spain wouldn't it all be in Spanish coinage?'

'No,it would be a selection from all the well-known European and New World mints of that time, which is what we've got here. That's how currency circulated in those days.'

I produced the button and brooch I had collected from Portsmouth and gave them the little information I had gathered, but I couldn't keep my eyes off the little pile of coins and the lump of corroded metal which I had been assured was part of an iron cannon. For the first time the treasure hunt was becoming real to me. It wasn't just an excited hypothesis. There was a wreck down there that was slowly yielding up its treasures and we were going to be the benefactors – hopefully.

'Mike, can nothing be done to keep other interested parties off?'

'Can't you claim "Salvor in Possession"?' Rory added to my plea.

Mike shrugged. 'We're back to the old identification problem. If we can only prove that we have found the *Merchant Royal* we have the legal means to stop anyone else from interfering.'

Magnus leant across the table and said something to him in a low voice. They had a quick conversation *sotto voce* and then Mike lunged to his feet and started to pace the floor, a look of devilment spreading across his face.

'There is a way round it; if we can prove we have found a wreck, not the *Merchant Royal*, of course, but another known wreck of archeological interest in the area we have pin-pointed, we can approach a local museum or well-known archaeologist and apply to the Runciman Committee for a licence under the Wreck Protection Act. If they think it is of enough interest they will issue a licence which gives us the sole rights to work, survey and excavate within an area of, say, 200 yards diameter from the co-ordinates given, excluding any other persons.'

'And that is better than claiming "Salvor in Possession"?' asked Rory.

'Yes. "Salvor in Possession" doesn't stop anyone else from diving; it's just supposed to stop them from touching or taking anything; but if they did you'd have to take out a private injunction against them. But a Wreck Protection Act licence stops anyone else from going near. You'd have exclusive diving rights in that area and could go on looking for the *Merchant Royal* under cover of salvaging this other wreck.'

'But that's cheating!'

'It's legal and has been done before.'

'But how do you produce another wreck in the given area?' Rory jabbed his pipe at Mike, excitement smouldering in his brown eyes.

'You fake it,' said Mike succinctly.

'Wh-at?'

'You "find" some artefact that proves you have located a wreck known to have sunk in that area.'

'Such as?'

'First we'll settle on a suitable wreck. Well lads, what shall we pick on? Something of great historical interest that could have gone down on Crim.'

'One of Sir Cloudesley Shovell's fleet?' said Tom, 'that would be an obvious one.'

'They've found the *Association*, the flagship,' added Bill, 'but several of the others were lost with all hands and have never been found.'

'Yes, I think one of them would do admirably,' said Mike slowly. 'Now let us see what have we got?' He rooted about amongst his books and found the one he was looking for. 'Here we are: the *Firebrand*, the *Romney*, the *Eagle*, all lost. What about the *Romney*? Forty-eight tons, 683 guns and her captain was a William Coney. I think she would fit the bill.'

186

'But how do you go about convincing a committee that you've found her?' I asked, intrigued in spite of myself.

'We draw up a site plan, longitude and latitude etc. That's easily done. Anyone who has done any diving at all could do that. You mark on this plan the positions of the anchors and cannons.' He saw my face and continued, 'There'd be practically nothing left of the original ship, you know. By the time it had been smashed on Crim and sunk to the bottom on a hard, rocky floor it would have mostly disintegrated.'

'What about artefacts?' said Rory.

'We know exactly when she went down – October 1707. We can easily get some cannonballs, say, from that period and some coins of the right year – there's still enough circulating from the salvaging of the *Association*. What we really want is a ship's bell with the name on or a silver spoon or fork with the family crest of the captain or some other wealthy passenger.'

'But how can you manage that?'

'It's easy enough. I'm sure we've got a piece of silver that we've already found somewhere else that we could use. Otherwise you could even buy something from an antique dealer or another diver and leave it in sea water for a period and somehow fake markings on it. You've heard of "distressing" reproduction furniture to make it appear antique, haven't you? This would be the same sort of thing.'

'But that's downright dishonesty!' I exclaimed, horrified.

Mike grinned. 'Having cold feet? Do you want to drop out?'

'No, of course not, but . . .'

They overruled my scruples and went into a huddle from which I was excluded. I sat back and the talk floated round the table whilst I tried to concentrate.

Sometime later Mike pushed back his chair and said: 'Well, that's settled then. We'll start putting it into action.'

I was very tired by this time and I stifled a yawn. Mike had noticed. 'Let's call it a day. I'll take you back to your place, Bethany.'

'There's no need,' said Rory rising to his feet and suddenly looking very formidable, 'it's on my way.'

Mike didn't argue and I was too tired to care either way. We didn't talk on the walk back. I was going over in my mind all that had been discussed that evening and Rory also seemed lost in thought. We reached Sallyport and I said goodnight and started up the steps.

'Just a minute, Bethany.' Rory reached up and pulled me back to his side. 'I haven't finished yet.'

'Finished what? I'm too tired too talk or argue any more.'

'I can see I've misjudged the situation and have been handling you far too gently. Mike's not having it all his own way.'

'What are you talking about?' I said crossly.

'This.' And he enfolded me in his arms and proceeded to kiss me very thoroughly. It was the kiss I had been waiting for, longing for, dreading, trying to avoid, and it was devastating. Against my will I found myself responding. A jumble of emotions was released in me and I felt as if I was being swept along by a tidal wave. I came to my senses and started to struggle.

'There's no need to struggle.' He ended the embrace and held me at arm's length. 'That's just to be going on with. Now go in quickly before I really forget myself.'

I stared at him transfixed for a few seconds and then turned and rushed blindly up to the cottage. As I opened the door I heard the clonk, clonk as he tapped his pipe out against the wall.

I sat on the bed and held my burning cheeks in out-stretched fingers and tried to marshall my whirling thoughts. To be kissed twice in one evening and what kisses! The first since Martin's death. Martin; I should be feeling guilty but I wasn't. Instead I felt free and light-headed. Martin was still there but at long last he had slotted into his correct place, the past, not my present or future. I had been awakened again, sexually and emotionally and now I was vulnerable again. I was not sure I welcomed it. Mike Carberry was quite stunning. It would be easy to fall for him; was this what I wanted? And Rory Patterson?

I groaned and fell back and buried my head in my pillow. I was so completely mixed-up over Rory Patterson. I had been quite aghast to discover that he might be gay and now, just when I was getting used to the idea, he did a thing like that. Why had he suddenly kissed me? Because, whispered that cautious little voice inside my head, he feared Mike Carberry's influence over you; he wants to keep control of you still, so he chose the weapon in hand having been pointed the way by Mike. He was a devious man and I couldn't believe he had kissed me for kissing's sake. Maybe he had had to subjugate his natural desires to achieve it; if so he had succeeded very well; I still felt quite shattered at the memory of that kiss and how it had affected me.

How would he behave when we next met? I decided as I got ready for bed that I was looking forward to that meeting with very mixed feelings.

The next morning Lisa phoned to say that she could get away earlier than expected and could she come down straight away. I hadn't yet mentioned the possibility of her coming to Mrs Pethick so I told her I would ring her

189

back. Mrs Pethick when approached seemed quite agreeable.

'You'll have to pay extra and she'll have to sleep in the studio but if that's all right with you she's welcome.'

Lisa was really keen to come. When I rang her back she had already made a reservation on the overnight sleeper and was crossing on the *Scillonian* the following day.

'I'll meet you off the boat tomorrow,' I promised, 'and don't bother to bring a lot of sophisticated clothes and gear. We live the simple life here.'

'Is the weather good? I can't wait to acquire a suntan like yours. Don't worry, I shan't cramp your style. You can go off and do your painting or whatever and I shall just find me a beach and lay and soak. By the way, how is your Rory Patterson?'

'When last I saw him he was in rude health. He has also altered his line of attack.'

'I wonder what you mean by that? Be careful, Bethany, and don't get involved. Bisexuals are an even worse bet than gays for us girls, you know. Still, from what you've told me, you're not short of male company. I can't wait to meet all those men you've been consorting with.'

She rang off and I mooched about the studio trying to tidy up, wondering ruefully whether her advent would set the island, or rather, the entire male population, by the ear.

I spent the rest of the day painting in the cottage garden. The Garrison Wall which formed the back boundary was rich in specimens. Every nook and crevice was stuffed with a variety of plant life and I eagerly tackled pennywort and spleenwort. Later, when the freshening winds made conditions unpleasant I retired indoors with sprigs of escallonia and periwinkle and continued my work. I saw and heard nothing of Rory Patterson for which I was thankful, not being sure how I was going to face him again

190

after what had happened the night before. I should have liked to have seen Mike Carberry; in comparison he seemed so straightforward and open; but I couldn't encroach on his spare time without an invitation and he hadn't suggested a meeting.

I was down at the harbour in good time the next day to meet the *Scillonian*. She was due in around midday but was not in sight as I strolled down to the quayside. To my surprise Mike Carberry was stowing equipment into a small outboard dinghy which was moored at the end of the old jetty.

'Hi, Mike!' I called out as I hurried towards him. 'Aren't you out diving today?' He straightened up and waved. He looked more piratical than ever with his black eye and the sun glinting off his gold earring.

'We're carrying out some running repairs on *Sea Wolf*, nothing serious but it will take all day. Did you want me?'

'I didn't know you were here. I'm meeting a friend off the *Scillonian*. She's coming to stay with me.' As if on cue the *Scillonian* hooted as she rounded the Hugh from Broad Sound.

'You didn't tell me you were expecting company. How long is she staying?'

'I'm not sure. She's an old friend – we were at school together.'

'Any friend of yours is welcome, especially if she's anything like you,' said Mike gallantly.

'She's not a bit like me,' I said wistfully. 'She's a quite famous journalist and very modern in her outlook. She wants to meet some of the local talent.'

'Well, I'm sure that can be arranged.' He grinned and screwed up those amazing blue eyes against the sun.

191

'Bring her down to the Mermaid this evening, we usually congregate there. Bring Rory as well.'

'Isn't he with you today?'

'No, I haven't seen him. I thought he was probably with you.'

'He must be writing.'

'Writing? Is he keeping a record of all our business?' Mike suddenly looked worried.

'He's supposed to be writing a book, a novel, but I haven't a clue what it's all about.'

'Good God! I didn't know he was a writer as well. No wonder he asked so many questions.'

'Mike, can I come with you one day when you go out to Crim? I promise I won't get in anyone's way.'

'Well . . .' He looked dubious and then his face cleared, 'I suppose we owe it to you, seeing as how you've got a stake in it. It can get pretty grim out there, but I'll choose a fine day and we'll take you along for the ride.'

'That's a promise?'

'That's a promise. I'm getting out of the way before the *Scillonian* docks. See you this evening.' And with a quick pull he fired the engine and zoomed off across the sparkling water.

Lisa sauntered down the gangway looking the very last word in what the Sunday glossies would call nautical elegance. She was wearing a reefer jacket that owed little to naval influence, and a pair of pleated trousers, cut off at the knees, in shocking pink. To complete the picture she wore a pair of enormous sunglasses that practically obscured her piquant, gamine face. When she saw me she flung herself at me and off-loaded some of her gear.

'So this is where it is all happening. Tell me, do I look the part?'

'You'll wow the natives,' I assured her.

She seemed genuinely interested and thrilled in all she saw as we made our way back to the cottage.

'No wonder you keep your figure,' she gasped as we toiled up the hill. 'I hope I'm not expected to do this many times in a day.'

'You know you're perfectly fit. What about all those aerobic classes?'

'Somehow it's not the same at all. Still, you must get a fantastic view from the top.'

'You wait till you see the one from the studio window, that's where you're sleeping.'

Mrs Pethick was flustered on being confronted by some-one as sophisticated as Lisa, but in her deft, amusing way Lisa soon put her at ease. In fact, so much did Lisa win her over that in no time at all she had produced a welcome meal and promised to prepare another one for us that evening.

Lisa was delighted with the studio. I had been rather worried about what her reaction to Percy would be. Lisa is not an animal lover, and cats come way down on her list of priorities; but beyond commenting on his size she showed no interest in him and Percy, for his part, simply ignored her.

We spent a delightful hour chatting and later in the afternoon I showed her round Hugh Town and we finished up lazing on Porthcressa beach. Lisa already had the beginnings of a suntan but I suspected that it came out of a bottle.

'Well, if the weather stays like this I shan't grumble.' She roused herself to apply another layer of oil. 'How is your commission coming along, have you much more to do?'

'Quite a bit, but a lot of the plants I can capture on the mainland – you know, the common ones like dandelion and daisy.'

'You sound almost regretful as you say that.'

'I like it here.' I dug my hands into the warm sand and let

it trickle through my fingers. 'I could live here permanently; London seems very remote.'

'Don't tell me you're turning into a hedonist.'

'I've been working very hard, I'd have you know.'

'This treasure hunt of yours – is it really big money?'

'It could run into millions.'

'Bethany, you're having me on!'

'That's what the salvage value could run to but don't forget it costs thousands to mount an operation like this.'

'No wonder you want to stay around. Does your Mike Carberry want any more financial backing?'

'You'll be able to ask him this evening.'

Rory Patterson was already in the Mermaid drinking with Mike and the others when we arrived. He greeted me casually and when introduced to Lisa afforded her the least attention that courtesy demanded. But Mike more than made up for it. It was like the meeting of two titans; you could feel the sparks sizzling between them.

You could have almost cut the atmosphere in the bar with a knife; it was hot, smoky, noisy and very crowded. Wedged tightly at our table I sipped my drink and listened to Lisa flirting outrageously with Mike, aided and abetted by Bill and Tom. She had asked for a Campari and soda but Mike dismissed this request: 'You don't want that stuff, have some cider.' So she and I drank cider whilst the others swilled beer and I digested the fact that I would probably receive no more kisses from Mike. Mixed in with the regret was a faint feeling of relief. Rory sat in the corner, his pipe clenched between his teeth, a smug grin on his face as he listened to the interchange.

I was goaded to ask: 'What is it about?'

He started elaborately as if he were only just aware of my presence. 'What is what about?'

'Your book, your *magnum opus* or whatever.'

'It's still in the planning stage. I think it's going to be a profound study of human relationships.'

'Then you'd better get together with Lisa; I'm sure she could throw some useful scraps of information in your way.'

'Bethany, if I didn't know you better, I would say there was just the touch of the little yellow god in your voice. Is she always like this?'

'It's automatic as far as the male sex is concerned; she can't help herself. I suppose she doesn't turn you on?'

'Even I can see that she is quite something.' He ogled her lasciviously and I gave up in disgust.

About an hour later when my head was reeling even more from the noise and smoke Magnus got up to leave.

'Magnus, you're not deserting us?' Lisa switched her full magnetism onto the black-visaged man, who, alone amongst us seemed immune to her charm.

'My wife will be wondering where I've got to.'

'Your wife?' I squeaked in surprise. 'I didn't know you were married.'

'Married with four children,' said Mike with a grin. 'We're not all footloose philanderers.'

I watched Magnus shoulder his way through the crowd and as he neared the door my eyes suddenly fell on the man sitting to the right of the doorway, partly obscured by a group of raucous teenagers. I gasped and icy fingers ran up my spine.

'Tom, move your head quickly!' Tom ducked and I got a clearer view of the man. I gulped.

'What's the matter, Bethany?'

'That man over there, the one in the dark suit – I know him.'

Their eyes all swung towards the door. It was easy enough to see whom I meant. He stood out like a sore thumb in his formal wear amongst all the other casually-attired customers.

'Who is it?' – Rory had been warned by my tone of voice and was instantly alert.

'You'll never believe this – but I think its "De Big Boss" himself.'

'Are you sure?'

'I'm sure it's the man who accosted me in London – at my exhibition, Lisa – and who made the threatening phone-calls.'

Mike started to get up but Rory pulled him back to his seat.

'You think this is the man in charge of Pete Walmsley and Co.?'

'Yes, the one who gives the orders and pulls the strings.'

He must have sensed we were talking about him. His heavy-lidded eyes rested on me for a few seconds and he moved a white hand in acknowledgement.

'Those two chaps with him – they're the ones who followed us out to Crim,' said Bill suddenly. 'I owe one,' and he indicated his bandaged arm.

'For heaven's sake don't start another fight in here!'

'I think someone should have a few words with your friend and warn him off,' Mike growled belligerently.

'Cool it,' snapped Rory, 'just keep on drinking and ignore them.'

Not long after this the man rose to his feet and left. Rory waited a couple of minutes and then casually followed him after first telling Mike to look after Lisa and I, and to wait for him. It was near closing time before he returned. He sauntered over to the bar and bought himself a drink before coming back to our table.

'Well . . ? What happened?' I demanded, as he seemed in no hurry to enlighten us.

'Control yourself, Bethany.'

'It hadn't occurred to you that we might be wondering whether your lifeless body would be washed up on Town Beach tomorrow?'

He sighed and addressed himself to Mike: 'His name is Albery, Robert Albery. He's booked in at the Godolphin and this is his third visit in the last few weeks.'

'He must be able to pull a few strings,' said Mike. 'You don't come and go casually at this time of the year. Accommodation is very tight at the height of the season.'

It occurred to me that the same thing might be said to apply to Rory Patterson; he appeared to have no trouble in booking in at Star Castle whenever he so desired. Under cover of the general conversation that this news promoted I hissed at him: 'Just what *is* your profession?'

'My profession? What *do* you mean, Bethany?'

'I mean', I said darkly, 'that I think you're probably an undercover agent for MI5.'

'As of the moment, I am an out-of-work budding writer.'

Mike had caught the word 'writer' and he turned to Lisa. 'I believe you're a journalist, Lisa. I hope you're not making copy out of this.'

'As if I would. I shall be discreet as the grave but I hope when it breaks you'll give me exclusive rights?'

She smiled at him beguilingly and I was moved to remark: 'You know you're not a reporting hack.'

'Darling, this is big – think of the wonderful human interest story it will make.'

'If you dare so much as to write up one word of it I shall personally see to it that you never make your way back to the mainlaind!'

'How long have you two been friends?' enquired Rory lazily, packing his pipe with nimble fingers.

'Don't worry about us,' said Lisa with a laugh,

197

'Bethany is my conscience. She keeps me on the straight and narrow – or at least she tries to.' She turned to me, 'Where are you taking me tomorrow?'

'The idea was that *you* would occupy yourself whilst I worked.'

'Girls, girls!' said Rory shaking his head in mock dismay, 'tomorrow I shall take you both to St Martin's. We haven't been there yet, have we?' he asked me pleasantly, ignoring the smouldering looks I was giving him. 'You shall show me round the island and Lisa may accompany us or spend the entire day on the beach, whichever she prefers. I make just one proviso – no painting, Bethany – tomorrow shall be a holiday.'

Lisa assured him she would love to visit St Martin's and I agreed with bad grace.

'You seem to have the future all wrapped up. I suggest Lisa and I retire now and catch up on our sleep in readiness for the big day. Don't bother to get up,' I added sweetly as he lolled back in his chair and regarded us with lazy brown eyes, 'I expect we shall manage to get home safely.'

Mike bounced to his feet but Lisa waved him back.

'We'll be okay, Mike, don't let us break up the party.'

'Lisa, me dear, if Rory's having the benefit of your company all day tomorrow, make sure you reserve yourself exclusively for me in the evening.'

He rolled his eyes suggestively and she laughed, 'Will do.'

'Well, you certainly seem to have made a hit,' I remarked as we walked back to Sallyport.

'You don't mind, do you?'

'Of course not. What do you think of them?'

'I'm not regretting the impulse to visit you. As for Rory Patterson, I haven't yet made up my mind about him. I sense undercurrents between you.'

'You do talk a lot of nonsense sometimes, Lisa.'

198

I suppose I had been in bed about half an hour and was just drifting off to sleep when there was a shriek and a thud from the studio above my head. I sat up in bed and listened. There was silence for a few seconds and then another thud and the sound of feet moving across the floor. I grabbed my dressing-gown and hurried up the stairs. Lisa was standing in the middle of the room clutching her pillow, and nearby Percy was crouched, his tail lashing.

'What's the matter? What's happened?'

'That cat – he lay on me! Do you understand, Bethany, he *lay* on me? I'm completely flattened!'

'Oh Lisa,' I said weakly, leaning against the doorpost.

'And that's not all' she said, lowering her voice dramatically, 'he dribbles!'

Lisa spent the rest of the night in my room and I slept on the studio couch. Percy made no attempt to share my bed.

Chapter Ten

We did not go direct to St Martin's the next day, but took a launch trip that detoured round the Eastern Isles. It was a blisteringly hot day without the hint of a breeze. We creamed over a crystal sea that lay mirrored beneath the arching blue sky. Lisa had chosen to wear a halter top and shorts in a blinding yellow and over them a short, swingy caftan in vivid swirls of orange and yellow and a sunhat as big as a cartwheel.

'You certainly don't intend to be upstaged by the flora,' I had remarked as we walked down the hill to the harbour, 'but for heaven's sake don't linger in front of a display of mesembryanthemums.' It was completely unsuitable wear for a boat trip, but she looked terrific and the weather was on her side. Rory certainly appreciated her appearance and had given a low wolf whistle when we met up on the quay.

We saw seals swimming near the rocks; their sleek grey heads bristling like periscopes out of the water. It was nearly full tide; at low tide we would have seen them basking in the sun. Rory lent me his binoculars and as we cruised in and out of the isles we saw a variety of seabirds; the usual gulls, guillemots, cormorants and shags; also whimbrel and several turnstones running along the rocky shore of Great Ganilly. The boatman assured us that the head peeping out of a crevasse in the rockface belonged to a stormy petrel. The names of the isles tripped off the tongue like a string of magic passwords – Great Ganilly, Little Granilly, Menawethan, Great Arthur, Little Arthur, Nornour. We saw a pair of ravens near the summit of Great Arthur after the fledglings. The guidebooks may insist that there are no birds of prey on the Scillies apart from the odd kestrel, but we saw ravens that day.

It was midday by the time we landed on St Martin's, and Lisa decided that all she wanted to do was to subside on the beach. She chose the beach edging St Martin's Flats as her resting place, and waved us on our way.

'Have fun, children. Rather you than me. I intend to do absolutely nothing all day except perhaps a little gentle beachcombing.'

'You'll find a good selection of shells when the tide goes out,' I said as she picked her way over the rocks to the shore.

'Watch the sun,' warned Rory, 'you'll end up getting very burnt if you're not careful.'

'I'll find me some rock-shadow if it gets too much.'

The road wound upwards and we trudged along, panting in the heat, past a row of cottages that had bags of bulbs for sale outside. I hesitated and Rory said hurriedly, 'Don't forget how heavy they are.'

'I've nowhere to plant them,' I said regretfully. By the time we reached the top I was in a state of exhaustion and my thin shirt was sticking to my shoulder blades. There was a cairn of rocks on the prow of the hill with a wooden seat at its base.

'Let's stop here and have our lunch,' commanded Rory. I sank onto the seat thankfully and gulped at the iced juice in the flask whilst he unpacked the sandwiches. The grass around us was parched and straggly and a flock of sparrows twitted in and out after our crumbs. We had a marvellous view of the Eastern Isles and beyond them Crow Sound. All the islands and rocks that had towered above us a short while ago as we approached them by sea were now spread out before us sailing serenely on a brilliantly turquoise sea – Great and Little Ganilly, Great and Little Innisvoulis, The Arthurs, The Hats and out on the far left, the mighty Hanjague like a galleon in full sail.

'It's no good, Rory,' I said as the sun beat down on us and I almost expected to hear my skin sizzling when I stretched out my legs, 'there's no way I'm going to hike round this island today. I shall have melted away completely before we're half-way there.' Was there relief in his eyes as he turned to me?

'What do you suggest?'

'We get back to the beach quick and then I shall fall into the sea.'

'Come on, then, what are we waiting for?'

Our progress down the hill was considerably faster than the ascent had been. As we reached the path leading down to the quay Rory led the way through the marram grass to Higher Town Bay which gleamed like a silver half-moon to the left of the jetty.

'Lisa's on the other beach to the right,' I said, holding back.

'I know she is. I'm sure she's perfectly happy on her own and we're going to spend the rest of the day on *this* beach.'

I was quite happy to acquiesce and we picked our way through the clumps of marram grass and I flung myself down onto the hot, soft sand. I quickly kicked off my sandals, wriggled out of my shorts and shirt and hurried down the beach into the water. It struck colder than usual because I was so hot, but it was wonderfully refreshing. I swam lazily around for a time and then rejoined Rory. He had stripped down to bathing shorts and was stretched out face downwards on a towel apparently asleep.

Undressed he didn't look as thin and gangling as his clothed appearance had suggested. True he was slim but there were muscles and bulges in the right places and he looked in good condition. I dried myself briefly and flopped down beside him. The sun beat down on my closed eyelids, painting a series of violent patterns inside my head, and I was just wondering how long I could bear to lay out under the burning rays when Rory pushed himself up onto his elbows, glared fixedly at the sea for a few minutes, then got to his feet, ran down the beach and plunged into the water. Under my astonished gaze he struck out in a competent crawl. There was nothing amateurish about the figure he presented in the water. He was a good, a *very* good swimmer, and he made my efforts look like the wallowings of a seal cub. He stayed in for about five minutes; then shaking the water out of his eyes and hair he walked back up the beach towards me.

'But I thought you couldn't swim?'

'I never said so.'

'No, you didn't. You said you hated the water. Why? Were you once fished out of the local pond?'

'My wife was – dead.'

'Rory!' I gasped at him. 'I didn't know . . . I mean . . .'

He made no attempt to help me out. He just sat there towelling his hair vigorously whilst I floundered on. 'I didn't know you had been married. Rory, I'm sorry, but please *tell* me!'

At first I thought he wouldn't comply but then he sighed and turning to face the sea he started to talk in low, disjointed tones.

'She killed herself. She didn't know what she was doing – she was unbalanced at the time. She came from an emotional, highly-strung family, and she couldn't accept

203

the truth – she went to pieces.' He paused and swung round to face me. 'I'm not making much sense, am I?' I slowly shook my head and he gave a little, humourless laugh. 'I'd better start from the beginning.' He sighed again and ran his fingers through his hair so that it stood up in damp peaks.

'We took it for granted when we first married that we would eventually have a family. Vanessa was very keen and I went along with it. Well, when we'd been married for several years and there was no sign of a baby she got more and more upset, so we both went through all the usual tests – you know, fertility clinics and all the works. The result was that Vanessa was told she couldn't ever bear a child.

'I was disappointed but I suppose I would have come to terms with it but Vanessa just could not accept it. I suppose it is always harder for the woman in cases like this. Anyway, she got more and more neurotic about it. It got to the state when she couldn't face a baby, couldn't even bear to see children playing, which you can imagine was most awkward as far as our friends were concerned – most of them young and active in producing families. She had several spells in a local mental hospital; she wasn't committed but went in as a voluntary patient and after a few weeks they'd usually sorted her out, temporarily anyway. The last time she went in she went missing. The hospital was situated in vast grounds including woods and wild areas. They searched for two days, even used tracker dogs, and then they found her body in a pond deep in one of the copses.'

'Oh Rory, how awful for you! I had no idea – you just let me blunder on about my own loss and all the while you. . . . Why didn't you *tell* me?'

'I suppose I still had my hang-ups'. He grimaced ruefully. 'I had no right to lecture you, had I?'

'How long ago did it happen?'

'It's six years since she died. I've got over it, but today is the first time I've been swimming since it happened.'

'Rory, I feel so inadequate. . . . I don't know what to say. You must have loved her a great deal. Has there been no-one since?'

'Not until recently, but I think I've made a mess-up over that.' He shrugged and I daren't ask him what he meant. Just as I was feeling relief at the thought that he was straight he came out with something that suggested that he was entangled with another woman.

'Thank you for telling me anyway. Is there anything else I should know before I jump in with both feet again?'

He took both my hands in his and smiled at me sweetly. 'I'd better come clean. Ned Donnelly was Vanessa's brother.'

'He was your *brother-in-law*?'

He nodded and I snatched my hands away. 'Why didn't you. . . . Why did you let me believe . . . I mean. . .'

'I suppose I wanted to see what your reaction would be, and I was furious that a stray rumour flung out by a flippant friend should impress you far more than anything that had happened between us.'

'You must admit, you rejected me, held me off.'

'I told you, I've made a mess of things. I'm sorry, Bethany.' Well, now you know, Bethany, my girl, I told myself sternly. He's as good as told you he's involved with another woman; he was momentarily distracted by you but he came to his senses in time.

'Well, now we know where we are, don't we?' I said brightly, 'you're straight and damned.'

'I believe I am. By the way, when Ned died he left everything to me – I'm living on his money at the

205

moment. I am still employed on a free-lance basis by M. & K. though. They were concerned about a security leak and I was asked to follow it through.'

'And were you trying to prove Martin's innocence or Martin's guilt?'

'Let's forget about Martin for the moment; it's Albery I'm interested in. I suspect skullduggery in high places. He seems to wield a lot of influence.'

'The same could be said of you. You seem to carry a lot of clout. You have no difficulty in getting any information as and when you require it – how do you manage it? Do you go around flashing an official card at doors like a police officer?'

'Not quite, but you're on the right tracks.'

'Rory Patterson, you're *not* a policeman of any sort, are you?'

'Good heavens, no, but I do work in close liaison with them when the occasion arises, and I have my contacts.'

I must have looked at him askance for he flipped a shell up and down in the air and gave me an aggravating smile.

'Still suspicious, Bethany? You really must control your curiosity.'

There seemed to be nothing to say after this and we lay side by side on the beach avoiding any contact until it was time to return to the quay. Lisa, looking very pink, was bubbling over with enthusiasm and her bright chatter made up for my silence. I sat on the edge of the jetty and gazed down into the water. There was another world down there; a forest of green and tawny seaweeds pulsating in the translucent water. Long fronds of some mahogany coloured weed, complete with rows of polyps on the underside, snaked to and fro like the tentacles of a giant octopus and shoals of small fish darted in and out and hovered over the sandy floor.

Later, back at the cottage Lisa tackled me about my

taciturnity. 'Have you had a row with Rory Patterson? You've been very quiet ever since we met this afternoon.'

'No, of course not.' I mooched round the studio and gave Percy a saucer of milk whilst Lisa repaired the damage to her nail varnish. 'By the way, he's a widower and his wife was Ned Donnelly's sister.' I tossed it off as casually as I could and had the satisfaction of seeing Lisa for once bereft of words. She dabbed at the large blob of pink varnish running down her ankle, shaken from a startled hand, and when she had recovered she drawled: 'Well, well, that's one nugget of information I missed out on. Perhaps he has honourable intentions towards you after all.'

'He has *no* intentions towards me,' I said shortly and hurriedly changed the subject.

The next few days passed uneventfully. The weather continued fine and I concentrated on the coast and shore plants. I re-visited Tresco and St Agnes and took Lisa with me, but for the most part she was quite happy to go off on her own. I saw little of Rory Patterson though I believe he spent one day initiating Lisa into the delights of Bryher. We had no more intimate little dinners together. The fact that he had been married and therefore proved to be a full-blooded male seemed somehow to have distanced him from me. I was prepared to believe now that his interest in me had not been prompted by self-interest and greed, but rather from a genuine desire to help me, the poor grieving widow, and also by his somewhat distorted sense of humour. This did nothing for my self-confidence. I usually saw him only in the evenings, either at Mike's place or in the Mermaid where we all met.

Lisa took to spending the occasional night with Mike. They were quite open about it, brazen almost. Tom and

Bill were envious, Magnus and I disapproving, and Rory amused. He rescued me one evening after Lisa announced that she was going back with Mike and not accompanying me to the cottage.

'Come on, Bethany, you and I have things to discuss.' He whisked me off and I was grateful enough to invite him in for coffee when we got back to Sallyport. He flopped down on the studio couch and patted the seat beside him as if he owned the place and I was the visitor. I plugged in the kettle and eyed him warily.

'What have we got to discuss?'

'That was really an exit line. However, I should like to know, do you mind?'

'Mind? About what?'

'Mike and Lisa.'

'What Mike and Lisa get up to is their business. I am not Lisa's keeper and neither are you Mike's.'

'I thought maybe Mike rang a bell for you.'

'Certainly not. All right, I'll be honest with you. Mike is quite something and he's a dear with it, but he's not my type.' To forestall him asking who was my type I hurriedly continued. 'I am worried about him though. I'm afraid he'll get hurt. Lisa thinks no more of sleeping with someone than, say, sharing a cup of coffee with them. To her it is an enjoyable experience with no involvement on either side. I suppose you could say she's completely amoral in this respect. She doesn't exactly collect scalps but she'll pass on to the next lover without a backward glance and no scruples about emotional bruising.'

'I don't think you need to worry on Mike's behalf,' said Rory slowly. 'You've heard of the Spanish Waiter Syndrome?'

'Are you likening Mike to a Spanish waiter?' I demanded angrily.

'Only to put my point across. I think he's had all his own

208

way in the bed-hopping stakes up to now. He may have met his match in Lisa. The results should be amusing to watch, but I don't think there'll be any broken hearts.'

I had to admit that he was probably right but I must still have looked uneasy.

'Are you very upset about it?'

'My greatest worry is coping with Mrs Pethick and her questions. *I* have to go on living here.'

He laughed. 'I'm sure you'll think of some way of appeasing her. How about coming to Tresco with me tomorrow? I should like to visit it again.'

'I *had* intended to go to Tresco tomorrow, but to work. I really can't spend it with you.'

'Let's compromise. Spend the morning painting and meet me after lunch and we'll have the afternoon together.'

I hesitated and he pressed home his point. 'I'll meet you at the little café just inside the entrance to the gardens at two o'clock.'

He left soon after that, having got his own way as usual, and as I prepared for bed I had to admit that I was looking forward to the next day.

I should have been warned. There should have been portents in the sky, omens to prepare me for what was to follow. As it was I fell asleep almost as soon as I got into bed and slept soundly, untroubled by dreams or any worrying visitation of the morrow.

The day started very early when an irate Mrs Pethick banged on my door to tell me that I was wanted on the phone. It was Mike Carberry on the other end.

'Do you know what time it is?' I demanded squinting at my watch.

'Just after six. Have you looked out of the window?'

'Not yet. I presume it is another glorious day.'

'How about coming out to Crim? I promised I'd take you and this is the perfect weather for it.'

'Today? Oh, I'd love to come, Mike, but I promised Rory I'd meet him on Tresco after lunch.'

'I don't suppose you'll want to spend all day on the *Sea Wolf*, it will be rather boring for you. I'll run you over to Tresco this afternoon.'

'I can't expect you to break off your diving and take me all the way to Tresco, it's a long way from Crim.'

'No problem. I've been planning to go to Tresco sometime in the next day or two – I have a chart to give to someone over there. I can do it today.'

I wondered whether Lisa was standing at his elbow and I was prompted to ask: 'Is Lisa there?'

'She's asleep.'

'Is she coming too?'

'No, she wouldn't thank me for dragging her out in the middle of the Atlantic. How soon can you be ready?'

'Give me half an hour. What do I bring?'

'Just yourself. We've got the food and oilskins in case the weather should turn nasty; not that I think that's at all likely. See you on the quay in thirty minutes.'

He rang off and I rushed round getting dressed and snatching some breakfast. I cursed the fact that I had lost my camera but I took my sketching things with me. There were very few people about at that hour of the morning. The water shimmered like shot silk under the hazy sky and gulls drifted lazily over the harbour wall. The *Sea Wolf* was a working boat and I was impressed by the equipment she carried when I was shown around. Mike and the others were already on board and we were soon under way and heading out into Broad Sound.

Annet dropped away to the south and then we were past Gunners and nearing Crim. Mike had lent me a pair of binoculars and I swept the sea looking for unusual seabirds and seals. I saw more than I had bargained for.

'Mike, we're being followed!'

'That's normal. We're under surveillance most days.'

'Is it . . ?'

'Almost certainly. They'll drop anchor about 150 yards from us and copy everything we do. When we dive they'll send someone down too. They've got a very nice little support vessel there – she cost a pretty penny, I can tell you. They've kept their distance on the last day or two – I don't think we need worry about any in-fighting today. The most we'll have to grapple with is amorous seals.'

'Really?'

'They can be quite a nuisance at this time of year. You must ask Bill to tell you about the time a great bull seal took a fancy to him.'

The next few hours passed quickly. I was fascinated by the whole process of diving; the procedures taken, the stringent safety precautions, the strict timing. I sat up in the bows sketching feverishly everything in sight; the men, the equipment, the rocks; even the Bishop Lighthouse jutting up out of a placid sea due south of us.

Magnus said afterwards it was my presence on board that brought them luck. I was brewing up tea in the galley when there was a shout and excited voices above me. I made it up on deck just in time to see Bill, water streaming off him, emptying out his sack whilst the others huddled round him. There was a cascade of golden coins, catching light as they rolled across the deck. Afterwards, when I described the scene to him, Rory declared that I was letting my imagination run away with me; that coins that had been under water for over three hundred years couldn't possibly glitter like that, but he was wrong.

'This is it, Bethany, me girl,' declared Mike, chuckling as he ran his fingers through the hoard.

211

'How many?' I breathed, quite overcome by the sight.

'These are just a few,' said Bill, 'there's a lot more down there.' There were mishapen cobs and other unidentifiable coins mixed in with the ducats and he also had a broken hinge and part of a lock – all that remained of the original chest that had housed them.

We celebrated there and then. There was no champagne; we made do with lukewarm beer, swigging it under the hot midday sun and there was much laughter and repartee tossed to and fro.

'Are you going to get a positive identification now so that you don't have to resort to that underhand business?' I asked.

'That's still worrying you, isn't it?' said Mike. 'Tom's going down this afternoon and let's hope he brings up something that will really pinpoint it. In the meanwhile we'll get this little lot to the Receiver of Wrecks.' He saw my puzzled look and grinned. 'The coastguard. Take them with you this afternoon and give them to Rory. He'll know what to do them them.'

The coins were scooped up into a leather drawstring bag, not unlike my shoulder bag, and Mike put it in the bottom of the dinghy after he had helped me into it. As we chugged away from the *Sea Wolf* another dinghy slipped away from our watchdog and followed at a discreet distance.

'Mike, we're being followed again.'

'Don't worry, it will just be one of their crew members seeing where we're going. When they realise it's Tresco and not St Mary's, they'll think it's nothing of any importance and soon return here. This is where the action is as far as they are concerned.'

The other dinghy kept its distance and I could not make out who or how many were manning it. As Mike took it as a matter of routine and appeared not to be worried, I soon forgot about it and settled back to enjoy the trip. As the green and gold mass of Tresco loomed nearer Mike swung the tiller and we swept round the southern tip of the island.

'If you're meeting Rory in the gardens I'll drop you off at Carn Near – that's the nearest landing place,' said Mike as we swept over The Road. 'I've got to go round to Old Grimsby Harbour.'

'Mike, are you expecting any more trouble from our friends?'

His face darkened. 'Yes, when they get to hear about this little find it's going to be open warfare. I think we'll have to mount a guard day and night at Crim.'

'But what can they do?'

'If they get their hands on this or bring up something themselves they could claim salvage.'

'I see. Then you must either make sure of the identification immediately, or put the other scheme into operation.'

'Yes, ma-am, I knew you'd come round to our way of thinking.'

I made a face at him and got a wicked wink in return. We glided alongside the jetty at Carn Near and I scrambled out.

'Hey, don't forget this!' Mike reached down for the leather bag and handed it up to me. He cast off, opened up the throttle and shot off round the eastern shore of Tresco. If he had only gone back the way he had come or gone towards New Grimsby Harbour on the west side of the island he would have met our pursuers face to face. As it was, he roared away without a backward glance and left me alone to face the occupants of the small, powerful motorboat homing in on Carn Near. There were two men in the boat, one of them the stocky middle-aged man I knew to be Robert Albery, the other was Pete Walmsley.

I turned and fled up the track which ran between tracts

213

of pungent bracken. They must not get hold of the bag of coins. With Mike's recent warning ringing in my ears I sped across the stretch of short grass that opened up in front of me, wondering which was the quickest route to the gardens. There were large clumps of marram grass and hottentot fig to my right and out of one of these clumps, looking ludicrously out of place, a single, slender catalpa tree arched gracefully.

For someone as heavily-built and unsuitably dressed, Albery moved surprisingly quickly. My one idea was to get inside the gardens and find Rory. He would be able to cope with the situation. They followed on my heels, silently but persistently. There were other people about in the distance and they obviously did not want to draw attention to themselves, but I knew they would not let me get away. I ran across the open space that did combined duty as cricket pitch and helicopter pad, fearing that if they didn't get me heat-stroke would.

At the entrance gate to the gardens I looked back. They were very close and I bolted into the little building that served as a souvenir shop and ticket office.

'Are you all right, miss?' The man behind the ticket counter looked at me with concern.

'Yes, I mean, no.' My brain hurriedly thought of a way to capitalise on the situation. 'There are two men who have been following me, making a nuisance of themselves.'

'Where?' He leaned over the counter to get a better look.

'Those two over there, just coming round that hedge. Can you warn them off, please?'

'I most certainly will. You go through to the restaurant and get yourself a cool drink – you look as if you could do with one. Leave them to me. I'll deal with them.'

I muttered my thanks and walked through to the little café that opened off the entrance building. There was a patio, partly under cover, set out with tables and chairs, and other tables and chairs were dotted about amongst the shrubs and flowerbeds. There was no sign of Rory but a glimpse at my watch told me it was only one-thirty. Surely he must be in the gardens somewhere? I did not stop for a drink. I wanted to get as far away as possible from my followers. If I couldn't find Rory I must hide the bag.

The men stepped out of the shop doorway but didn't see me as I hovered behind a stand of bamboo. The man in the ticket office had not had much success in stopping them. I slipped down a pathway with the idea of reaching Valhalla, the little museum that housed a collection of figureheads from the shipwrecks, and which ran alongside the southern boundary of the gardens. They saw me, my scarlet shirt as good as a signal, and they pounded after me. I ran across the lawn in front of Valhalla. The short grass was bleached fawn and was as slippery as an ice-rink. I dodged amongst the figureheads rearing up around me in majestic splendour but could find no place to hide my booty.

It was hopeless, they were right on my heels; so I turned and ran back into the gardens. I shot up a path that tunnelled beneath arched, aromatic pines. I must elude them somehow. I twisted and turned up flights of steps and along a maze of paths that dissected the terraces. There were plenty of people about; visitors taking in the beauty of the gardens, sauntering gently in the blistering heat. What they must have thought about the crazy woman charging precipitously amongst them I do not know. I dare not enlist anyone's help and Rory was not in evidence. I paused behind a group of giant aloes. The men were nowhere to be seen, I had succeeded in evading them temporarily. Where could I hide the bag? I dare not drop it amongst the clumps of flowers, I should never find

215

it again; each floral display looked identical to its neighbour, stretching in riotous colour beneath the blazing red blossoms of the New Zealand flame trees that were now in their full glory.

I was near the top tier of terraces by now and above me the statue of Neptune reigned supreme at the head of the flight of steps that cascaded down to the bottom layer. There was no-one about up here. I left the path and pushed through the scrubby geraniums that flanked the statue. Behind it was a little hollow of bare soil where I carefully laid the bag and pulled over it some foliage. Then I regained the path and fled down the steps, past the tall sentinel palms and stone arbours. Before I reached the bottom I turned left and slipped along the gravel walk easing my pace. I sat down on the edge of one of the large rock stones to get my breath back and plan my next move. I *must* find Rory and take care that my two seekers did not find me.

In front of me was a most exotic-looking plant. Out of massed sedge-like leaves, tall slender stalks arose carrying sprays of pink blossoms. They looked like miniature fishing rods carrying strings of fluorescent fishes. Nearby was a bird of paradise plant. The red blossoms really did look like birds poised for flight. I sat there admiring it and then a scrunching on the gravel behind me made me spin round. A hand came down on my shoulder and I was jerked to my feet to meet the implacable gaze of Robert Albery.

'What have you done with it, Mrs Carr?' he snarled. Yes, he really did snarl. His top lip lifted away from his too-white teeth and he hissed from behind them.

'What are you talking about?'

'Don't play with me. I want the bag that Carberry gave you. Where is it?'

Pete Walmsley, hardly able to contain himself,

snatched at my shoulder bag and quickly searched it, tossing aside my sketching block and paints and pencils.

'I dropped it somewhere down there.' I nodded vaguely towards the lower stretch of gardens.

'Mrs Carr, we intend to have that bag. You'd better recover your memory.'

'I'm so hot and thirsty; I must rest . . .'

He glanced round; there was no-one in sight and he casually brought his hand out of his pocket and I found myself staring at a gun. I gasped.

'I don't want to use it in here. This is just to show you that we mean business. We will go down to the café and I will buy you a drink and perhaps that will prompt your memory. For your own sake I suggest you be very careful how you behave.'

'I've already reported you to the man at the gate for molesting me.' Anything to keep them away from the café and Rory.

He gave his humourless chuckle. 'That's all been smoothed out. He now thinks you had a tiff with your boyfriend and his father and were being bloody-minded. Hold her hand, Walmsley, that will look more friendly.'

I snatched my hand away from any contact with Walmsley, and Albery laughed again. We were back at the café by now. There was no sign of Rory although it must have been well past two. I dare not look at my watch in case I alerted them to the fact that I was due to meet someone. We sat down at the table at the far end of the patio and Walmsley was despatched to buy three cups of tea. My eyes were mesmerised by the bulge in Albery's jacket pocket. Surely it was obvious to everyone that he was carrying a gun? But no, I was getting hysterical; I must pull myself together. Walmsley returned with the tea and slopped it in the saucers whilst handing it round. He and Albery sat facing the patio and serving hatch where they could keep an eye on the other customers. I sat round the other side of the table looking out across the café gardens and was able to see Rory when he sauntered round the corner. He saw me at the same instant, quickened his stride enthusiastically, then saw my companions and stopped dead.

I shook my head violently and gesticulated with my hand to stop his approaching; and then jerked my head and flapped my hand again at an obliging fly that was buzzing round the table. My gestures fooled the two men and Albery also slapped out at the fly. I made a business of stirring my cup and mopping up the spilt tea and watched Rory out of the corner of my eye. He moved forward stealthily and then ducked down behind the escallonia hedge that guarded the edge of the patio. He was only a couple of feet away from the two men facing me but quite invisible to anyone looking in that direction. Hope sparked through me. If only I could convey to him that I had hidden something vitally important and where I had hidden it, I could leave him to retrieve it whilst I led the men on a wild goose chase round this part of the garden.

'Well, Mrs Carr, you had the bag with you when you bought your ticket, and as you now seem to have mislaid it we must presume you have hidden it somewhere in the gardens. How can we jog your memory?'

'I didn't hide it, I dropped it in fright when you started to chase me. I don't know exactly where. What do you want it for?'

'I think it contains something very important; something we have all been looking for, am I right?'

If he was expecting me to deny this he got a surprise. 'You're quite right,' I said defiantly, raising my voice. 'It contains the real thing – gold ducats and proof of the ship they came from.'

'Keep your voice down,' snapped Albery.

'Why? It will soon be common knowledge over all the islands.' Inspiration came to me in a flash and I continued in as loud a voice as I dared: 'Poseidon's treasure, found at last.'

'Who's Poseidon?' enquired Walmsley suspiciously.

'Poseidon is the god of the sea. All shipwreck treasure belongs to him but he will yield it up if you look.' As I spoke I willed Rory to understand; to make the connection between Poseidon and his Roman counterpart Neptune and to get my message.

'I am not interested in Greek mythology, Mrs Carr, only in the present. We shall now re-trace your footsteps and I hope for your sake we find it.'

'I should like another cup of tea first.' He gave in with bad grace and as Walmsley went to fetch it I saw a movement in the escallonia bush. For a few seconds the branches at one side threshed to and fro as if Rory had shaken them as a signal, and shortly afterwards I caught a glimpse of him sidling furtively away from the scene.

When I had drunk my tea I insisted on visiting the toilet and after this I could stop them no longer.

'Where do we start, my dear?' Albery helped me to my feet solicitously, but his fingers were like steel claws on my elbow.

'Valhalla.' Valhalla was about as far from the statue of Neptune as it was possible to get in the gardens. I led the way under the colonnade, cool in shadow, and walked as slowly as I dared past the rows of figureheads and then searched the ground beneath the giant cannon positioned on the edge of the lawn.

I shook my head in puzzlement. 'No, I still had it when I left here. I think I went up here next.' I led them up the path under the pines that I had fled along so short a while ago and I hesitated and fumbled and retraced my steps and changed my mind and did all I could to delay them. I poked in clumps of flowers, searched behind rock and bush, and even looked carefully in a water-lily covered pond as if I could have dropped it in there by accident.

'Mrs Carr, my patience is nearly exhausted. I suggest you find it very quickly.'

I dragged them up and down another couple of paths and tried to present a picture of genuine bewilderment, and all the while my thoughts were racing away. How long was it since we'd left the café? Surely at least fifteen minutes. Would Rory have had the time to retrieve the bag by now, always supposing he had understood my cryptic message? I hoped against hope he would have the sense to get away with it and not entertain any thoughts of rescuing me.

Then I realised that instead of leading the way I was being edged along a path that led to a part of the gardens not open to the public. There was a board pinned to a tree saying 'Private' and beyond it, half-hidden by foliage, I could see a greenhouse and what looked like a potting shed.

'This section is private, I didn't come along here.' I said, alarm whipping like a frisson through me. Their answer was to grab me by the arms and bundle me along the path till we reached the shadow of the shed.

'I have been a very patient man,' said Albery, 'but I think you have been making a fool of us.'

'I can't remember where I dropped it.'

'Perhaps this will help you to remember,' said Walmsley and there was a glint of metal as he brought up his hand which was holding a knife and pressed it against my neck. I shrank back against the wall and tried to turn away.

'It would be pointless to put a bullet through you at the moment,' said Albery, looking very nasty, 'but Walmsley is an expert with the blade. Unless you want your pretty face carved up so that your own mother won't recognise you, you'd better start singing.'

'I don't . . .'

'I'm serious'. He nodded at Walmsley who gently ran the tip of the knife from my neck round the curve of my jaw and up to my cheekbone. There was an animal excitement in his green eyes and an unhealthy sheen on his face, and I was more afraid than I had ever been in my life before.

'Well, Mrs Carr?'

I opened my mouth to scream and I felt the point jabbing into my cheek, breaking the skin. There was no pain but I could feel the blood trickling down the side of my face. I knew that they would have no compunction in carving me up; that Walmsley would positively enjoy it. I talked.

'It's not here,' I whispered, mopping at my face with a grubby hand.

'What do you mean, not here?' snapped Albery.

'You don't think I'm on my own, do you? There was a friend with me. I told him where I had left the bag and he has taken it away.'

'What are you talking about? You haven't left these gardens, haven't spoken to anyone.'

I decided I might as well come clean. Rory should be well away by now and I wanted to rub in how I had tricked them.

'I hid the bag behind the statue of Neptune.'

'Oh, very clever, Mrs Carr,' snarled Albery, 'Neptune, Poseidon, I see it now. But how did you tell your accomplice – where was he?'

'Just behind you in the bushes by the café. He'll be far away by now.'

'Who was it? Not Mike Carberry. I suppose it was our interfering friend, Mr Patterson?'

221

I didn't reply but stared trimphantly at them both.

'Shall I . . . .?' Walmsley, nearly beside himself with rage, lunged at me with the knife but Albery knocked the blow aside.

'No. He must still be on the island, we can catch up with him. He'll make for New Grimsby Harbour; you go along the path by the Great Pool and we'll go along the coast path. Hurry up, and if you get to him first don't let him get away!'

He grabbed my arm and swung me against him. 'You're coming with me, Mrs Carr. Any attempts at further tricks and I really will shoot. Now, get moving!' I could feel the gun pressing against my side through the thickness of his jacket and I moved.

Never had the distance between the gardens and New Grimsby Harbour seemed so far. True, I hung back as much as possible and tried to spin it out but I was not allowed to dawdle much. Every time I slackened my pace Albery made me aware of the gun, and out in the open on the isolated path I wasn't so sure that he wouldn't shoot me out of hand. I had served my part, Rory was now their quarry. I should have known better.

We reached New Grimsby harbour. There were very few people about. The afternoon launches had come and gone and there was an air of siesta time about the scene, heightened by the intense heat that was more reminiscent of the Mediterranean than the Atlantic coast. Rory was not about.

'You're too late,' I said triumphantly. 'He's left the island and that bag will now be in the hands of the Receiver of Wrecks.' His reply was to jab me viciously in the back and hurry me on past the quay and the buildings that backed the harbour. We scrambled up the footpath

222

that followed the coast round Castle Down, and when we were well away from New Grimsby he stopped.

'I don't think it is possible for Patterson to have got away in that short time. I think he is still on Tresco so we will wait for him.' I subsided onto a ledge of rock and Albery fixed his sights on the harbour below us. 'Of course,' he continued, 'Walmsley may already have dealt with him. I wonder who will appear first – Walmsley or friend Patterson?'

It was Rory. But he didn't come from the direction expected. He came loping down the path to the left of us that led from Dolphin Town, the settlement that straddled the centre of Tresco between New and Old Grimsby. We both saw him at the same time and as Albery gave a grunt of satisfaction I opened my mouth to shout a warning.

Chapter Eleven

I discovered later that Rory had been in contact with Mike and knew that he had planned to visit someone at Old Grimsby that afternoon. When he had found the bag he made for Old Grimsby harbour in the hope of catching him, but Mike had aleady left and there was no other boat around on which he could get a lift. He had immediately struck inland in the hope of being luckier at New Grimsby harbour.

He swung down the track looking hot and worried, the bag slung over one shoulder and he saw us just as Albery pulled me against him. He hesitated fractionally and then plunged towards us and I yelled despairingly: 'Rory, get away, he's got a gun!' He didn't pause, but hurtled towards us and Albery drew out the gun and I heard the click as he slipped off the safety catch. 'Rory!' I screamed expecting to see him blasted down at any second but Albery grabbed my arm and I felt the barrel cold against my heaving bosom. That stopped Rory.

He shot to a standstill a few yards from us and Albery spoke gloatingly: 'That's better, Mr Patterson. I think you have something I want. Just hand the bag over very carefully and no funny business or else . . .' He jabbed the gun hard into me and I could not stop myself from crying out.

Rory slipped the bag off his shoulder and stepped slowly towards us. He stared directly at me, not at Albery, and there was a bleak look in his eyes, and something else. I knew suddenly what I had to do. As he swung the bag towards Albery's outstretched hand, I moaned and slumped against Albery in a mock faint. He was momentarily distracted by my dead weight and in those few seconds Rory acted. The bag gained astonishing momentum and cracked against Albery's jaw sending him staggering backwards. Rory sprang forwards knocking me out of the way and grabbed his gun arm forcing it upwards.

There was an explosion and I screamed and the gun flew upwards and landed somewhere in the heather. Rory was really vicious. He smashed and slashed at Albery and got in some kicks that were well below the belt in more ways than one.

Albery slumped to the ground out cold and Rory snapped at me: 'The gun!' We dropped to our hands and knees and searched feverishly, scrabbling through the heather and gorse. There was no sign of it. 'It must have gone down a rabbit hole; quick, come on!' He pulled me to my feet and I glanced down at Albery stretched out pale at our feet. Even as I looked a little groan burst from him as he stirred.

'Come *on!*' Rory tugged at my arm.

'Pete Walmsley's about somewhere gunning for you.'

'Then we'll go this way.' He dragged me up the track to Castle Down and I tried to match his pace. When we had put a short distance between us and the unconscious man he paused and pulled me behind a bush.

'Are you all right?' His voice was harsh but the way he looked at me made me melt. 'What's happened to your cheek?'

225

My hand flew up to the cut on my face. I had forgotten all about it.

'Pete Walmsley had a knife.'

'My God!' He sounded thoroughly shaken. 'I never thought they'd harm you. From what I overheard you appeared to be having a civilised exchange. I didn't think . . . I should never have left you!'

'It's all right, Rory. They didn't really hurt me and you got away with the bag.'

'When I meet up with Pete Walmsley he'll be very sorry he laid a finger on you.' He looked so dangerous that I almost felt sorry for Walmsley. Then he gently kissed my damaged cheek.

'They really *are* gold ducats,' I touched the bag lightly, and he said: 'Then we had better get them back to St Mary's quickly.'

He cautiously raised his head and I started to get to my feet. There was a retort and something whistled close by and tore through the bushes. I yelped and he jerked me back beside him.

'He's found the gun!'

Rory cursed savagely. 'How could I have been so careless, I should have made sure . . !'

'It wasn't there. He must have fallen on it. It was lying underneath him all the time.'

'We can't stay here, we're just a sitting target. We must get up to those rocks – they'll provide a bit of cover. Can you crawl round that side?'

'Where are you going?' I asked in alarm.

'I'll crawl up from the other side. Keep down below the cover of the bracken and for God's sake don't put your head up. Why on earth did you have to wear a red shirt today. Take it off.'

'But . . .'

'Don't argue. Take it off quickly.' I did as he com-

226

manded and stuffed it in my bag. 'That's right. Now off you go and *keep down*.' He gave me a little push and I flattened out and started the long crawl. The bracken and heather pricked my bare skin as I wriggled upwards. Somewhere to my right Rory was hopefully also making progress. I reached the rocks and dragged myself behind them. Where was Rory? Then I saw him; snaking through the undergrowth which ended abruptly a few yards from the edge of the rocks.

He'd never get across that open space without being seen. As he hesitated by the last gorse bush I deliberately bobbed up into sight to draw attention away from him. There was a whine and a crack and a shower of rock fragments spattered me and then Rory had reached me and rolled me down beside him.

'You crazy little fool! When we're married I shan't let you out of my sight.'

'*What* did you say?' In my astonishment I sat up again and immediately another shot rang out and ricocheted round the rocks. He grabbed me and lay on top of me pinning me beneath him.

'I said, when we're married I can see I'll have to keep you on leading reins.'

'You choose your moments,' I managed to get out in a shaky whisper. He eased his crushing weight off me and actually grinned.

'When and if we get out of this I promise I'll do it properly. In the meanwhile you'll have to make do with this.' And he proceeded to kiss me very thoroughly. There, as we lay huddled behind the rock, in danger of being blown to oblivion at any second, he embraced me and the ground rocked beneath me and the sky whirled overhead and it was nothing to do with the imminent danger threatening us.

He finally desisted and when I came down to earth

again I saw he was counting on his fingers. 'Have you still got your shirt? Give it to me.' A long branch of charred gorse was lying nearby and he poked the end through my shirt and then hurled the burdened stick sideways. There was a flash of scarlet as the shirt flapped briefly beyond the fringe of rock and another shot rang out.

'Good, five. Now what shall we do?' He ignored my puzzled face and scooped up a piece of rock and handed it to me. 'I am going to crawl out over there. When I move throw that as hard as you can in the opposite direction where your shirt fell.'

'Rory, what are you going to do? Don't be crazy!'

'Do what I tell you – *now*!' He moved out from the shelter of the rock and I hurled the rock over the other side. There was another flash and crack and I saw Rory grab his arm. I screamed and stood up.

'I'm all right – nothing serious.'

'Rory, for God's sake get down!'

'It's OK now. He's used up his six bullets.'

Albery charged towards us clicking furiously at his empty gun and I pulled at Rory, 'Come on, let's get out of the way!'

'No, I'm going to finish this'. He turned to face Albery and they met head-on. Rory didn't have it all his own way this time. Albery had changed his grip on the gun and he lashed out at Rory with the butt and caught him on the elbow of his damaged arm. Rory gave a grunt and lost his grip on the bag and his arm swung useless at his side. Albery grabbed the bag and as Rory lunged at him he put out a foot and tripped him up. Rory crashed heavily to the ground and I hovered anxiously nearby, wanting to help but not knowing what to do. Albery shot past me and Rory got to his feet and stampeded after him. They stormed along the footpath towards Cromwell's Castle and I followed on their heels, forgotten and unheeded.

Twice Rory caught up with him and a short tussle ensued before Albery broke away, the bag still in his grasp. The thick-set, middle-aged man seemed suddenly possessed of superhuman strength, impervious to the heat or the injuries he had suffered at Rory's hand. The path strayed dangerously close to the cliff-top that curved round the little bay south of the promotory carrying Cromwell's Castle and as Rory tackled him for the third time they swayed close to the edge. I pressed a hand over my mouth to stifle the scream that was rising in my throat, fearful of distracting Rory. He had got hold of the bag but Albery still retained his hold on the strap and they tugged it too and fro like dogs fighting over a bone.

Albery gave a sudden jerk and Rory let go his end, but the sudden release threw Albery off-balance. He staggered back, tripped over a rock, teetered almost in slow-motion on the edge of the cliff and then plunged backwards with a scream.

Rory, gasping and winded, dragged himself to the spot from where he had fallen and I hurriedly joined him. The cliff was not particularly high but it fell away in a series of jagged rock formations. Albery lay spreadeagled on the beach just below the bottom clump.

'Is he . . ?' I asked fearfully.

'I must get down.' Rory looked around for a way down the cliff face. It was a perfect little bay, private and secretive, and seemingly inaccessible from the cliff top.

'Your arm, Rory?'

'He got me on the funny bone and it went numb but it's coming round now.'

'You've got blood all over it.'

'That last shot showered me with rock fragments – it's only a graze; but remember, I got it climbing down this cliff to rescue Albery.' And with that he swung himself over the edge and felt for toe- and hand-holds as he worked out a way of getting down to the beach. I clung to the top and looked around to see if there was anyone else in the vicinity who could have witnessed the fight and fall. It seemed utterly incredible that we were the only people on that part of Tresco. I can only suppose that because of the intense heat all the other holidaymakers were either prostrate on the beaches or huddled in the shade in the gardens. There was the sound of falling scree and Rory slithered the last few yards in a flurry of rocks and pebbles.

He bent over Albery, then straightened up and shouted back to me: 'He's broken his neck. There's nothing we can do.'

He prowled round the body and picked up the gun which had fallen a few feet away. He wiped it carefully with his handkerchief and then hurled it out into the water as far away as he could.

'Throw your handbag down,' he shouted.

'What . . ?'

'Quickly, chuck it to me and take this in exchange.' He picked up the bag containing the coins and threw it up to me. As I still hesitated he explained: 'The two bags are similar. You take the coins and get rid of them. I'll leave your handbag beside him. Listen, he snatched your handbag and I chased after him and he tripped and went over the edge. It was an accident – do you understand?'

'Yes, but what do we do now?'

'I'll stay here with the body. You must go back and alert the authorities. The police will have to be involved. Remember, it was an accident – no mention of the coins or his real purpose.'

I threw my handbag down to him. 'I suppose so, do you think we'll get away with it?'

'Why not. It was an accident, wasn't it? You saw him fall.'

'Pete Walmsley?'

'If he turns up he'll be only too eager to hold his tongue and disappear discreetly from the scene, I should imagine. Off you go.'

I turned away but he called me back. 'Bethany, I love you!'

The words echoed round the little bay as I looked down into his upturned face framed by tousled hair. 'Think of this as an eye for an eye.' Of course, two accidental deaths, one on either side, what a waste. I did not trust myself to reply so I just waved and started back along the footpath.

The first people I met as I got back to New Grimsby harbour were Magnus and Lisa. I couldn't believe my good luck as I ran towards them.

'Magnus, thank God! How on earth do you happen to be here?'

'I noticed you were being followed when you left *Sea Wolf* and I was worried so I decided to come after you and I met up with Lisa on the way. What's happened?'

'Oh it's awful – I think Rory is going to be charged with murder!'

Lisa gave a little shriek and Magnus put his arm round me and helped me to a seat. 'Steady on; try and tell me what has happened.' So I spilled it all out and he listened with varying expressions of worry, incredulity and admiration chasing across his face.

'Trust me to miss all the action!' Lisa's eyes were practically coming out on stalks.

'It was an experience I for one would have been quite happy to have missed,' I said coldly. 'What do we do now?'

'What Rory suggested,' said Magnus. 'He's obviously kept his wits about him. We'll hide that bag of coins in the dinghy. Lisa, you do that – tuck it away out of sight somewhere – and Bethany and I will give the alarm.'

'The police?'

'There is no policeman stationed on Tresco. It's privately owned, remember? But most of the male population are auxilliary coastguards, so we'll soon get things moving.'

Reaction was setting in and I was only too glad to have things taken out of my hands. Once I had got over the initial shock I realised that there was no way Rory could be accused of murder. He had acted in self-defence, it was an accidental death, but I could not rid myself of the picture of Albery lying there, smashed on the rocks, his head at an unnatural angle. It brought back to me Martin's death. I saw Martin lying there lifeless, not Albery, and I clung to Magnus feeling sick and shaky.

Events moved quickly after that and I have only a confused memory of what actually happened. Looking back afterwards everything was jumbled up in my mind, out of order of sequence. I remember the stretchered body of Albery being carried across the beach to a dinghy lurking at the water's edge, this being easier than trying to winch it up the cliff-face, from whence it was taken to St Mary's Hospital before being conveyed to Penzance by the *Scillonian*. I remember Rory insisting on his story that his fiancée had been the victim of an intended mugging and, as luck would have it, my original complaint to the attendant at the gardens of being followed and molested added weight to his story. Walmsley was found hiding in the interior of Tresco, initially picked up because of some complaint over unpaid landing fees.

I remember the welcome coolness of the interior of the police station on St Mary's, not far from the cottage where I was living; and being positively cosseted by a sympathetic sergeant whilst I told my side of the story and Rory

232

talking his way quietly but emphatically out of an awkward situation and emerging practically a hero.

The Coroner for West Cornwall and the Isles of Scilly was summoned and an inquest held in the Town Hall. Evidence of identification was accepted and then the inquest was adjourned for further police investigation. After exhaustive enquiries in which many details of the treasure hunt came to light, Rory was completely exonerated from being responsible for Albery's death and eventually a verdict of accidental death was brought in. Pete Walmsley had denied all knowledge of Albery's attack on Rory and as we didn't want the true tale to come out we were forced to hold our tongues so he got off with a caution. Amazingly nothing ever came out about the gun and even more extraordinarily, nobody seemed to have heard the gun shots.

But all these happenings were to be spread out over a considerable period of time. Immediately after the accident I was filled by a great feeling of revulsion and shock. Albery had been responsible for Martin's death, for almost drowning Mike; he had been prepared to disfigure me to achieve his own ends, and when that failed he had tried to shoot Rory and myself in cold blood. But all I could think of was his body lying stretched out on the silver sand, the head snapped sideways at an unnatural angle whilst Rory tossed bags to and fro. How insignificant that handful of coins seemed to me in the light of what had followed their discovery; another man dead and Rory implicated in his death.

At Rory's insistence I was allowed to go back to the cottage whilst he stayed behind at the police station. I collapsed onto the studio couch, too apathetic to even make myself a cup of tea or coffee, and there Lisa found me some time later when she returned with the welcome news that Rory had been released.

'He's gone to the hospital.'

'The hospital?' I started up, all sorts of fearsome thoughts whirling around in my head, but she reassured me.

'Presumably to be patched up. He sent his love. Mike's just come ashore. They've found something else on the last dive but he doesn't seem very happy about it. He refused to say what it was, only that he's got to confer with Magnus and that it would mean a complete re-think of the whole business. We're all summoned to his place this evening. He was shocked to hear what had happened and I imagine he and the others will also get involved with the police enquiries; they'll have to if anything is to be done about settling Pete Walmsley's hash.'

Lisa fussed around me whilst I gradually managed to pull myself together and I even ate at the snack she produced. Later, as we changed and prepared for the coming evening, I brought up the subject that had been nagging away at me over the last few hours. 'Has Rory really managed to talk himself out of any trouble – the police are satisfied with his explanations?'

'It would appear so. He seems to bear a charmed life as far as extricating himself from difficult situations is concerned. Are you going to marry him?'

Lisa certainly jumped in where angels fear and all the rest of it.

'He hasn't asked me yet,' I said carefully.

'I thought from the way he was shooting his mouth off about his fiancée that it was all cut and dried.'

'He seems to take it for granted that I'm going to marry him.'

'Well, what are you waiting for? Not an official proposal on bended knee surely? You don't know how lucky you are, Bethany. Twice you've managed to entice some gorgeous man into wedded bliss, or at least the contemplation of it, and yet you're dithering.'

'Lisa, that sounds strange coming from you!'

'You think I have eschewed such old-fashioned ideals as marriage and a permanent partner? It's quite true that I know it's not for me, but that doesn't stop me from being envious. Grab your chance, Bethany, and be happy.'

'What about you and Mike?'

'Don't be ridiculous darling. Perhaps one day in the far distant future I may want to be tied down, but not yet, not yet. Anyway, you haven't answered my question; are you going to marry him?'

'I don't think I could bear not to.' The words came unbidden but as soon as I had spoken them I knew they were the truth; that life without Rory did not bear contemplation.

'Oh, my God, Bethany, don't let the gods hear you! Well, I shall dance at your wedding yet again and I promise to be a model godmother.'

'That's jumping the gun.' I was suddenly daunted by the thought of Rory's previous childless marriage and of all that we both had to put behind us; to forget. Was I mad to think that he and I could be happy together? Had he really meant those words thrown out so casually as we had huddled in fear of our lives on Tresco, or had I imagined it all?

'You look as if you're having second thoughts already.'

'Just the proverbial goose walking.' I quickly changed the subject. 'What do you think Mike meant?'

'We'll soon find out. If you've finished primping I suggest we get over there and find out.'

Rory looked none the worse for his ordeal. His arm was neatly bandaged and sticky plaster covered the worst of the cuts and bruises on his face and hands. He was his usual laconic self and greeted us casually when we arrived at Mike's, and I began to believe I really had suffered a mental aberration on Tresco. Then his lips brushed the nape of my neck as he helped me to my seat and I saw the look he bent on me and I knew everything was all right.

The scene around the table reminded me of the time before when we had met here and examined the coins and pieces of cannon. Now there were different exhibits. Magnus was handling what looked like a piece of earthenware pottery and he handed it to Lisa and I. It was quite large and curved in before swelling out to a rim. I guessed it had come from the neck of a vase of some sort. Stamped in relief on one side was the head of a monk and I looked enquiringly at Magnus.

'It's come from a Bellarmine jar. Named after a certain Cardinal Bellarmine, hence the monk's head which was always placed on the neck of each jar. They were used by the Dutch East India Company to transport oil and wine and mercury etc. I think this one originally contained mercury – it was used for the refining of silver. So, what have we got?'

'Not the *Merchant Royal*?' I looked from one to the other in dismay.

'I'm afraid not,' Mike looked rueful but not unduly disappointed. He tipped out the contents of a bag onto the table. 'And this clinches it.' The silver coins, quite a large amount of them, rolled across the surface of the table and Lisa picked one up.

'What are they?' she asked sharply.

'Pillar-dollars. Pieces of eight, if you want to be fanciful.'

'And these couldn't have come from the *Merchant Royal*?'

'Pillar-dollars such as these were first minted in 1732. Before the pieces of eight were cobs – all odd-shaped

236

coins minted in Potosi, Lima or Mexico City – or there were screw-pressed pieces which were minted in metropolitan Spain.'

'So coins like these couldn't have come from a ship that went down in the middle of the seventeenth century?'

'Lisa, my dear,' said Rory gently, picking up a coin, 'they are dated – look.' He turned it over in his hand and we saw the date clearly: 1742. The coins were in pristine condition and could have been minted yesterday; the design of two pillars flanking the twin globes with crowns on top were clearly discernible on each coin and they were all dated between 1735 and 1744.

'It's almost certainly the *Maria Johanna*,' said Mike, producing the rest of their finds; a little ring made of twisted strands of gold, badly bent out of shape, a pewter flagon lid, and a pair of brass dividers.

'And is she of much less value than the *Merchant Royal*?' I asked.

'The *Merchant Royal* was literally a fabulous treasure ship, a floating goldmine; but I suppose it was always rather pie in the sky. She may be out there somewhere, maybe one day we'll find her, but the *Maria Johanna* has to be the most valuable Dutch East Indiaman ever recorded lost. What do you think one of these coins is worth?'

He turned to Lisa who looked at the coin still in her hand and replied cautiously: 'A hundred pounds?'

'In this condition they could fetch up to £2,000 each.'

'You're joking!' Lisa gasped at him and then looked round at the other faces grinning back at her. 'You're not joking. Ye gods! This is for real! Then what are we waiting for?'

'Don't forget we don't get everything. The cost of mounting this operation eats into any subsequent profit. The Dutch Government claim twenty-five per cent from

237

any salvaged Dutch East Indiaman, and there is a certain London solicitor who owns the rights of salvage to many of these ships – he bought the contract off the Dutch Government – and will have to be contacted about this one. Hopefully he has no claim on it. Rory . . ?.

'I'll deal with that side of it.'

'We're not going to become millionaires overnight but you'll have a little more pin-money to juggle with than before. Tomorrow we set things in motion. The coastguard has already been informed. Now we claim Salvor in Possession, apply for a Wreck Protection Licence, publicise it – the full works – and let's hope we get final proof that it really *is* the *Maria Johanna*.'

They got that proof later in the week. Firstly, in the shape of a silver spoon with the A-VOS logo of the Dutch East India Company on the stem and then, unbelievably, they brought up the ship's bell itself, bearing the name *Maria Johanna* faintly but still visibly inscribed on the dull bronze. The story broke then. There was no more need or hope of keeping it secret. Mike and his team became the focal point of interest, but Rory and I came in for quite a lot of attention too and Lisa, her professional self taking over, kept the telephone line to the mainland almost permanently engaged as she made the most of her unique position. I vacillated between the urge to personally throttle her and getting carried away by all the excitement engendered by the discovery.

But that was not the end of the story. There was to be another night of drama and death before I was completely free of the nightmare that had haunted me since Martin's death. Rory kept a very low profile as far as I was concerned in the days that followed. I think he was trying to keep the pressure off me, what with the police enquiries into Albery's death still continuing, and the fear of which way Pete Walmsley and his team might jump now that their leader was permanently out of the way. I was grateful to him but could not help wondering whether he was already regretting his involvement with me.

The spell of fine weather ended with a thunderstorm and it turned considerably cooler with strengthening westerly winds. I found it difficult to get down to any serious painting, and I was restless and filled with vague misgivings. Lisa was making plans to return to London. I knew she would have liked to prolong her stay but had working commitments in the city which she could no longer ignore. We were sitting in the studio about ten-thirty one evening talking over the latest developments when the first rocket went up. We rushed to the window and I ripped back the curtains as the second burst showered the sky.

'My God! Don't tell me they celebrate *Juillet Quatorze* here,' gasped Lisa.

'They're life-boat maroons. They're summoning the life-boat crew – look!' Even as we watched a pair of headlights swung down the hill opposite us and stopped in the vicinity of the life-boat shed, quickly followed by others, all converging on the same point. I pushed open the window and the wind snatched at the curtains and tossed them back in our faces. There was a glow in the shed and Lisa pressed against my shoulder.

'Are they going to launch the life-boat?'

'It's not berthed there now. The new one's too big, it's moored out in the bay. There is a small, fast launch in there which they use to get out to the real life-boat.'

We strained to see what was happening out there in the dark and heard rather than saw the passage of the launch down the slip into the black, turbulent water. A little while later, above the sound of the wind we heard the deeper snarl of a powerful engine surging into life.

'Shut the window before we get sucked out into the

elements!' We struggled with the catch and when we had secured it we looked at each other warily.

'Where do you think it has gone?'

'Probably to some yacht that's got into difficulties – it's easy enough to imagine on a night like this.'

'I hope it's not . . .' I checked myself and mooched round the room unable to throw off the feeling of foreboding that was encircling me. Lisa for once seemed to share my feelings.

'It couldn't be Mike? No, that's ridiculous.'

'It couldn't possible be, but I'm worried, Lisa.'

'My thumbs are pricking too.' We stared at each other across the room and I made a sudden decision. 'I'm going down there. I must find out what's happening.'

'It's utter madness, but I'm coming too.'

We wrapped up in thick sweaters and anoraks and let ourselves quietly out of the cottage. The wind tore around us in powerful gusts and a three-quarter moon sailed fitfully between ragged clouds. By the time we reached the harbour we were both out of breath. There appeared to be nobody else about and we walked cautiously down the quay, straining to see if we could detect any activity across the water. The moon emerged from behind a bank of cloud and for a few seconds the scene was bathed in silver light.

'Lisa,' I clutched her arm, 'The *Sea Wolf*'s not there.'

'You can't possibly see from here.'

'Wait till the moon comes out again – look! There's a gap where she should be moored.'

'I believe you're right.' She sounded shaky. 'My God, whatever can be happening?'

'I'm going to get Rory.'

'You can't knock up the entire hotel and besides, what good could he do if he were here?'

'I don't know but I must do something.'

'It's all right, I'm here.' Rory loomed up out of the darkness and I gave a little squeak and rushed towards him.

'You made me jump,' accused Lisa crossly; 'do you have to sneak up on a person like that?'

'I can assure you I'm making my normal amount of noise – you wouldn't hear a brass band playing on a night like this. What are you girls doing down here?'

He wrapped his arms round me and and I nestled in their shelter whilst Lisa explained about our fears.

'I suppose you heard the maroons too,' she ended. 'Do you know what's happening?' Rory shook his head but I thought he looked particularly grim.

'I'm going to Mike's place to make sure. I can't stand the suspense,' said Lisa moving away from us.

'He's not there,' said Rory and when we both rounded on him, continued, 'I've been trying to ring him, there's no reply.'

'So he *is* on the *Sea Wolf* and it *is* missing, isn't it?' said Lisa, gesticulating wildly in the direction where the *Sea Wolf* was normally moored.

'It doesn't appear to be there,' said Rory, squinting out to sea, 'but that doesn't mean the distress signal came from him. They may be standing by, guarding the site.'

'On a night like this?'

'Come on, I'll take you back to the cottage. You can't do any good hanging around here.' Lisa agreed but I refused to go and they left me standing alone at the end of the quay as he escorted her home.

The water slurped and slapped against the jetty and now that my eyes were becoming accustomed to the gloom I could see there were lights shining from several of the boats moored out in the harbour; I even thought I could hear voices across the water in the bay but decided I must be imagining it. It seemed a very long time before

Rory returned and I was shivering and numb with cold when I heard the scrunch of his feet and turned round to be pulled into his embrace.

'Lisa's tucked up safely. I've found out something – there were two lots of distress signals – one of them from the *Sea Wolf*.'

'Oh Rory, where?'

'From somewhere out towards the Western Rocks.'

'Oh God!'

'Don't worry, it's probably not as bad as it sounds. They managed to let off a distress signal, so whatever has happened there's hope.'

'Rory, how do they know it was the *Sea Wolf*?'

'They must have been in radio contact with them so there's even more cause for hope. You ought to be back indoors. We can't do anything – it's in the hands of the life-boat crew now.'

But we stayed, pacing the quayside and I clung tightly to Rory's hand. By this time a small crowd had gathered and an ambulance waited ominously in the background. Nobody spoke. We waited, enacting a scene that had been played many times before down the centuries. I was transported back in time; I was wearing long skirts and a shawl round my head and around me women similarly dressed with crying children clinging to their skirts keened as they waited without hope for their fishermen husbands adrift somewhere on the storm-wracked seas. But there were few women and no children in this crowd, just a tight knot of people waiting tense and expectant whilst in the background the radio telephone of the ambulance burbled senselessly.

We were still there when the life-boat returned some time later. It stopped only long enough to discharge its four passengers and then roared off to sea again. Mike, Magnus, Tom and Bill, cold, wet and exhausted but very much alive, were rushed of to the hospital but not before we had managed to get the gist of what had happened. Apparently someone had alerted Mike to the fact that a diver had been seen nosing around the *Sea Wolf* as she swung at her moorings. Mike had summoned the others and they had put to sea in the *Sea Wolf*, recklessly ignoring the weather signals, fearful when they discovered that his boat was missing, that Pete Walmsley and his team might be trying to sabotage the site of the *Maria Johanna*. They had got out into Broad Sound before realising that they were taking in water badly. They had tried to put back but the situation had rapidly deteriorated, and more by luck than judgement they had managed to ground themselves on a shelf of rock off Annet. They had sent off distress signals and a short while later had heard further signals going up beyond them out towards the Western Rocks and knew that the rival team was also in trouble.

As Rory remarked later, it took some skill and know-ledge to sabotage a ship like the *Sea Wolf*. It wasn't just a case of stoving in a plank. She had been deliberately crippled by underwater drilling in the bottom of the hull. But all this came out later when yet another enquiry was underway. As soon as I had ascertained that Mike and the others were safe I was persuaded to return to the cottage and I was not there when the life-boat returned as dawn was striating the sky.

Rory had remained and he gave me details later. The life-boat had spent hours sweeping the sea in a fruitless search, hampered by the high winds and rough seas. Eventually they had found one survivor clinging to rocks near Little Crebawethan. It turned out to be Pete Walmsley, half drowned and nearly dead from exposure. Of the rest of the crew or the boat itself which, incidentally, had been called the *Star Voyager*, there was no trace.

Later in the week a lifebelt was washed up on St Agnes, and spars of wood were found floating in the sea between the Crebawethan groups of rocks. The mystery of why she foundered was never really solved. Mike's theory was that the crew had been so eager to watch the *Sea Wolf* come to grief that it hadn't kept a proper look-out itself, and *Star Voyager* had become impaled on a submerged rock and been pounded to pieces by the enormous seas. Pete Walmsley confirmed this later when he recovered enough to be questioned. He was so shocked and dazed at first that he was quite incoherent but later he talked, hoping to save his skin.

What he told confirmed a lot of what we had suspected. He had originally met up with Martin when working as a diver in the Celtic Sea. Martin had mistakenly thought he was a friend and colleague of Mike's and discussed the find with him. Realising that this was something big Walmsley had lost no time in alerting his employer to the significance of this information. Robert Albery had been an important businessman, albeit crooked, with a string of useful, dubious contacts. He had got at the police; he had had some sort of hold over the Chief Constable in my manor, something to do with corruption and a crooked deal, and had applied blackmail to get my pleas and complaints squashed and 'forgotten'. Martin had been approached by him, but quickly sensing his original mistake, had refused to cooperate in what he saw as a crooked venture. Martin had died accidentally when Albery was trying to put pressure on him. In fact, all the deaths, in the eyes of the law, had been accidental. If Robert Albery were still alive he would not have had to answer a murder reckoning. However, when Pete Walmsley was eventually brought to trial, enough charges were made, including piracy and grievous bodily harm, to put him away for a long time.

Shock waves reverberated round the islands at the disaster and were intensified when the skullduggery was revealed. We were all subdued and the pleasure had gone out of the treasure hunt. Several men had died in a week, albeit through their own scheming and malice, and it threw a blight over the proceedings. I felt particularly affected, having been personally involved with one of the dead men right from the beginning. I eased the tension by painting violently in oils a picture of how I imagined the Crim Rocks to look in a storm. I applied the paint with a knife in thick slabs of colour suggesting the wedged formation of the rock and high-lighting the foam-capped waves with splatters of flake-white. I felt better when I had finished and Rory said that the psychiatrists would have a field-day analysing my picture if they were let loose on it.

Gradually we each in our own way came to terms with the situation. The *Sea Wolf* was easily recovered and repaired, and on their first dive after the tragedy Tom and Bill brought up a chest containing hundreds of gold ducats. After that we were caught up in the excitement again. Lisa was due back in London by the end of the week, and Mike had arranged a celebration meal for all of us in the Mermaid on the evening before her departure. He declared his intention of getting thoroughly drunk before the night was through and I could tell by her reaction to this that they had both become more involved with each other than either had intended.

I felt I was living in a no-man's land; neither engaged nor footloose. My marriage to Martin would always remain an important part of my life but I now accepted that it was in the past. I was no longer content to live on memories. I wanted a real flesh and blood man; I wanted Rory.

The meal was arranged for late evening but Rory came early to the cottage to collect us.

'I'm not ready yet,' complained Lisa. She was wearing white. There was nothing virginal about it, but the contrast with her suntan and exotic make-up was startling to say the least.

'You, my dear Lisa, must make your own way to the Mermaid later. Bethany and I have things to do first.' And he whisked me out of the cottage.

'Where are we going and what have we got to do?' I demanded.

'We are going to watch the sunset,' he said and marched me up Garrison Hill. It looked as if we were going to get our sunset too. The evening was golden and balmy and the shimmering water already reflected the path of the sun as it sunk towards Samson. I was reminded of that first evening of my arrival when I had trod this same path and wept from bitter-sweet memories. Such a lot had happened since then, it was quite unbelievable. We sauntered along the rough, dusty path arm in arm and I leant my head against Rory's shoulder and let the peacefulness of the scene seep into me.

'Do you want to go back to London?' he asked abruptly and I stared at him in dismay.

'No, I should like to stay here, at least for the time being.'

'Good, so would I. We'll rent a place whilst we look around for a cottage to buy. You can finish off your commission and I shall make a start on my bestseller.'

'Rory Patterson!' I exclaimed, whilst relief flooded through. 'Aren't you taking a lot for granted?'

'Well, you are going to marry me, aren't you?'

'Yes please, if you're sure that's what you want . . .'

'But of course, what else did you think I had in mind?'

'I wasn't sure whether you meant marriage, living in sin

246

or whether you were trying to give me a polite brush-off.'

'My God! I'm not very good at this, am I? Perhaps this will help convince you.' It certainly did. When I broke from his embrace some time later I felt dizzy and light-hearted. We strolled a little further exchanging the universal language of lovers and I was moved to ask: 'Rory, I still don't know how you got caught up with me in the first place; what M. & K. thought I was involved in and why?'

'As I've told you, there was a panic about a security leak at the beginning, but that was soon cleared up. However by that time I had met you and I was hooked.'

'You mean . . ?

'I fell for you completely and utterly at first sight. Do you believe me?'

I looked into those dancing eyes, which were for once serious and supplicating and I said slowly: 'I believe I do.'

'I'm just an old-fashioned romantic at heart. You were so vulnerable and lost and I felt you were in some danger. The only thing I could do was to stick around and try and protect you.'

'You certainly did that. I felt I had a bodyguard, a shadow and *doppelganger* all rolled into one, but I didn't know you were interested in me in that way.'

'I was afraid of putting a foot wrong. I knew how you felt about Martin – after all, it was early days since your bereavement – and I knew I had to handle you gently in case I scared you away permanently. Also at first I was afraid Martin really was involved in something under-hand. That's why I tried to blacken him in your eyes, why I taunted you about him. I wanted to implant doubts in your mind so that if he did fall from his pedestal in your eyes, at least you would have been warned. Actually I think my actions had the opposite effect, hadn't they?

'You don't know how hard it was to keep my hands off you, but I wanted you to come to me of your own free will.

Not because you were sorry for me, or trying to pretend I was Martin or using me as a sex substitute. I've never been so frustrated in my life and I don't know how I managed to keep my baser instincts under control.'

'And I thought I left you cold and you were just sorry for me – I even thought at one stage that you preferred the boys!'

'I'll never forgive you for that. You've got a lot to make up for, you know.'

'Will this do for starters?' and I went eagerly into his arms again.

When I surfaced it was considerably darker.

'Rory,' I wailed, 'we've missed the sunset!' The sun had indeed disappeared and there was just a gleam left in the sky above the twin hills of Samson across the shadowed water.

'There'll be other sunsets.'

We retraced our steps down the hill and across the Bank but Rory led me past the Mermaid and along the quay. It was getting dark rapidly now that the sun had gone down and the first stars were sprinkling the sky. The water glowed strangely as far as the eye could see.

'Rory – look!' I clutched his arm, 'the sea – it's phos-phorescent!'

'I believe it does happen from time to time. There is a perfectly logical scientific explanation for it but it's certainly a sight, isn't it? We must look on it as a display put on especially for our benefit, a good omen.'

He dug into his pocket and held out something towards me. It was the gold ring that had been found in the wreck of the *Maria Johanna*. Then it had been twisted and bent, now it gleamed in perfect symmetry.

'Magnus has been working on it all the week. You shall have a proper one later but this is just to be getting on with.'

'Oh Rory,' I breathed, 'it's beautiful. But isn't it treasure trove or something? Are we supposed to have it yet?'

'I don't think anyone is going to quibble if this is missing from the official record. How is it for a fit?'

'Just a moment, there is something I have to do first.'

I walked to the edge of the quay and twisted at the wedding ring on my left hand. Its removal left an indentation in my finger and I held it gently in my palm for a few seconds.

Rory spoke at my shoulder: 'Wear it on your other hand.'

'No, this is where it belongs,' and I hurled it out into the luminous water.

'My God, I almost expected a hand to come up and catch it. Are you sure . . ?'

'Yes, quite,' I said firmly. 'Martin would have approved. Who knows, perhaps in another hundred years' time some other diver will find it and wonder from what wreck it came.'

I slipped the new ring on my finger and Rory bent and brushed his lips across the back of my hand.

'You're committed now, you know, I shan't let you go.'

'There's no escape clause for you either.'

We smiled at each other and walked back towards the Mermaid which spilled squares of light onto the shadowed cobbles. In front of us the whole of Hugh Town was silhouetted against a star-shot sky, and behind us a lambent sea whispered in approval as we strolled back to the awaiting company.

Epilogue

The Scillies are beautiful in winter when the low-slung sun highlights the purple rocks and picks out the green and gold burgeoning bulb-fields. However, the storms can be horrendous and after two years I am still afraid that one day the Atlantic will triumph and sweep across the narrow isthmus separating Hugh Town from the Hugh and swallow up most of the town. We are safe on our hill though. After we were married Rory and I came back to St Mary's. Mrs Pethick had decided to sell up and join her daughter on the mainland and we were lucky enough to be able to buy the cottage in Sallyport.

Rory wrote his first book; it turned out to be a psychological thriller and was very well received by the critics. He is not a bestseller yet but his next volume is eagerly awaited, and his tribute to Ned Donnelly has achieved coffee-table status. I finished my flower commission and I now paint locally. I shall never get tired of recording the ever-changing beauty of these islands, and I am to have another exhibition in London soon. Lisa is acting as the go-between.

But we are not reliant on the results of our toil. We are rich – filthy rich. The salvaging of the *Maria Johanna*, or rather what was left of her, is nearly complete and the sum realised has run into millions of pounds, outdoing even Mike's wildest expectations. Of course, not all this is profit. The salvaging operation to date has cost about £100,000 pounds and the Dutch Government, who had taken over from the old Dutch East India Company, have claimed 20 per cent as all Dutch East Indiamen still officially belong to it.

At first Mike and the boys struggled with their existing divers-support boat and gear, but it soon became obvious that a much bigger rescue operation needed to be mounted. At that depth divers could only stay down between four and ten minutes a day and it looked as if the salvage operation was going to drag on for years. But as the precious artefacts, including gold, silver and jewellery, were brought to the surface and auctioned off (the Dutch Government getting first refusal) we were able to invest in the latest equipment; a super boat with a decompression chamber and oxygen helium gas for the divers so that they could stay down much longer. The vastness of the undertaking has meant that we have had to bring more people into the consortium and there has been a good deal of publicity, adverse as well as good. We can still only dive in the summer and each day's work costs between two and three hundred pounds. I still can't get used to thinking in such vast sums but Mike says we have to think big.

He and Lisa still have something going for each other. They both insist that there can never be a steady relationship between them, and they go their own ways, but they can't stay apart for long. I hope they will eventually realise they can't live without each other but Rory says I am indulging in the realms of fantasy and that any sort of permanent arrangement between them would be absolutely fatal – to them and their nearest and dearest. However, Lisa has even wintered here and from time to time Mike goes swanning off to London and the bright lights, and I haven't given up hope of them making a go of it.

They have both agreed to be godparents to our first-born who should put in an appearance in about four months' time. Mike has promised a pristine piece of silver from the *Maria Johanna* as a christening mug, and it will take pride of place on our sideboard with the perfect Ballarmine jug, the pewter flagon and the original pieces of crud which Rory has had mounted.

Rory reckons we shall have behaviour problems and an identity crisis with Percy whom we took over with the cottage. He mutters darkly of sibling jealousy and noses being put out of joint, but I think Percy will adapt very well, and the presence of a baby in the household is hardly likely to make a dent in his supreme self-possession. Rory insists that if it is a girl she shall be called Mary Joanne, but I'm sure it will be a boy and what is wrong with Ned?